To my Parents, who raised a Author

To my Family, who nurtured one

CW00523464

Special thanks to:

Johanna, without which this would never have happened

Manuel, who made art of thought

Amy, who stoked the embers of my writing and put my
words in order

1.

The long shadows of Winter were finally over.

Snow was still thick and heavy over the hills and valleys, heavier still from melting in the mild early spring sun, shrouding the lands in a cool white blanket.

Basking in the rays in front of the roughly hewn shack on the hill sat a dark haired and bearded man. With a grimacing smile he squinted toward the rejuvenating morning sun taking in the twitter of birdsong and the misleading peace of the small valley he called home.

Feeling alive and kept in that moment the cold steel of Kharagh, the mythical Tuakk axe, brought him temporary bliss like a lovers' touch across his stubbled chin. He realised just how much he needed a good shave.

A figure was warily approaching from the south, stalking towards the building, regularly stopping to observe the man before moving closer. She was a tall and broad woman dressed in thick furs and carrying a wicked bow at half draw. She wasn't actively sneaking up on the man but not announcing her presence in any way either.

She paused a dozen feet from the man, donned a disapproving frown under her wild hair then boldly stepped up to the man effectively blocking his light.

She almost seemed to pull back from him as she saw a glimmer of annoyance cross his face but still he didn't open his eyes.

She couldn't expect anything other than a brazen, almost suicidal attitude from him but having known him all her life she had never considered him careless. Vexed, she let the arrow knock against the bow to get his attention.

Still there was no acknowledgement of her presence.

"Wolves and plagues Ulmar! Has the winter made you content to become goblin-bait or has old age finally caught up to you?"

"I saw you stalk the valley, Hild," Ulmar said, still not opening his eyes, "I saw you from the second you crossed the brook."

"I might have been here to kill you. We have a debt of blood to settle, you and I."

The man smiled as he spoke. "But you aren't. Tell me kinsman, what do you want?"

Finally deciding that the man wasn't about to pounce Hild relaxed her draw.

"Your chieftain calls for you. The Winter is past. Now is the time for council before the season of war. Chief Brlac needs you in the talks with the Marrodar."

-"Does my uncle really need me, Bearpaw?" Ulmar queried, opening his eyes to see Hilds' reaction to the nickname he knew she hated. He still felt it appropriate, the woman had the soft, rolling gait of a great brown bear. She even looked the part in her shaggy furs.

The bearlike woman visibly composed herself, as he suspected she'd do and changed the subject.

"You look unwell cousin, much thinner than last we met. I half expected you to be dead by the hand of Troll or frost, it's been a long and hard winter. How have you fared?"

She almost seemed to be concerned, he mused. Maybe the last bitter years had been washed away by this spring's smelting, reemerging the tight friendship of their youth.

"It has been a hard winter. The snows were as thick as I've ever seen them while some lesser plague haunted me. It sucked my fat and melted my strength while the black wolf shared terrible visions with me during the nights. But that is in the past. I was granted another spring and I will regain my strength."

"Ill news cousin, yet I suspect that if the black wolf would ever pass your threshold it would spit you out. Your fate is not to wilt from sickness nor die in battle against mortal men. I'd not be half surprised if you'll live forever purely because the black wolf does not want you."

Ulmar scoffed in amusement. Hild was always a blunt speaker and he wasn't sure if he'd been complemented, mocked, taunted or all of the above.

"Does it bother you so, that my uncle calls for me? Neither of us thinks that he should bother when he has fierce warriors such as yourself at his side. Why don't you claim your right and take your place at his side as his strongest blade?"

"He doesn't want me", there was a bitter tinge in her voice, "He has made that abundantly clear. You can stay here and test your fate, but by the look of it you'll be starving in a matter of days or you can answer the call of your chieftain as honour demands. Your choice."

With that as abruptly as she came the woman stepped away from the shack starting her trek back to the hold.

"Briac doesn't know what he wants", Ulmar called after her.

"He does", Hild disagreed only halfway turning back to him but not stopping, "He wants the Doomwolf."

It did not take long for Ulmar to gather the few belongings he needed for the journey. What little he still had in the way of provisions was, as Hild had suspected, long gone. Parts of what was left had started to warp and rot from the harsh tear of weather. He had managed to keep his strange axe Kharagh from rust and wear but most other things had fared badly from the long days and nights he had been ill.

With his small bundle tossed over his shoulder he travelled across the wooded valley floor pondering what his uncles', Chieftain Briac of the Tuakk, request could mean.

The Tuakk and the Marrodar had been locked in a blood feud for a generation now, killing and avenging without any of them ever gaining any real ground towards the other. Ulmar himself had lost a brother to the Marrodar and by all rights he should be consumed by the need to avenge his kin. Yet he didn't. His brother had taken two Marrodar lives before they found and slew him. They in turn had probably themselves Tuakk blood on their hands and so forth. This was just how life was among the hills of the true men. Once the tribes had been allies sharing in blood and battle before a simple dispute at a gathering had led to blood being spilt which in turn had lit the fires of revenge. As his kin told it the spark was ignited when Dovod of the Marrodar had insulted Ragnvar of the Tuakks drinking prowess. The Marrodar probably told it differently.

From what he heard Ragnvar had been an incorrigible drunkard.

Could this mean that Briac was considering peace with the Marrodar?

Ulmar hoped so as he slogged through the sloshy snowy water of the brook. He hoped that peace was on the horizon and that he could be there to help bring it into being.

2.

The House of the Hold of Tuakk crowned its small valley with all the majesty of a watchful bloodhawk. The hall was old, older than any village or keep within leagues of its location, only beaten by the dark ruins that littered the countryside. It was almost unheard of to see a hall of the True folk unburnt for such a span of time and with the years the hall had seen many expansions and reparations.

Ulmar stopped at the height of Chills Pass to behold his ancestral home once again. Memories of his broken life swept bitterly across his mind. From that hill he had set forth time and time again to bring the axe to the enemies of the Tuakk. Mortal men, monsters and unspeakable things had been crushed, driven before him and cast into oblivion.

On that hill he had felt the pride of his bloodline and sung songs in honor of his ancestors amongst the warriors.

He had met happiness, sorrow and anguish, but always with a bitter taint.

Ulmar had never accepted the title of Doomwolf but had never cast it off. It was who he was and for a moment he hated it. His kin were busy in preparation around the hold as he strolled through the valley. The dust and grime of winter had to be cleared out of the buildings to keep the black wolf away, the season of death now being past.

What animals had survived the frosts were goaded down into the valley to feast upon the first blossoming of new life.

Even from when he stood in the Pass he had heard the sound of the warriors testing their mettle against each other, stretching stiff limbs and rebuilding their strength. As he passed the clearing of old oaks he heard rustling and the bleating goats. Probably a dozen of the brownish animals were being methodically driven toward the now probably open upper pond by two young boys. The animals ignored the arrival of this stranger in the valley but as the two goat herders came into view from behind a bare blackcurrant shrub they stopped in their tracks. Tensing up, staring wide eyed at him, they froze like deer before Ulmar. He recognized them as Thrynkattlas young ones, around eight or ten years of age. He remembered them as slightly spoiled but good lads though he was somewhat worried by the scrawny look of them. He moved to speak and the spell was broken. The two boys ran flailing back towards the hold, screaming of strangers and raiders, leaving the goats to fend for themselves.

Ulmar swore at their craven reaction as he picked up their stout quarterstaffs and moved to guard the flock in their place. This time of year there were far too many hungry things stalking the hills that would rejoice at the sight of such a succulent bounty. They should have blown their horns and stood their ground at the sight of a single stranger. Help was after all, nearby, and if he knew Chief Briac, he would value the lives of the goats more than the boys.

Ulmar followed the flock patting the side of a nearby nannie absentmindedly. At least his presence would be announced now which he was happy to be done with.

The glade by the pond was still partially covered with melting snow. What plants had appeared from under it were sparse, though probably brimming in sustenance. Ulmar took the opportunity to scoop up some of the revitalizing icy water to quench his thirst before he found a rock to sit on that the sun had managed to dry the top of. The goats needed no tending, routinely foraging the glade only too happy to be out of the confines of the buildings. There was a simple joy in just watching the animals play in the sunlight, bounding and running about in a celebration of life.

He himself had never had to tend goats, yet, he imagined that it was something which would have brought him satisfaction in a way his life had never done.

The barking of dogs brought the games of the animals to an abrupt halt. Clumping together for protection the herd gathered at the shore of the pond restlessly awaiting the arrival of their would-be tormentors.

Hearing the thudding of the feet and the voices of warriors Ulmar prepared himself. It was always precarious business to reenter the hold, depending on whom he encountered first. He hoped that this year it wouldn't at least end with him having to spill blood. He gently balanced Kharagh in his lap, ready at a moment's notice but not overtly threatening.

First to enter the glade were two of Briacs hounds, barking loudly but not fully understanding what the excitement was about. Too excited to greet Ulmar, the hounds ran around the glade mostly terrifying the goats.

Then Vroth, Hild and Greldir entered the glade followed by the two children.

Of course it had to be hot-headed Vroth. The pockmarked man held no claim of vengeance against Ulmar, but he had no love for him either. This was a man that had single handedly started no more than two wars with their neighbors simply by being obnoxious.

-"Welcome kinsmen. I come as called."

The three warriors didn't relax at the sight of him. Ulmar understood that he had to do something to break the tension, or risk goading Vroth into doing something rash. As he was moving towards telling the trio a joke Vroth preceded him, of course letting his temper get the better of him.

-"You left the goats for this?" He bellowed at the now cowering boys. "I'll have your ears!"

As the man raised his fist and stepped towards the two boys, Ulmar felt rage boil in his gut. More reacting than acting he stood up menacingly and proclaimed;

-"Vroth! You scar those boys and I'll thrash you."

Vroth froze in his tracks. Something between fear and bewilderment rippled across him.

-"The fools left the herd."

-"Better they leave the herd and warn the hold, than be gutted by raiders for the sake of pride."

Ulmar half agreed with Vroth, the boys had acted foolishly, but he wouldn't see them harmed.

-"Spoken like one who doesn't need to tend to the herds. Too few animals survived when the white wolf spread frost across the world. To lose this herd to childish foolishness would bring starvation to the hold."

-"They understand that they would have starved. My warning stands."

Ulmar detested that he had so swiftly been forced into a confrontation with his kin. Now it was all too late to hesitate. Vroth would certainly risk going too far disciplining the boys, but this was about something more than concern for their safety. Ulmar wouldn't back down. He couldn't.

He wondered how the other two would react. He mostly saw them fuzzily in the background.

It seemed as if Greldir was unsure how to react, fidgeting. Hild was as likely to help him as she was to join Vroth. So they stood there, Vroth and Ulmar, neither willing to back down and neither ready to take the first swing.

-"Seems like he means it Vroth," Hild said in a hushed voice, "I'm not going to try to stop you from challenging him, but you'd be a gelded fool to go up against the Doomwolf. Do what you will, but I'm not dragging your stupid corpse to the hold. Die, and I'll leave you for the ravens."

-"Besides, Briac has called for me."

At Ulmars statement Vroth nodded ever so slowly, not breaking his gaze. There was a way out now and a glimmer in the corner of Vroths eyes told Ulmar that he'd accepted it.

Vroth started backing away, not turning his back to him till they a good bit past the glade. Mostly communicating through body language and vague gestures, the warriors had wordlessly decided to escort Ulmar to the hold. The situation was somewhat diffused but he gained another enemy, and for what? A dozen goats and the hides of two craven boys.

Looking at their shamed and grateful faces, Ulmar knew he might have come to blows with Vroth and never regretted his choice, even for a single moment. He followed the trio, and left the bleating flock of goats behind him.

3.

The outer buildings had not weathered the winter well. As Ulmar was led up the soft slope of the hill he could study their condition quite closely. The rough square storage shed he'd helped build as a boy was sagging over the ridge. A crack in the beam gossiped that the heavy snow had damaged the roof as surely as if the white wolf had stepped on it and in a way he had. The new chicken coop that had once been a curse for the clan to build, lay abandoned and rotting. Maybe it was for the best - Ulmar wasn't completely convinced the blasted construction wasn't cursed, and yet it was a shame to see it in its current state.

All around him, people that mere moments ago were deep in chores, now stared at him whispering that the Doomwolf had returned home.

Eldrig, Krat, Volda, Hethweg, Yldra, Bolbata, Ulfwu and Nenneth, were all staring at him in a mix of fear and adulation. Some abandoned their chores, following the trio of warriors that plowed through the forest of curious kinsmen.Though, some familiar faces were missing, as Dasra and old man Hod were nowhere to be seen. By all rights they should have been basking in the sun. They passed Hods' timeworn bench, which was empty of any sign that the wrinkled half blind man had claimed it from winters' hold. There should be half worked wicker, cloths, whittling and the odd assortment of bric-a-brac gathered all around the bench.

Collecting his wits for what was ahead, Ulmar raised his gaze and took in the impressive sight of the Hall of Tuakk. The height of several stout men, and the towering form of the hall was a constant reminder of what the True Folk should be. Aged timber shaped its frame into a triple archway whispering of a time long past, when the people of the hills mastered skills now long forgotten. Its supporting pillars, every single one having the girth of a stout man, were chiseled with shapes and creatures from the clans long past. A gate that three men could enter shoulder to shoulder, stood ajar letting in the cold fresh wind and stoking the fire-pit in its midst. The few warriors that had been sharpening their skills on the mustering field now flocked to the door awaiting the trio.

Without hesitation they led him into the dim hall and straight to the seat of the chieftain.

There he sat, Briac, Chieftain of the Tuakk, Ulmars uncle. Haunched on the decorated seat was the large balding man surrounded by his hounds and even posed much like he was when Ulmar left for his little neighboring valley. Briacs' famously massive red beard was braided into a single plait and decorated with rings of detailed silver matching the descriptions Ulmar had heard of the men from within the mountains. The man still had silver streaks veining across his temples just as Ulmar remembered, the only sign that the chieftain was aging was a sunken look around his eyes.

Wanting to get things over with, Ulmar stepped towards his uncle stopping two arm lengths from him and proclaimed,

-"Chieftan Briac, I, Ulmar of the Tuakk have heard the call and heeded your summons. What does the clan need of me?"

Briac sat up, straightening his back, and seemingly growing in stature, he tilted his head and smiled a crocodile smile.

-"Welcome Ulmar of the Tuakk, to the hall of your kin. Your presence has been missed this long winter. The clan needs all of its able bodied members in these trying times. As chieftain I grant you the rights of your blood, to retake your place in the hold as one of its warriors."

Ulmar sincerely doubted that Briac had missed him. His blade maybe, but in the midst of winter a warrior was a costly mouth to feed.

-"Show me then, to whatever chores need doing. My back is as strong as it was before the snow fell."

Briac shook his head slowly, producing a faint clinking sound from the silver rings in his beard. Taking the time to pat one of his hounds he then continued:

-"I have much greater things to ask of you than the strength of your back, kinsman. Long has there been bad blood between the Tuakk and the Marrodar", at the mention of the blood enemies, there was upset muttering and hissing from the assembled clansmen which was swiftly hushed by a lazy hand gesture from the chieftain.

-"This has gone on long enough. The wolven ones have been hard on the people of the hills, no matter what blood runs in their veins. Once there was peace between our people, we even called each other friends, and now, the time has come to retie our bonds.You Ulmar will be there at my side when we speak with the Marrodar. I require your voice and your strength in these matters, so now I ask you, does your blood still run thick?"

Ulmar might have been told by Hild that the chieftain was going to discuss peace with the Marrodar, but even hearing Briacs own words, he had a hard time believing it. An actual end to conflict was unusual. Most often peace between the True folk was mostly because the warring factions focused on other matters.

-"It runs thick and my heart still beats for the Tuakk."

At the sound of Ulmars declaration of fealty, his kinsmen cheered. He couldn't help wondering what Briac hadn't told him. There was a glint of secrecy to the older mans' eyes making Ulmar very uncomfortable. Yet he wouldn't pass the opportunity of actually putting a stop to a conflict, and it wasn't as if he would have broken his bond to his kin anyway. Though, uncertainty still itched in him.

-"Now that that is over, let's discuss details uncle."

Briacs nostrils flared slightly as his lips kept smiling. Ulmar knew how much Briac detested being reminded of their bond in public. There was more, though.

-"Later, later. There are times for details, and there are times for feasting and tonight we feast."

Yet again the hold broke out in cheers. Ulmar guessed that the hold hadn't seen a good feast since the midwinter solstice, nor a good meal since that very same feast. He knew he wouldn't be able to pry any details out of Briac. Besides, there was much to do before the feast. When it had started he would count on strong drink and late night bragging to work in his favour.

4.

The people of the hold were quick to make use of a pair of strong and willing arms. It didn't take long before he was emptying the crumbling storage one back-breakingly heavy load at a time. It was dirty work in the dark and dank building, but it wasn't without its benefits. He chose to help there so he'd get close to Volda. During their childhood, Volda had been closest to him in age and something of a friend to him, but more importantly he knew that she had always been enamoured with him. When they had been young, they had been engaged to be wed for two long years before the would-be engagement was finalized. Time had passed, Volda had wed Rohad though he disappeared never to be seen several winters ago while Ulmar had never had a wife. Volda was now wed to Vroth, an unfortunate situation which he was almost tempted to use to sow misfortune into the man's life, if it weren't for the fact that misery would spill onto Volda as well. Now they were working busily side by side without speaking to each other except for short instructions.

In the murky building he studied her from the corner of his eye. Voldas body language was stiff, nervous. She rose from her crouching stance, straightened her back and shook thick dust from her hair. She stared at him, not knowing that he was studying her every move.

Hethweg was still stubbornly hovering close by, frustrating his efforts to have a lone moment with Volda. Maybe the stern woman was worried that he was scheming, she was close to Vroth or maybe she wanted to keep Briacs secrets. Fate would have it though, that he would get his way.

A great while into their work Maulagh showed up at the threshold with news of rot amongst Hethwegs riding equipment. Water had somehow seeped through to her gear, warping her saddle and destroying several reins. Anxious to assess the damages as soon as possible, Hethweg rushed out of the storage in a huff leaving Ulmar and Volda to their own devices.

Volda fidgeted with a couple of sacks and blushed intensely.

-"I heard winter has been hard." Ulmar stated matter of factly.

Volda nodded.

-"Winter is always hard. There is no mercy in a wolf's jaw."

-"From what I've seen, this winter has been harder than any has been for many years."

Volda met his eyes for the first time.

-"What have you heard?"

-"It's not what I've heard, I have eyes. Houses cracked and thin kin. Few animals and missing faces." Ulmar put a hand on her shoulder, and mustered sympathy in his voice. "Tell me all about it."

Sighing, Volda kept her hands busy with the sacks and focused on the task. It seemed as though she wasn't going to tell Ulmar anything more before she cleared her throat and started speaking in a monotone voice.

-"I wouldn't say you've been spared from our plight by the look of things. Your clothes droop and your eyes sag, and it cuts into me like a knife to see you this way. This winter might have been more merciful for a lot of us if it had come as a single vicious cut across the throat. By the first moon it was apparent the white wolf was hunting us with reckless abandon. The snow fell so thick that any who left the hall risked losing their way even an arms length from the threshold. Hail smattered in the crib of winter and then, the frost of the white wolf's breath was so strong that icicles almost touched the flames of our fire. We had to burn what we could spare in the hall and some that we couldn't.

I still wonder what curse brought us the ire of the wolves this winter. Some ill deed done by us must have spurned them to feed on the clan. Some wronged soul must have put them on our scent.

The food gathered turned out to be vastly too little for what was to come, a lot of what grain and greens we had was spoiled by moisture seeping into the stores. Had the white wolf stayed away for another week things might have been different. To look to what the mind can imagine could have been is folly and I have no use for folly. We can only live with what we are faced with and this was our lot.

As the white wolf howled in the wind gushing snow over the world his dark brother sneaked across our threshold. The animals caught that plague first, dropping weak and sweating to the floor. Many died, only adding to misery. Then the wolf stalked the children. Nightmares gripped them, then fever burned them. Sol, and Dagni, both stolen away long before midwinter. The nightmares spread among us, and with them, the fever. Not one was left unscathed. I was lucky, I was only stalked by the demon beast for a single week. Dasra was old and could not keep away from the wolf, he hunted her till her heart simply gave up. Yldra lost her child under the new moon just before midwinter, had Kallabra not been quick at our threshold we would have lost her too.

Three clear days was the respite that allowed us to survive this winter. As promised by Kallabra as she stood with Yldras blood all over her hands, the weather cleared for three days just after midwinter. We took the time to store the dead and forage what we could. We didn't find much but it was enough to keep us a while longer.

There are no horses left in the hold. Our lives will be that much harder without Homneth and Thilla. Their death meant many days of life for the rest of us.

There's been no joy this winter. I thought it would be the last winter of the world, that the white wolf had finally sunk the world in the endless winter and his brother had swallowed the sun. I'm glad I was wrong."

Ulmar let her story sink in. Seemed that he wasn't the only one the black wolf had stalked that winter.

-"Where is Hod?"

Volda clenched her jaw, as he insisted while not trying to sound all too pushy.

-Volda, where is old man Hod?"

She turned away from him disguising her feelings with the pretense of hanging sacks on hooks.

-"He walked out into the snows."

Ulmar tensed, a knot forming in his stomach. Truly the Hold had suffered but Hods' disappearance meant that Briac had condemned the old man to death.

-"I know what you're thinking Ulmar, I wish you wouldn't. Hod walked out of the Hold of his own free will. I'm not going to pretend that Briac didn't make it clear that he was a weight on the Holds resources, but he didn't force him. It was Hods' own choice."

-"And Kallabra? Does the bone woman still live?"

Volda seemed only too happy to change the subject, her words were spoken more or less before Ulmar was finished with his.

-"Alive and well, or well enough at least. Who knows what devils or demons she summons to keep her feet planted on mortal soil. She's older, frailer, but she survived without us in her little house. It's a shame she can't teach us more of her ways because she seems to have fared better than all the rest of us."

-"No raids then?" Ulmar was pretty sure of the answer, but had a hard time imagining the good fortune that a Hold that cursed wouldn't be picked off by man or monster.

Volda shook her head.

-"No. There at least is a ray of light. What manner of beast could have survived the ravishes of both wolves? No, would there have been I doubt we could have survived. Though there might be something new out there. I could swear that I heard the howls of some unknown beast during the dark nights."

5.

-"On this eve we cast off the chains of winter. These have been dark times for the Tuakk but as the sun grows brighter so does the future of our clan.

Heralding this new dawn, we welcome back Ulmar of the Tuakk, who will lend his strength to our efforts. Fear not, for I have a plan that we will together fulfill great deeds the next coming days. Raise your horns for the glory of the clan, Tuakk!"

Paired with Hild, Ulmar raised his chipped drinking horn in a ceremonial toast. They looked each other deeply in the eyes and much was said without words in that moment. Hild wasn't content with things but the look she gave him almost dared him to make some sort of challenge.

She was still unflinching in her loyalty to Briac, and she would fight Ulmar in a heartbeat if it came to it.

As he drank deeply from the horn, he wondered if everyone had a soul like Hild in their life, someone you would just as easily gladly die beside in hopeless battle, as have as a mortal enemy till the day you died.

-"And to fallen kin."

Stone-faced, Briac poured the rest of the content of his silvered horn out, upon the floor in honor of those that didn't make it through the winter. At least he admits that much, Ulmar thought bitterly. He still had many questions for his chieftain, and was itching to confront him.

His horn was swiftly refilled by the bogvale boy who scuttled back into the background as soon as his chore was done.

Ulmar glanced over to Briac and Hild, postured almost like a threatening bear in front of him.

Ulmar tried not to make a face as he took another deep swig of the content of his horn. It wasn't the sweet mead that it should have been but ale so watered-down that it was more akin to stale water. No one would be losing their head to drink this evening.

The diminutive Bogvale boy served them their helping of food from a great tray. Ulmar couldn't help feeling outright sadness about the contents of the promised feast. One of the goats, a goat which he had only a few hours ago patted, had paid with its life to feed them. The animal was garnished with so much ground bark that even the strong taste of licklatter root couldn't hide it. Smiling happily at the boy, he took a bite and was dismayed to feel the taste of ground bone in the mix. The Hold was basically sustaining itself on bark and bone. If he hadn't understood how dire things were, this would definitely divulge it.

Keeping to their tradition of sharing few words, Ulmar focused on shoveling down his helping over talking to Hild.

Getting up after he had fed himself, Briac immediately gestured for him to be seated again. Hammering the pommel of his dagger against the table, he started reciting the chronicle of the True Folk in a deep rhythmic voice.

-"We are the True Folk, to us was given the heritage of the world."

-"We are the True Folk", the hold answered ritualistically. Briac had invoked the ancient retelling of the history of the people of the hills. It was long since the tale had been told in the Hold of the Tuakk. Last it had been, was last summer, when a travelling skald had recited the length of the tale in such a clear and compelling manner, that he might just as easily have burned pride into their hearts. It had been an inspiring rendition, from which most in the hold had grasped pieces of the tale and made it their own, bearing a striking resemblance to how he felt that they as a people were grasping at a past that was slipping through their fingers like fine sand.

It was custom to recite the tale of their people, the chronicle of the True men at least at a feast at every full moon. Even that was slipping through their fingers.

Now that Briac had invoked the tradition, Ulmar could not interrupt him until he had told as much as he chose to. Maybe it was a way to keep Ulmar from confronting him, but there seemed to be more at stake here. The hall was full of attentive kinsmen eager to listen to Briacs words and relive history. He saw in them, a clan that was inspired instead of a flock of tattered souls. So Ulmar listened, he listened when the chieftain recited the song of glory, the song of the fall of the great throne, the breaking of the world and the long march to the hills. He spoke of heroes whose names were long forgotten, of Chethondre the keeper of the words and High King Trimboldumn, The Bearfaced One.

According to tradition there had been a time when the people of the hills thrived. They had built a great kingdom that stretched between the two seas, and the word of man had been the law of the land.

Ulmar wondered if that really was true. He knew of many signs that the hill clans had long forgotten. There were ancient ruins carved in thick stone that tools would not chip. There were rings and amulets, forged in metals none among the true men could name. There were a handful of scrolls written in a tongue long forgotten.

He sighed and listened to his uncle passionately uphold the revered oral tradition of the true men, and dreamt of an ancient time when his kin had ruled the world.

6.

It was late night when the hold was finally done rebonding with their past. Most had withdrawn to their beds, while some of the kinsmen had simply slumped in their seats at the table.

Hild had stubbornly fought sleep but had just lost and was snoring ever so softly, her chin lightly resting against her chest. With the smooth movements of a mountain lion stalking its prey, Ulmar got slowly to his feet and walked over to Briac who was abstractedly stoking the embers of a ashen log.

-"I figured you were going to seek me out."

Ulmar crossed his arms and growled more than whispered.

-"I figured you were trying to avoid that. "

Briac smiled a wolfish smile.

-"You have always been more soft of heart than hard of head, you can't blame me for that boy. Sometimes you need to let a blaze burn hot before there is anything to be done about it."

-"Watch your words, uncle. You may be chieftain, but you are not beyond reproach."

Ulmar wondered if he had gone too far as the older man gave a hard chuckle.

-"No son of my brother, you watch yours. You may be an ill omen with an unstoppable blade, but I will not run from you with my tail between my legs. I could banter and bawl threats but let us instead cut to the heart of the issue. You feel righteous disdain over Hods fate, it moves you to action. If you had been here, you could see just how laughable that is. Did you have a hard winter in your fox den? If you think you did, I can promise you that ours was worse. I didn't force him. He understood his time was past. He was a burden to the clan, and in our time of need he did what countless of our elders have done before him. Don't you dare question his sacrifice."

-"I wonder if you will be as brave when the burden of time breaks you?"

-"I doubt you will be alive to see it, Doomwolf. Those who are will sing songs to the manner I made my passing. "

Briac stretched out his hand and held Ulmars clenched fist in something half restraint and half gesture of affection.

-"Ulmar of the Tuakk, don't lose yourself in the past. It was his choice, you know you cannot argue it. Help your kin instead. You must see how desperate things truly are. Follow me and I can give the children of the clan a future beyond that of the next winter not to speak of the here and now."

Ulmar crouched down before his chieftain, he was still pained by the fate of the old man, but these were the ways of these harsh lands. This was something he had never been able to accept and truly thought he never would.

-"Then tell me. What is your plan? What am I to do?"

-"I intend to cease war with the Marrodar. I need you there as my right-hand as I negotiate with them. No longer will we claim death by the right of blood. The killings must stop, for both our bloodlines. I know how you detest the feuding, so help me stop them."

-"So I am to speak by your side?"

-"You are feared and venerated by the clans of the true people. Do not be surprised if your name has carried all the way to the sea and the cities of the muck-dwelling lowlanders. With you by my side I can be given the time to talk with them. With you by my side I can promise you that I can break the cycle of death."

It was a strange thing to hear the traditionalist Briac propose something Ulmar had longed for over the course of several long years. It was an opportunity too precious to pass up.

-"So when do we leave?"

-"Tomorrow. Get what sleep you can, we need to be on our way shortly after dawn."

Ulmar nodded, leaving for his bed. Somewhere out in the wilds of a nearby valley something large, ferocious and new roared its defiance to the oncoming dawn making the hounds at Briacs' feet whine, disturbed in their sleep.

7.

Seven of the Tuakk were to meet seven of the Marrodar in the Dell of Turundar. Vroth argued that the Tuakk should muster all their warriors and hide all but seven a shout from the meeting place. Briac was inclined to agree with him, before Ulmar put his foot down. It would be a poor olive branch indeed, to prepare to betray the trust of their would-be allies.

He and Briac were a given, and Hild was a universally accepted choice to go on the journey. Ulmar refused Vroth which meant that Volda was out of the running. Briac insisted on Hethweg and Greldir. The other choices were Krat and Bolbata.

Before they could leave, the gathered warriors were to visit Kallabra, the bone-woman.

On the very edge of the hold, in a crooked building that was a little farther away from any building was to the other lived the revered and feared bonewoman. Kallabra was the oldest member of the Tuakk by a decade or more. The shriveled woman was a sharer of wisdom to any who would visit her to gain it. As a counselor, she had averted many social catastrophes, as a midwife she had saved many of the Holds women and children. But it was as the Seer, the layer of bones, that she retained her status.

The gift of seers' sight was a useful one for the Hold, which had helped them avert many disasters, but any delving into the arcane, however useful, was treated with a great measure of apprehension among the true folk.

What manner of unnatural powers had the woman at her disposal? What horrible lord of the unknown had empowered her? What curse strengthened her?

Images of the eating of stillborn children, and the stealing of the strength of warriors flashed before Ulmars eyes as he studied the strange fetishes that hung from the rafters of the building.

At the same time Kallabra had never been anything but kind and helpful towards Ulmar, even if he was uncomfortable around her. There was no procrastinating the matter, with a knot in his stomach he opened the door and stepped over the threshold.

The single room of the building was dim and smelt of spicy smoke. Ancient utensils were strewn around as if a giant chicken had picked them up and discarded them at random.

Kallabra, strange and powerful, was crouched like a crow in front of the fire. Muttering to herself she was doing her best to ladle some broth-like liquid from a small pot into a ceramic bowl.

Avoiding the bones hanging in rough twine hanging in seemingly random locations, Ulmar carefully approached the fire and sat down cross legged. Winter had not been too kind to the old woman either. Her skin was thin as the wing of a dragonfly. It was wrinkled and sagging and the bright fire that used to shine in her eyes was a cooling ember.

-"I know, I know, but not yet..." The bone-woman cooed. Ulmar raised his eyebrow, unsure of what to ask her when she raised her head, stared him directly in his eyes and leered.

-"You were wondering if my mind was gone and if death was near."

Taken aback Ulmar just muttered, "Not really, well almost."

-"No?" She croned, "It used to be that they'd gasp and say something like, *"how did you know that"*, it seems I've really lost my touch, at last."

Saddened, she shook her head quickly moving into action as she realized she was spilling the liquid into the fire. Kallabra put away the half empty bowl, shook her hand dry, scooped up more liquid in a second bowl and motioned it toward Ulmar.

-"Soup?"

A little hungry Ulmar accepted the bowl and responded in a jest.

-"Is it magic soup?"

-"Oh yes", she nodded seriously, "it will keep you from starving if you eat it regularly. There's great magic in that!"

It was a strange thing, he reflected as he tasted what seemed to be some kind of mild broth, that he could be so intimidated by the old womans' powers, and yet have such playful jargon with her. He couldn't help smiling broadly. She in turn, smiled a toothless smile back at him.

-"You have always been such a good soul. Others would see it as well, if you weren't carrying the cursed circumstances of your birth. You are as little to blame as a child born with a cloven tongue or crippled arm. I'm happy to see you again and I know you have questions, so just do an old woman a favor and let her ramble on for a while."

Ulmar nodded ever so softly.

-"Good, good. It's good that we two, the stormcrows, should have the chance to reacquaint ourselves again. You know it's not often I just get to talk. Sure, they fetch me to ease their pains and ask me their fate, but to talk? No. They ask a question and I answer, that's as far as that will go. So speak with me for a short while. How is Ulmar doing this fine day in early spring?"

Ulmar cleared his throat.

-"I came yesterday on the summons of..."

-"No, no, no," The old woman reproached him, "all duty and weighty news. You young people are given a forest of days, yet have no idea how to use them. I know all of Briacs spiderwebs. There will be time for heavy words and sorrow, but joy, ah, you need to make room for joy or it'll flutter and flee. So tell me, young one, of some happy thing."

Ulmar stroked his beard for a while trying to decide on some ray of light to share with the old woman.

-"Spring is finally here. I don't know if you've been out much, but the sun has been quite kind the last few days while I've been sitting in front of the house. That's when I noticed a pair of Greysocks that are nesting, down by the creek. Most would call them grey and dull, but that's for people who have no wit or patience. When they fly close I sit still, not moving a muscle and it's then that they sing. And how they sing! Never have I heard any voice so free nor dance as lively. They weave through the air voicing their love for each other and for the waking land."

Ulmar then told the old woman about the hum of the first bees, the colors of the sunrise and the smell of a world being reborn from under the snow. He told her of his little peaceful valley and what he had created there and found himself to be much more content.

As he spoke, she smiled and chuckled, not at all the frightening spellcaster to be feared but an old woman with a good heart.

Light of spirit and carrying an honest smile, the old lady gripped his hands softly.

-"I'm sorry to cut our time short but you came with a question in your heart and you need an answer before you set off."

Kallabra let go of his hands ,and moved to get a heavy skin that was inscribed with thin, sprawling mystical symbols. With a wide swoop she placed the mat by the fire, moving all the hanging bones with a rush of air. Smoke from the fire spríralled and danced as the old woman muttered some strange incantation. Next, she grabbed a deep skin bag which she started shaking rhythmically, matching her chant. With the quickness of a striking snake she thrust her hand into the bag and strew out a number of rune inscribed bone amulets.

Quietly settling into a rapt focus, Kallabra crouched down and studied the runes.

Ulmar crept in front of her, fascinated and apprehensive about the many colored bone pieces.

-"Tell me, what news of our undertaking?"

With a sharp intake of breath Kallabra shushed him. Gliding her hand over the bones the old womans' mutterings had a harsh edge. Wind crept in around them, keeping the bones banging into each other.

-"You ask the wrong questions. I see you walk in the shadow of the king, bent to his will but that is only the beginning. Here," she said jabbing at a sharp s-like rune drawn white on a charred bone, "See here, this is the lightning rune. I see lightning and thunder, change. What you think is only mist before your eyes. I see you follow the steps of an apprentice of the man-made mountain. There is danger and battle, it has always been your path and always will be, but there is..."

The old woman froze with a look of surprise carved into her slender features. For a moment Ulmar almost thought that time had stopped before she blinked. Lodged firmly between her crooked thumb and forefinger she was grasping a single white tile depicting a blazing yellow sun. A single ray of light shone in on her hand from a gap in the ceiling creating the illusion that it was glowing brightly. Kallabra strook her hand affectionately across his chin and smiled.

-"I will tell no more futures. Your glimpse is the last. Now go and bend the world after your will."

Confused yet wanting to put on a straight face Ulmar stepped out of the bone-womans' house. At a respectful distance, Briac and the warriors waited for him silently. When he didn't say anything Briac simply barked,

-"Well? What did she tell you?"

Not wanting to share anything, he raised Kharagh towards the heavens and looked confident.

The warriors raised their own weapons in response and bellowed a short battlecry, then set off. Briac seemed to hesitate a moment, Ulmar could see his uncles' mind roll into motion, weighing Ulmars response then he set forth to catch up.

Hild waited for him. He tried not to look at her, for fear of being read by the taciturn warrior.

-"No." He simply stated to her. In this case, meaning he wasn't going to share the old womans' words with her. She squinted her eyes slightly and stared at him inscrutably, all the way down to the outer buildings.

-"Do you know what she told me? " Greldir, the youngest of the warriors, asked while walking backwards facing Ulmar and Hild.

-"She said that if I don't watch my step Vroth will kill me with an arrow! Have you heard how daft that is? I think the crazy bat's gone into second childhood."

-"Knowing you", Hethweg growled, stopping to pull his bushy sideburn so that only shock kept him from awkwardly dropping his vicious war club, "You probably deserved it."

Hethweg let go of Greldirs' hair, slapped his ass and joined the other warriors in a hearty laugh at the young ones' expense. Even Hild chuckled.

Ulmar on the other hand, was staring at Hods empty bench which they were now passing. With a dull rage in the pit of his stomach, he committed the benches lines to memory, trying to keep the image of old man Hod as clear as midnight ice.

None of the residents of the Hold followed them to the outskirts of the valley on strict orders of the chieftain. He had explained to them that enough time was wasted and if they weren't intending to starve while he paved the way for their salvation, they'd better work hard every waking hour. Trying to give the clansmen every thinkable advantage, he had left his hounds to help with the hunting. As the small company stood looking back at the hold he could see that his uncle already missed the hounds, something he'd never admit.

8.

The way to the Dell of Turundar was like most travels in the hills - a perilous one. Only a day or so away if a man was in a hurry, it wasn't so much about the distance but the weather and what dangers lurked in the valleys between the Hold of the Tuakk and the dell. Walking along the open path running from their valley, they were debating what road to take.

-"We should walk the wide valley and camp in one of the passes to some of the other valleys when night falls, like the entry to Red Mist or Dead Man's Rising.We'll be able to see danger from afar and have a defendable position at night."

Briac swung his great mace, testing it against the wind or imagined enemies. Ulmar cringed at the thought of trooping down the open, soft earth of the wide valley. He cursed that Hild and Krat were scouting ahead, too far to have a say in the matter - he surely needed an ally in the debate against his uncle.

-"Walking the wide valley will leave us exposed to the horses of the Holumngar. If they find us on open ground, we'll feed the crows by nightfall. Not to mention the earth is ripe and soft for death delvers. Last Fall I saw their mounds litter the valley and you know they aren't keen to leave a rich hunting ground like that for a good long while," Ulmar motioned and snapped his hand imitating the murderous bite of the feared burrowing creatures.

-"Let's instead cut over the southern ridge into Five-Fingers and from there we head straight west following the rocky stream. Safe, subtle and will give us the advantage when getting into the Dell."

Briac huffed.

-"Slow. Too slow. We need to be there with only one nights rest. For that matter you aren't even counting in the castle of madmen that have fortified the ridge of FiveFingers. I'd rather risk something unlikely, than face the guarantee of getting shot at by those crackpots."

Ulmar growled internally. Briac was making a rash move journeying the wide valley this early in spring. Chances were, that the snow was completely melted in its midst which more or less guaranteed that there would be ravenous death delvers just awoken from the winters' slumber. The end of frost wasn't only a blessing.

-"We should all have a say in the matter", Ulmar challenged.

-"Why?" Briac snapped. "Do you see me as so weak a chieftain, that I should keep the council of the entire clan? I'd not walk that road with me, Doomwolf or not."

The mood in the small party grew instantly tense. Greldir looked openly worried and Hethweg gave Ulmar dark looks. Not a promising start, he thought to himself.

-"Then what do you say, warriors of the Tuakk? Will you trust the word of your chieftain?"

Briac motioned at Greldir, who muttered his allegiance and Hethweg, who stated a simple "always" in answer. Briac stepped in Ulmars way, making the younger man stop for a moment before they trudged on. This was the chieftains' way of asserting his rule Ulmar told himself, but in his mind that rule might very well be cut short.

Further ahead Hild and Krat waited at a distance to see which way the party would travel. Briac forcefully pointed towards the soft slope into the wide valley. Hild tilted her head then slowly nodded, Krat shook his head and laughed. Whatever he told Hild, Ulmar could only imagine that it wasn't polite. Ulmar cursed yet again that the two hadn't been part of their discussion.

As Ulmar expected, the wide valley was clear of most of Winter's snow. In its midst a cold brook ran thicker than he had expected with the smeltwater. From where they stood they could see for several miles. Nothing sinister could be seen as far as the eye could see, but among the hills of the true folk, danger had a way of creeping up on you due to its craggy nature and myriad of hills. He took in the sight, marveling at the view just enjoying the moment before setting off.

They descended into the wide valley, warily fully expecting enemies to burst out from everywhere,but nothing happened. Growing brazen, the group quickened their pace, driving the scouts to keep a speed well over their preferred trot. Briac strode on, the undisputed king of the valley while the warriors started chatting behind him. Greldir strolled up to Ulmar and in a infuriatingly taunting tone proclaimed,

-"So where are these dangers you promised us? Can't see I'm dodging death delvers or heavy cavalry or am I just missing some fine point that you see and I don't?"

The young man seemed so pleased with himself, that Ulmar didn't know if he wanted to joke with him or throttle him.

-"See there", Ulmar pointed over to an earthen mound like that of a giant mole. .

-"That's a death delver mound. That's where one of the beasts broke through the surface, probably hunting. I'll wager you my last meal in this world, that if we start poking around them, we'll find the bones of its kill half buried in the dirt. When they attack they break the surface so hard that whatever's stupid enough to walk it's territory never has a chance to react. Your last moment will be the toothy grin of one of those monsters snapping shut, shearing off limbs so it doesn't get into its mouth like when you shear the wool of a sheep."

Greldirs' cocky demeanor broke into a more paranoid gait. The young man tried hiding the wind seeping out of him faster than a broken bellows but to no avail. Ulmar, feeling slightly more testy than he should, kept on going, pointing the mounds out to Greldir as they walked on.

-"There's one, and there's another. I'll wager that we'll be able to count a hundred of them before we set up camp for the night."

The color had faded a bit from the young mans' face and was not any better when Ulmar grabbed him and pointed to a nearby mound where the cloven hoof of a deer stuck out of the soil. The mound, Ulmar observed, was disturbingly fresh. If they'd make it in one piece through the valley it would be a miracle.

-"Maybe you should start sneaking", Ulmar whispered to Greldir who tried his best to do just that while keeping to the tempo of the group. Ulmar gripped Kharagh in both hands and tried to watch out for signs of the beasts before it was too late.

Further on, Hild and Krat had stopped, waiting for the party on top of a flat slab of a boulder. Seeing them, the band of warriors grew wary and quiet. Ulmar and Briac crept up on the boulder as well, stopping at arms length from the scouts.

-"Danger?", Briac inquired.

Krat nodded, whispering softly in response.

-"Fresh signs of death delvers. Mounds not more than a day or two old, retchings piled in a few places along them, and blood.

The beasts would often vomit up things too poisonous or difficult to digest. These stinking cone-shaped piles, called retchings, were easy to date. A fresh Retching would be wet with the stomach juices of the beast and filled with almost identifiable chunks. After two days the strong juices would melt all but the hardiest materials into a snot-like blob. After five days, the retching would have dried out leaving a porous rocklike material that was overgrown with plant life at an extraordinary rate.

-"Did you see any of the beasts?"

-"No", Krat answered Briac and was quick to continue, "But they'll be here. We should move out of the valley and on to rockier ground as soon as possible."

Briac stroked his beard in contemplation.

-"They'll be sluggish now. We'd best move on quickly and quietly."

-"There's no such thing as a sluggish death delver and you know it", Krat objected, seeming to instantly regret contradicting the chieftain, "I'll do it if you deem it necessary, but I don't like it."

-"We've moved too far to turn back now. The sides are too steep to climb here and the other paths won't be without their own perils. We trust in fate and push on."

So they did at an excruciatingly slow pace flinching at every unexpected sound.

Bolbata joined Ulmar when they were at a respectable distance from Briac.

-"Just so you know I agreed with you from the start", she whispered, "walking the valley was madness. You did well to tell him so."

It is so like Bolbata, giving council after the fact, Ulmar thought to himself. The warrior was constantly whispering words of rebellion against anyone who took authority and never one to protest to that persons' face.

-"Shut up, before you lure one of them over here."

Not caring about the reprimand, she slipped off to Greldirs' side. She had said what she wanted so now she'd wait to reap her reward later.

The sun kept its journey across the sky as they inched through the valley. No new signs of the beasts were discovered making the band increasingly more relaxed. Ulmar was tired from the strain of vigilance, but refused to slip into complacency. He was looking straight at Hild as she raised her hand quickly. More reactive, than thinking, he lifted his hands and crouched. He could hear his pulse thumping in his ears and realised that he was on a large stretch of soft dirt. There was a sizable boulder fifty feet behind him and a smaller one only twenty feet in front of him. It was too far for comfort. Would the death delvers move to attack he might have three or five seconds to get to a boulder, if he was lucky. Slowly looking around with as little movement as possible he realised that the band had seen the warning and had stopped. Drifting up toward him like wail from a bad dream he heard the haunting lamentation of a single wild goat. By the tone of the animals bleating, he could hear its fear.

Not knowing what Hild had spotted, he stood there like a very vulnerable statue, listening to the frightened bleating. Moments passed like hours.

Slowly Hild crept up on a nearby boulder informing Ulmar by her action that his premonition had really come to pass. Standing where he was, it was only a matter of time before one of the lured monstrosities would feel him through the ground or even just accidentally stumble across him. He had to chance it. He tried putting his foot down and easing his weight ever so slightly on it. Still alive he moved another step. He managed three feet, five feet and when he was only ten feet away he started believing that he might just make it.

Then the dirt shifted subtly beneath him. It was like a movement in the earth, like a wave, when the death delver pushed through the soil underneath him, more swimming than digging. Any movement would reveal him to the hunter beneath him, if it didn't already understand that he was there.

His heart hammered so hard that he suspected that the beast must hear it. What should he do? One or two leaping bounds would take him to the side of the rock. He imagined himself making the run for it only to be buried in the rain of dirt from a pouncing death delver swiftly crushed in its maw.

He chose to stay put. Fighting every instinct in his belly, he tried telling himself that it hadn't found him yet. He started repeating it like a mantra, only hoping it was true.

The others seemed to have had a lot more luck, all of them atop cliffs and boulders, all of them staring at him where he stood more or less literally on top of one of the monsters. Sitting firmly atop the boulder he was aiming for, was Hethweg, calm and with a strange twinkle in her eye. Ulmar wondered if she'd actually help him if he tried to make a run for it. It wasn't hard for him to imagine him bounding towards the rock, stretching out his hand, meeting hers and feeling that she was purposefully letting him go, letting him fall to the death that lurked in the soft soil. Waiting an eternity of heartbeats, Ulmar took a large step toward her and then stopped. He felt a slight tremor in the soil, or he at least imagined that he could feel the thing twist, sensing him. Moving one nerve wracking step at a time he stood by the boulder. Hethweg extended her arm towards him and gripped his firmly, almost single handedly hoisting him off the ground. In safety on the rock he now saw that the twinkle in her eye was concern. Somewhat surprised, he sat down on the boulder and looked over to the scene that had initiated their predicament.

On a rocky outcropping about ninety feet from his own safe haven a terrified little goat was bleating and jumping to and fro. The face of the rock was splattered with red stains located directly over a fresh death delver mound. Just beneath the outcropping the dirt moved slightly revealing the extreme of a huge snout. With a mighty huff that sprayed the rock with a thin cloud of wet dirt the beast started sniffing the air. Backing away from the impending doom the goat stumbled to the furthest part of the rock. The warriors were spread across their relatively safety all rapt witnesses to the scene before them.

-"Why aren't they just leaping on top of the rock?"

Hethweg was right to wonder. Ulmar had seen one of the monsters leap over a boulder in a single mighty movement straight from the earth, snapping several goblins from their imagined safety. Clambering onto the rocks made the band harder targets and made it impossible for the beasts to attack them from under their feet, but they were far from safe. They had made an impossible situation into a dangerous yet survivable one.

-"I think they're using that one to lure in other prey."

-"Can they really do that? I didn't think they were smart enough for that."

Ulmar shrugged in answer before he realised that Hethweg wasn't even looking at him.

-"Maybe. If the thing really wanted to eat the goat all it needs' to do is to stretch itself out of the earth and snap its jaws around it."

Beyond any ability to do anything else other than wait they kept watching the scene in front of them. Every time the poor animal was quieting down, a death delver would spray the rock with dirt from its nostrils then disappear under the ground. The goat started to sway after a while and then lay panting on the stone surface apparently too exhausted to keep on its feet. The subterranean beast sprayed the rock several times in what had to be an attempt to keep it going. Annoyed that its lure wasn't performing its intended duty the beast pushed a large part of its maw overground and let out a bellowing roar. It was instantly rewarded with the panicked animal scurrying to its feet and bleating weakly.

-"Sard! We have to do something. Why hasn't Hild shot the damn goat by now? They'll leave if it quiets down."

Frustrated that Hild hadn't come to her conclusion, Hethweg started waving at Hild, trying to get her attention. It didn't take long before Hild had spotted the movement and Hethweg was motioning towards her to draw her great bow and shoot the animal. It was such a strange reaction but Ulmar couldn't help feeling for the terrified animal and just wasn't ready to see it die. He wasn't sure why but as Hild drew her bow Ulmar quickly picked a rock and hurled it a mere moment before Hild loosed her arrow. The rock nearly hit the animal, startling it into jumping, ruining the shot. As the goat was in the air, jumping far out into the dirt Ulmar had grabbed a second rock and sent it flying into the air and then a third. His rocks hit the now empty outcropping with sharp snapping crashes. The goat was on the ground, its feet a flurry of movement as it ran for its life. The death delver should have struck by now and for a moment it seemed like the animal would get away without incident. In the middle of a bound the earth opened and the massive jaws of a death delver opened at the animal. The death delver had a triangular snout and a massive body covered in armor like plates. Its four limbs were clutched to its side as it moved through the air. The hulking beast seemed to have made a miscalculation, as it very nearly missed the goat who was gliding down the delvers' body. Crashing down into the ground again the death delver fell flat while the goat seemed to be mustering energy from pure desperation as it outdistanced the deadly predator. Ulmar and the rest of the warriors were pushing themselves against the surface of their rocks trying to make themselves as small as possible to avoid detection. By the time that the death delver was on its stubby feat the goat was leaping up the rocky side of the slope of the valley quite obviously out of reach from the burrowing beast. Letting out a massive bellow of frustration the beast slid into the earth with three shuffles of its massive limbs in a way that would be natural for a water living animal moving through water but was an unbelievable sight when it came to an animal on land.

-"Fool!" Hethweg growled at him. "What were you thinking? You condemn us to death!"

-"Better it get away than kill it. Shooting it would have added more blood and likely attracted either death delvers or carrion eaters. This way the death delvers will be more inclined to move off in search of other prey."

He meant every word of what he said but wasn't inclined to share his first and strongest motive. There was too much death and suffering as it was.

-"You can only hope that Briac sees it your way, though I'm pretty sure he won't."

There was a threat in the air that Hethweg for some reason chose not to vocalize instead growing quiet for a while before asking.

-"So what now?"

-"Now we shut up and wait."

9.

The night came all too quickly and with it a nip of frost. The band was hard pressed in their exposed positions, and were feeling every shift in the breeze down into their spines. Any temptation to leave the safety of the rocks was quashed several times that night, when they could hear movements and grunts that could only be made by the monsters. Grudgingly, Ulmar and Hethweg crept close together for warmth. The woman muttered a "don't get any ideas" to him as they crept under the same fabric. The warmth and proximity of another human being was a very welcome boon after a winter alone. Though the smell of a human unbathed for an entire winter was a stunning experience that he could have done without. He could only suspect that his own bodily odor was just as pungent. There wouldn't have been any risk of Ulmar sharing his bed with her in lust even in any other circumstance, but with the monsters only feet away and the stench of their bodies any would-be heated thought was whipped from his mind.

The sun rose cold and almost white behind a veil of fog. The kind spring day was a pleasant memory that kept away from them now that they needed it. They stayed where they were all through the early morning, surveying the still ground around them. Stretching their legs the morning turned to noon and still none of them wanted to test their fates.

At last there wasn't any other choice than to try their luck.

Hild took the first step so slowly that if you weren't looking at her you'd have sworn she stood still. Her feet were now firmly on the ground and still nothing happened.

The others joined her on the uncertain security of the soft earth. Instead of moving as a troupe they spread out sneaking along the valley floor. Led by the scouts they moved up a far part of the valley till they found a passable place to climb the side of it.

Gathering in a rough circle on the windy ridge no one was keen on being the first to speak up. Briac had the hostile demeanor of a storm on a mountaintop, with all the thunderous rumbling of one as well.

-"We're all alive. Let's be off. We camp at the pass to Dead Mans' Rising before dark."

A smattering of agreeable mumblings followed the chieftains statement. It wasn't what Ulmar would have done, it wasn't something that Ulmar would have thought anyone would have chosen to do. The dead didn't rest easy in Dead Mans' Rising and Ulmar felt a pang of fear at the thought of getting dragged into some terrible pit of some burning hell by the restless dead. From what he could see of the others, they felt very much the same.

They travelled on the ridge, battered by the wind and lack of rest, pleased to be on rockier ground. From the ridge there was an unusually open far reaching view of the hill-lands. There was a clear view of several of the low valleys of the hill-lands, most of them covered by gnarled forests. Ulmar could also count the imposing silhouettes of maybe half a dozen castles along the higher ground of the hill-lands. Far on the horizon he could see the outlines of massive mountains, the strangely formed one known as "The Throne" the most prominent among them. Watching that huge and aptly named mountain, brought a chill along your spine.

A couple of times the band hid as the scouts ascertained possible dangers ahead of them. These parts were claimed by many, but controlled by none. By the look of things, Hild and Krat had both discovered several potential enemies along the route and steered the band clear of them. The spring had made all those who lived in the hills of the true folk restless.

10.

The pass to Dead Mans' Rising was located higher than the nearby surrounding valley and was littered with old campsites. They quickly brought together what dry wood they had gathered on their journey and lit a hearty fire. Usually travelling the wilderness meant trying to hide your fire from potential enemies, but here, fire was the first bulwark towards what awaited in the nearby valley. As the sky darkened cold mist started gathering beneath them in that very mentioned valley. Two at a time would keep watch, both facing Dead Mans' Rising and both tasked with never letting the fire die out. Ulmar was gathering what he could for a makeshift bed as Briac walked past telling him without any ritual that Ulmar would take the first watch because he needed him rested and clear of mind tomorrow. Typically the first watch was for the inexperienced or the sick. He didn't argue the fact, but was somewhat fuddled when he took his place at Greldirs' side.

The young man didn't take his eyes from the entrance to the valley for a single second, as he was whipped into a watchful fear. He shifted uncomfortably trying to get warm under his ragged cloak resting his wicked war-club over his shoulder.

-"Go get more wood boy before it gets too dark."

Greldir was only too quick to comply with Ulmars order, his shoulders visibly showing how thankful he was for getting away from their vigil with every step he took. Ulmar on the other hand was almost thankful that he had something specific to do. He sat down, weighing Kharagh in his arms and studied the entry to the cursed valley. There wasn't much to see, only a narrowing path leading to who knew what within. Unless it crept in the mist like an evil cat, nothing would be getting the drop on them. The stubborn wind was a nuisance but the relative safety of their position was worth the chill. After all, who would be so dumb as to be there except them. A fair number of the band was still awake bandying stories between them. He heard Hild curse Greldirs skittishness before he explained that it was Ulmars idea to send him for more wood. It seemed that Hild was expecting more trouble during the night, he pondered.

By the time the night was too dark to allow for hunting for fuel for the fire, Greldir retook his place at Ulmars side.

-"Have you seen them?"

-"Do you really expect that I'd keep it to myself?" Ulmar let enough disbelief into his voice to instill the lad with confidence but not so much that he might take offence.

Greldir shook beneath his cloak repositioning his wicked club over his shoulder.

-"I heard that Briac and Hethweg have seen them."

-"So have I. But not tonight"

The boy was clearly fishing. Better to keep him in an adventurous mood than instill him with too much fear. Ulmar was undecided what he felt about the lad, mostly that he was very, very young. Barely more than a child really. So, why not share some of his war-stories with him, it might even help Ulmar get a better perspective on things.

-"Some summers ago, just after the giants burnt the second hold of the Grimgallagh, we were out this way recapturing cattle from the Durhaadi. We had been ambushed by lowland brigands and our band was scattered. Most of us were fine, but we had to get out of the ambush and we moved to rally over in Five Fingers as we had agreed to, if something like that happened. Lowland scum might not be stout of heart, but they carry wicked crossbows and are often laden with armor. So me, Briac, Hethweg and Hild staggered our way out unchased thanks to Hilds bow. Briac had taken a wicked gash to the temple and it was only a matter of time before the scum would be trying to chase us down so we had no time to spare. Instead of running out into the open we trekked into the valley, better that, than to be ridden down. The day was bright in general, it wasn't even noon, but as soon as we entered the valley we were greeted with heavy mists. Somewhere further down I swore I saw a building of some sort but deciding on what it was was difficult owing to how it was kept hazy by the mist. So we pushed on trying to keep our bearings and our wits. It's like that all over there", Ulmar said, pointing generally in the direction in front of him, "hazy, cold, clammy and unnaturally quiet. So we pushed on further into that place like it was a world of its own. Someone was standing in front of us. Very quiet like, almost mistook him for a tree before I realised what I was looking at. Tattered and thinner than I remember him, it was Ourin of the Marrodar, the young lad that had tried besting Tothreg at running. I remembered his brown moss of hair and his silver buckle. I also remember how I had cut him dead when the Marrodar tried to box us in at Longtooth Gulch. He still carried the wound though his flesh was now more akin to dried meat, a deep cut in his chest that if he'd been breathing should be bubbling and spurting. By the look of his dried eyes he hadn't been breathing or any other thing akin to life since that eve. Imagine then, what it was for us to find him there and him moving against us. Hild was quick to do what she does, the arrow stuck through his skull like a horn sticking out through both ends. That's all that did, gave the damned boy a strange piece of jewelry. Didn't stop him walking up towards us."

Falling for the temptation of a storyteller Ulmar quieted and stared into the mists feeling a little less apprehension of the place.

-"What happened next?"

The young man's expression, at least what Ulmar could make out of it, was truly that of a child and not a full grown warrior. He lifted Kharagh for the younger warrior to see, the dark metal of the axe caught the soft light of the moon while the same light reflected on the silvery runes which almost glowed.

-"What do you think? I've never met a foe or fiend that Kharagh hasn't been able to fell. I cut the boy to ribbons. It's strange killing a man for the second time. So don't worry, if they come they'll share Ourins fate."

The young man snickered. Ulmar on the other hand was not relieved in the slightest. He was remembering that when they left the valley he could see Ourins parts move, almost like he was reassembling himself. If the dead truly came Ulmar didn't expect the gathered warriors to be able to do much except flee. Greldir didn't need to know that on the other hand.

11.

The dell of Turundar looked so peaceful from where they stood, on the top of the ridge. A true borderland, the dell was often used as a thoroughfare by travellers and the migrating clans tended to drive their cattle through it. It was relatively small, easily traversed in a matter of an hour, with steep sides that were covered with downy birch and a calm stream running through the bottom. What was unexpected was the rough log homestead that was erected by said stream. The structures were alien to the true folk way of building and could only mean that some of those insane lowlanders had tried claiming ancient True Folk land. Maybe they didn't know the customs of the land or didn't care, whatever the answer, the party of Tuakk warriors were less than thrilled to see it.

Ulmar wasn't overjoyed but wasn't against a new neighbor either. The lowlanders had no roots, no common sense, but also lacked the True Folk bitterness. Instead their hearts were filled with the impulse for naive adventure, a quality he couldn't help admiring.

-"They have to be there, where else would they be?"

Bolbata wasn't wrong in her statement. There was no sign of any Marrodar camp nor assembled warriors. Not a great sign when it came to a peace negotiation.

-"We'll scout the flanks and then give you the positions of the Marrodar as soon as we find them", Krat was moving away even as he spoke.

-"No", Ulmars' objection stopped the scout in his tracks, "We approach openly, without any pretense or trickery. These are supposed to be negotiations to end bloodshed and mistrust between our people. We cannot hold out one hand and grasp a dagger in the other."

Krat and the others looked to Briac. The chieftain nodded his agreement. Whatever misgivings the warriors had felt toward the decision they swallowed them.

They openly made for the small farmstead. Smoke from burnt birch greeted them from half way through the valley, implying that the buildings were indeed populated. Moving up to the small farmstead they started seeing small signs of violence. A broken gate, a cracked pot, scrapes and fresh cuts. Some baskets and household items were haphazardly strewn in front of the main building implying to the trained eye that it had been discreetly looted.

Ulmar felt a chill down his spine as he studied the signs.

Walking brazenly out of the main building came Schilti, warrior of the Marrodar, flanked by four Marrodar warriors. Tattooed, shaven heads with only knots and tufts of hair, the Marrodar were very different in appearance than the Tuakk. Schilti openly carried a massive sword of lowland design that he playfully tried in the air as the Tuakk approached.

-"Well, well", the man declared in his infamous hoarse whispering voice, "so the Tuakk deign to show up. We were half convinced this was some childish faint to draw us out for you to butcher us. Well met, Clan Tuakk."

The four warriors spread out like a fan at his side clutching a wicked assortment of arms, staring down the Tuakk with grim determination.

Briac stepped to the front of the band, confident while towering over the Marrodar warrior.

"-We came just as we told you we would. Now, where is Menw? We have much to discuss, he and I."

From the low birch forest, from three directions, Marrodar warriors emerged. Numbering more in the numbers of fifty instead of seven it was clear that the Marrodar had broken the promise of only bringing seven warriors to the meeting. The Tuakk band gathered behind their chieftain ready to defend him to the death. They were effectively surrounded. Ulmars kinsmen glared at him the little chance they got, it had been he that insisted on not bringing more warriors after all.

-"You can ask for Menw all you want, Tuakk dog, you now stand before Schilti son of Menw, chieftain of the Marrodar."

-"I share the sorrow of the passing of your father. He was a fierce and worthy foe."

Schiliti gestured to his warriors to fully surround their old enemies, tightening the noose.

-"Your words ring hollow old man. It's too bad that your going into childhood will cost the Tuakk their best warriors."

As Schilti started poised to let loose his warriors, Briac mostly raised his hand. When the older warrior hesitated, Schilti waited long enough to let Briac continue.

-"Do you fear me so much that you won't let me speak my piece? Has Marrodar blood become so watered down that you forsake the traditions of the True Folk?"

-"It's your death", the chieftain of the Marrodar shrugged, "if you want to drag it out by bandying insults then fine by me, we have all day."

Briac casually lumbered over to a log and sat down motioning to Schilti to do the same. The rival chieftain sat down, removed his helm and rubbed his scalp.

-"Winter has been hard on the world. You can't deny that the twin demon wolves have been snapping at the throats of the living, your people as well as mine. Once, the halls of the Tuakk were open to the people of the Marrodar as your halls were a safe haven for us. We feasted, hunted, battled and lived together. Our young fell in love and bound our people together through blood, something you surely can't deny?"

Schilti looked bored.

-"I don't deny ancient history, why would I? Is there a point to your rambling or are you just talking to keep your head a moment longer?"

Briac just smiled a cold smile at the younger man.

-"I wouldn't be so hasty. You've already proved craven when you brought a warband to a peace talk. Though it wouldn't surprise me that your father simply never taught you to count."

The younger man was getting up, ashen faced and angry before Briac growled a simple "sit down", which he amazingly did.

-"Yes you might be able to cut us down at a cost of half your warriors. Then the skalds will fill the hills with songs of your treachery. I have of course taken precautions by telling where we were going and what we were going to do. Then of course, you can listen to me and both our people will not only survive but we will thrive."

-"Weave your words then wyrmtongue. But stay your insults or face our wrath."

Briac didn't even bother looking intimidated, instead he leaned towards Schilti speaking softly so that only those nearest to the men could hear him.

-"I respected your father. I was hoping to meet him here so that he and I could do what we both planned to do on many occasions. Instead of bleeding ourselves against each other, I say that the Tuakk and the Marrodar renew their oaths of blood and set out together as brothers. With our numbers we can grasp that which we need from those that stand against us. There is food and treasure to be had a-plenty if you only are fierce enough to take it."

-What's in it for us?"

-"You mean, besides enough food to keep you until summer? Enough to grow fat instead of having the wolf at your door? How about glory and riches?"

-"You promise too much"

-"And I claim the right given to me by blood to lead the combined forces of the Tuakk and the Marrodar as their warchief," Briac claimed brazenly, "I hail from the union between Sindri Halfshield, the Marrodar warchief that slew the giant Sifsgam and of Oifa Deodach shieldmaiden of the Marrodar. Mine is a lineage of Kings and I challenge you Schilti son of Menw for the control of our forces as your distant kinsman as is our unbroken tradition among the true folk."

Apart from outraged gasps and mutterings there wasn't much of a response to Briacs challenge. Schilti seemed to be swaying to and from different emotions, mostly anger and amusement.

-"You boar-mating age-addled loon!" He managed to spit out, "what mare-ridden mushroom spawned nightmare makes you think that I'd just give in to you and give away our strength? It will be a dark day on the verge of the jaws of the wolves themselves, when mud-munching rantallions as you do anything other than die before true rulers of the hills as the Marrodar. I've had enough of this!"

Schilti raised his weapon and was on the verge of attacking when Ulmar roared into motion. He was furious at Briac. The older man had never intended to do anything other than dominate the Marrodar, to cow them into submission while taking advantage of someone else's misfortune to fill the bellies of the clan. He didn't know why he had expected anything else. More than that he realised that Briac had placed the fate of the entire clan on Ulmars shoulders. He knew what his uncle was planning. The Tuakk and the Marrodar would choose champions to fight it out and that was the only reason Ulmar was here. Finding the opportunity to vent his anger Ulmar snapped hold of the Marrodar chieftains throat and dragged him into a lethal hold in a flurry of motion. On the other hand he held Kharagh ready to brain the first adversary that came into striking distance. Clinging for life the human shield that was Schilti choked and flailed his arms in an attempt to hold back the Marrodar warriors. Roaring half in his prisoners' ear and half at the gathered warriors Ulmar boomed, "You will listen!" Briac had yet to raise his guard instead idling up next to the pair before exclaiming.

-"These are our ways and they are generous. If the Tuakk beat the Marrodar in battle at the hand of champions in single combat, we claim the right to lead you onward for riches and glory. If the Tuakk lose, the Tuakk yield their freedom and willingly become thralls to the Marrodar. Our property, our labor and our bodies will be yours to do with however you choose to use them."

Ulmar let go of Schilti letting him slump, coughing, to the ground. He was stunned to hear what his chieftain was betting. If Ulmar lost, his people would effectively cease to be.

-"We choose Karnae as our champion", the chieftain was still sitting on the ground coughing, his hoarse voices more so than ever. At the sound of his name a lean and muscular brute of a warrior stepped from the Marrodar ranks. His face was smeared ritually in what could only be blood, a cut on the root of his nose only enhancing his visage of brutality. As the chieftain continued he stood up unsteadily.

-"Son of Belwouda, son of Thrash, Karnae,The Bloody Handed has never been defeated. When the Holumngar rode against the Marrodar, he stood like a mountain in the face of their charges, breaking their lances with his mighty axe, Wusraad. When we raided the men of the lowlands, he bested giants in the size of the rocks he hurled against them. When fire flees and winter wins there Karnae stands unopposed. He is the warrior that singlehandedly slew the lowland scum that defiled this dell with their homestead and shoved their quartered remains into the latrine - to face him, is to face death."

Ulmar took in the orderly homestead and all its details that had been painstakingly and lovingly crafted. He imagined a family trying to claim a part of these savage lands, trying to bring peace and order where there had only been wilderness and hardship. Then he imagined the animal Karnae and what he had done to them. A cold fire burned in the bottom of his stomach. He might be furious at Briacs' machinations, but that was dwarfed in comparison to what he felt toward Karnae. The man was hoisting his rusted weapon in the air to the roaring approval of his comrades. He looked proud and ruthless yet as Ulmar focused on him with the heat of his rage Karnae wouldn't look at him.

-"The Tuakk choose Ulmar the Doomwolf!" The jubilant roars of the Marrodar were outmatched by the strength of Briacs' voice. The noise died down when the Tuakk chieftain introduced their champion. From their curious looks it was obvious that they had all heard of Ulmar.

-"Touched by the twin wolves themselves, no man can fell Briac in battle. No blade can cut him down, no club can crush him. This man survived when all others perished, even as a newborn infant he bested death. Follow him and you will be victorious, oppose him and be destroyed. In his hand he wields Kharagh, the blade that cannot be dulled or broken, heirloom of the age when our people ruled the world. The axe of the long gone kings whose names we have forgotten."

Briac stood before Schilti, who was only a breath away.

-"You are challenged, choose your terms."

-"To the death," Schilti exclaimed, touching his sore throat. "At the setting of the sun, the champions will fight and then we will toast our fate, whatever that may be."

As the terms were now set, the two forces moved to opposite sides of the homestead. Even with all the betrayal and treachery that was rampant in the hills of the True Folk, none but the worst oathbreakers would break an accord struck over a duel to the death. Any who did, risked to curse their people or to be haunted by restless spirits of vengeance. Sealing the oath, Briac and Schilti stayed in the middle of the battlefield each drawing a dagger and cut their forearm then they gripped the others forearm and shook trying to keep from getting too close to the other while they held open blades. The oath was now set in blood and all the stronger because of it.

Ulmar sat down on the stump the homesteaders had been using to cut wood, feeling his anger give way to exhaustion. Winter, sickness and a rough trip to the dell had left him at a definite disadvantage for the upcoming duel. The Tuakk gathered around him looking tired and miserable, all except Briac who looked all too excited. To maximise the chance of their champion they gathered their meager supplies and tried to have Ulmar eat and drink the best they had. The Marrodar were chanting on their side of the homestead, working themselves into a froth.

-"Can you do this? Greldir sounded frightened, "I don't want to become a slave."

Hild grabbed the boy by the scruff and unceremoniously asked him to shut up. None of the warriors wanted to consider the possibility that Ulmar could lose the duel ending his life and condemning them all to slavery. Briac, not addressing the fact that the boy had just been manhandled, put his arm around his shoulders.

-"Not to worry, he can't lose. You know how things are, it's just a matter of getting on with things."

Hild muttered and started rubbing Ulmars' stale shoulders and arms.

-"I hope he's right," she said, addressing Ulmar directly ,"You've gotten old and brittle over the winter, old man. No games, just cut him in size and be done with it."

Ulmar on the other hand was busy studying his opponent. Karnae was obviously heavily right handed but favored angling his left side toward what was facing him. The man had a quick way about him, however, he didn't seem all too bright. Ulmar was counting on the Marrodar champion being a little slow on the uptake as he sat there nurturing his anger at the man. The Marrodar might have been whipping the warrior into a frenzy, Ulmar reflected, but Karnae was no true berserker. He would tire from the excitement leaving him vulnerable to Ulmar, who was mostly keeping from getting cold and sluggish. Ulmar ate a little and awaited the setting of the sun.

There wasn't a lot of time until darkness fell. The warriors had lit torches in preparation for a lengthy battle.

The two men faced each other with their own brutal axe gripped firmly. There wasn't any bell or toll to start the battle, instead it started as soon as one of them made a move. Ulmar was crouching slightly, legs firmly placed and far apart. Karnae was huffing, preparing himself for a ferocious charge in an attempt to overwhelm Ulmar. It was easy to read the man as he lacked tact but Ulmar suspected that it would still be a tough battle that he wasn't sure he'd win. Ulmar was fine with his foe rushing in on him, it just opened up the opportunity of Karnae making a mistake.

-"Tell me then brother of the True Folk", Ulmar snarled, "Why did you kill the lowlanders that lived here?"

-"Why not slaughter the weak sheep that invade our lands? They were easy to kill Doomwolf, hardly a battle at all. Only the woman fought me, a pity because it meant that I had to kill her quickly. Her man wasn't a man at all, he started crying and begging for mercy in that vomit of a language they speak. He was more fun when I gelded him. Oh, how he screamed."

Using his story, Karnae rushed in, making a wide upward arching blow aimed at Ulmars groin. Expecting a dirty move like that Ulmar stepped into the blow, whacking the handles against each other and then delivering a nasty jab to Karnaes nose with his left fist. Reeling in pain, the Marrodar brute backed away while senselessly flailing with his axe. Blood flowed freely from the broken appendage, making him snort in frustration. Ulmar swung his axe in slow arcs, getting the feel of it, goading Karnae into attacking again.

-"If slaughtering those weaker than you is what you believe in, then you won't mind dying."

Antagonised, Karnae bellowed and charged in with a massive overhead blow that Ulmar dodged by the width of a strand of hair. By pure momentum, the charging man crashed straight into Ulmars side, knocking them both painfully off their feet.

The world spun as they rolled, kicking and screaming on the grassy ground. Summoning strength his body told him he didn't have, Ulmar got his feet onto the raging brutes chest and pushed. His legs stretched, Karnae flew through the air leaving only the pain of stretched muscles in his wake. Rolling on his side to get to his feet, Ulmar could feel that he had indeed wrenched or torn the muscles in his right leg, something that just might cost him his life. In a battle of the great axes among the lightly armored warriors in the hills of the True Folk you had to move quickly, or die. Ulmars hope to get to Karnae before he was back on his feet was instantly soured. Karnae was already leaping towards him with his axe in full swing. Blood was pouring from the mans' nose, his teeth were chipped and he wore the snarling grimace of a man lost to rage. Reacting more than thinking Ulmar ducked down under the blow catching his foes legs with his back and pushed upward. Karnae was flung uncontrollably into the side of the stump where Ulmar had just minutes ago prepared for his battle. Pained but not maimed, Karnae was already on his way back towards Ulmar. He should be feeling the same kind of unchecked rage, he should have been putting every shred of his essence into a mighty blow that would slay anything that came in his way, instead he felt tired but filled with a steely feeling of righteous injustice. He knew that if he kept letting Karnae swing at him, a blow would sooner or later carry through into his flesh. He had had enough of this duel. Measuring his blow, it must have looked like he was filled with casual indifference when Ulmar made a single quick blow to his adversary's axe head. With a metallic crack the head shattered like frail ice, leaving Karnae swinging an unbalanced club. Swinging around, Ulmar caught the onrushing man by the elbow, twisted and pushed simultaneously, disarming him and pushing him face down in the grass. Not wasting a single moment

Ulmar stomped his foot between the downed mans' shoulder blades and then let loose a single low blow. In his mind he was punishing the downed warrior, he longed to make him beg for mercy just like Karnae had done to the innocent homesteaders but no good would come of it. Instead he finished the fight by neatly decapitating his foe.

With the same quick brutality the fight had started, it was now over. Ulmars surroundings were now coming into focus again taking in the mournful outbursts of the Marrodar and the Tuakks triumphant yells. Not knowing if the Marrodar would attack them out of desperate rage, Ulmar took up a fierce battle stance glaring at the assembled Marrodar warriors.

 Schilti had dropped his weapon and drooped, crestfallen at what had happened before him.

-"No mortal man can fell the Doomwolf!" Briac stated loudly in a matter-of-fact tone. "It didn't have to come to this Marrodar, now yield and fulfill your promise."

Having Ulmar stand battle ready before them as a terrifying reminder of the fate of those who opposed the Tuakk couldn't have hurt their cause. No Marrodar dared meet his gaze, no challenges were issued.

-"We yield." Schiltis voice was hollow.

-"Good, then tonight we feast like brothers", Briac stated and laid his arm around the younger mans' shoulders.

"Now show me what in the way of food you recovered before we got here."

12.

It was a strange thing in Ulmars mind that those who had been enemies for generations were now to be expected to be comrades in arms. There was a sort of probing tenseness in the air as the two groups dissolved into one. Ulmar tried to hide his limp as he made for the stump and sat heavily down. He felt old and ragged. His leg pained him and he was both nauseated and hungry. Briac and Schilti were heading into the homestead side by side, the elder chieftain acting like there couldn't be plunged a dagger into his back at any moment. It was true that breaking an oath given in blood most certainly would bring curses or the vengeful dead but on the other hand life was cheap among the true folk, even one's own. Ulmar was fully expecting blood to be shed at any moment. Mostly trying not to droop too much, Ulmar leaned his weight on Kharagh and waited.

The Tuakk and the Marrodar thoroughly looted the homestead, taking every edible, drinkable or usable scrap they could find. While most of the warriors were busy with that, three especially heartbroken Marrodar were seeing to the body of their fallen champion. The eldest of the three resembled the fallen man in a way that only a close relative could. The man shuffled helplessly around the body moaning in anguish. Even if Ulmar had felt no sympathy for Karnae when he was alive, his heart stung a bit at the aftereffects of his actions. The Bloody Handed killer as he had been, he wasn't without people that cared for him, his friends and his family. There was at least another soul that would seek retribution against the Doomwolf, maybe even an entire clan. Hopefully they would stay their hand at him and not refuel the hatred between the bloodlines, that way this death might have some kind of meaning.

The second man seemed to be trying to reattach the severed head before leaving it at the body or more likely he was trying to create some kind of order to the scene, to restore normalcy to his fallen friend. They spoke softly over the fallen man before carrying his body, and head, into a low outbuilding. What manner of fate awaited the body, Ulmar was unsure of. Tradition among the true folk was to inter the dead in one of the many cities of the dead that littered the hills but rumors persisted that some clans would eat their dead. He wasn't sure if the Marrodar actually did,, but he had heard rumors of it, though it might as well be slander. He was reasonably sure that they at least didn't burn their dead like the lowlanders did.

13.

The night grew longer while the two bands feasted trying their best not to fan the flames of their old hatreds. The Tuakk stayed close to each other, but, to Ulmars surprise, not all too close. Greldir, too young to have experienced much conflict with the Marrodar first hand, was best at blending into the gathering. As he sat there watching the young man smile and laugh, he wondered if that might be the way of ending this vicious circle of death. Would the young simply forget the sins of the past and move on with their lives? Could they? He really felt that the young were the hope of the land. There was probably too much passed on from the older generations for it to work. Grudges were imprinted into the children to be acted on later in life, suspicion was always there and then blood was spilt. He wished there could be some great magic that swept through the lands and swept away all their memories like a cleansing river leaving them open and innocent. It felt strange that the misdeeds of ancestors dead for four generations could live on like tangible things, but the secret of steel was all but forgotten among the true folk.

Nearer to midnight than sunset, Hild walked over to Ulmar, a simple earthenware plate in her hand. The smell of fried meat stirred his hunger again. Silently, the woman handed him the plate which he gratefully accepted. On it he found a bounty the likes of which he hadn't seen since before winter. A lot of hard rye bread with salted butter, flakey cheese, raisins, nuts, onions, beans, a couple of eggs and a slab of meat, it was enough to fill the belly and might even make for breakfast. Ulmar started chomping into the bread without a moment's notice.

-"You're getting slower."

Hilds statement might have been true, but coming from her at that moment it oddly stung his pride a bit.

-"I take it that we won't be murdered in revenge then," he stated more than asked.

Hild shrugged.

-"They fear you and wouldn't want whatever demons sit on your shoulders to claim them in your stead. Me and Bolbata will stay awake till we leave in the morning but we should be safe enough."

Ulmar couldn't help noticing that she wasn't carrying her bow at the moment. It was a visible display of easing hostilities though he also noted that her hand was never far from the small axe she had strapped to the small of her back. Ulmar realised there was something that he had never asked Hild that he had at the time wondered about, so he just blurted the question out.

-"So, do you think I'm cursed?"

Hild shifted her large frame looking straight at him.

-"I think we're all cursed. You might be more than others."

They sat in silence while Ulmar ate some more while they watched the warriors drink every drop of liquid they found in the homestead. Answering a question he never got the opportunity of asking, Hild handed him a wineskin from which he took a large gulp. Water. Considering the circumstances water might have been the wisest choice though Ulmar sighed a bit over drinking something with a fuller taste.

-"What meat is this?"

-"Dog. From the one Karnae killed."

Ulmar was appalled. It was a spoiled luxury to be picky about what you ate in the hills of the true folk, especially after a hard winter but this was a member of the household that had taken up residence in the dell. Yesterday this had been someone's friend and companion, now it was meat. Feeling nauseated by the thought of eating it he held it toward Hild and proposed a deal.

-"I'll trade you this in exchange for you rubbing my back and shoulders. I'm getting stiff and sore from the cold and could really use some blood in my arms."

-"Do you really trust me at your back then?"

The comment might have been meant in jest, but was uncomfortably close to a truth they were both well aware of. He could never completely trust her, one day she would move to kill him.

-"Well I am frightened that you'll maul me bloody and raw with those big old bear arms of yours", he said, continuing the humorous tone of the shift in their conversation, "but it's a risk I'm willing to take."

Hild snorted, the closest she would come to laughing, sat behind him and started kneading his stiff muscles. He reflected that she smelt more of soil and fur, than of sweat and dirt. He imagined the towering woman being a bearshifter, from one of the strange stories he'd heard of people turning into animals under the full moon and allowed himself to imagine the strange idea of Bearpaw turning into an actual bear. Jesting with himself he wondered if people would actually notice. They sat there a while under the spectacular star-studded night sky, just two distant relatives surviving the hardships of the land and taking a moment to enjoy life in that moment.

14.

Just before dawn, the two bands started stirring. Ulmar
woke stiff and sore from where he had slept during the
night with his back against the stump. It had been
harrowing to get to sleep, bitterly cold and wet, before he
had managed to scrounge up a caparison to cover himself.
Getting up he felt that his leg was still quite painful, and
getting back to the hold would be twice the bother
because of it. Briac and Schilti were up and about rousing
those that hadn't gotten up yet in anything but a delicate
manner.

-"Maccus, Eloch, Weylin and Truich will be accompanying
the Tuakk to the hold until Schilti and his family can join us
there for a feast to commemorate our blood bond four
days hence. Farewell warriors of the Marrodar, we will
rejoin you in a week at the stones of Broughdouilgh."

With that statement from Briac, they marched off,
homeward bound with four crestfallen Marrodar warriors in
tow. Ulmar didn't envy their fate, if Schilti intended to
break his allegiance to Briac he'd undoubtedly do it now,
before his own family would be kept at the Tuakk hold as
hostages. Tradition dictated that hostages were quartered
alive if it came to that, something the four men were
obviously painfully aware of.

Walking up to Ulmar, Briac slapped his shoulder painfully.

-"Our fate is changed, largely thanks to you, my boy. I told you it would be."

The man's broad smile felt like salt strewn in an open wound. He was less than happy with how these "peace talks" had progressed. Ulmar was thankful that the Tuakk and the Marrodar were on better footing, but he was suspicious of what Briacs' plan was. He hoped that it wouldn't be to raid other clans or the lowlanders instead focusing on nastier menaces like the Redshield Goblins.

-"What now, uncle?"

-"Now we get back home and wait until Schilti gets there."

-"No, what's the plan?"

Briac started walking off only in passing answering with a cryptic

-"You'll see."

15.

The trip back took them two days and was thankfully uneventful. Hild and Krat were instrumental in keeping the band from stumbling into any more dire encounters and the two kept them up on rockier terrain where it was much less likely that death delvers would attack them. The Marrodar "guests" turned out to be pleasant and likeable young men who apart from their alien appearance and some strange habits could just as well have been Tuakk warriors. Among them Ulmar came to especially enjoy the company of Weylin, a sanguine storyteller who had more passion than talent for the craft. If it would come to it, Ulmar swore to himself that he would defy Briac if he tried to kill the hostages. His leg kept him firmly in the rear ranks of the band doing his best to try to keep the fast pace. He was determined not to show that he was hampered, fully embracing the role of the unstoppable warrior. The night they camped at the mouth of Sunsnow Pass, he was truly grateful to just rest his aching body. He'd be fine in a week or so, but just getting to the hold was a gruelling trial.

Back at the hold, they were received like conquering heroes, their kinsman showering them with praise. At first, the Marrodar warriors were met with mocking comments as if they indeed were prisoners before Briac with a short bellowing reprimand ended the assailment. These were honored guests of the hold he explained. These were friends and allies. A good thing that the guests never wandered out into dark corners of the settlement alone, for the look in several Tuakk eyes spoke of vicious murder.

True to his word, Schilti arrived early the fourth day with his family and a modest number of warriors in tow. The four men that had originally followed the Tuakk band were overjoyed to see their leader and kin but mostly to not be gruesomely murdered by their hosts. Tentatively the Tuakk and the Marrodar socialized shallowly, not certain of how to proceed. Even if it had cost a life and might just be paid in others' blood, this new found cooperation between the people was a balm for Ulmars soul. He hoped this was an end to an age of bloodshed and the beginning of a long and fruitful cooperation.

At the arrival of the foreign chieftain there was a certain amount of ritual that had to be performed. The two ceremoniously greeted each other and then shared in drinking deeply from the great horn of the Tuakk. Before Briac and Shilti were caught up in the upcoming feast, Ulmar managed to corner the two while they were already deep in planning their next move. Boldly, Ulmar made use of his exalted status and suggested quite firmly that the tribes should deal with the threat of the Redshield Goblins, seeing how both clans had been raided by the creatures for several years. Surely he suggested there has to be a fair amount of loot, lost heirlooms and food that the ill-willed creatures had amassed. Both chieftains had firmly agreed that the goblins would make a natural target and had to be dealt with. Then the proceedings of the feast had swept them up. Full on the meat of another goat and watered down ale Ulmar sat at his corner seat fully content to let the feast fizzle out by itself without his intervention.

Fate on the other hand, had other ideas.

Nothing but a pack of wolves, Vroth, Hethweg and Herkeld made their way up to him. They had been talking to Bolbata who seemed just a little too pleased with herself and was now taking a place in the corner to assess the damages she'd helped inflict. Greldir was with them for the first ten steps or so but was luckily distracted by Maulagh. Sliding into seats next to his, Ulmar made sure that he kept his back free and that none of them got too close.

-"Another head at the feet of the invincible Doomwolf eh." Vroth sat down with his elbows on the table and did a terrible job of hiding the fact that he was hiding a dagger behind his forearms. The man must have virtually bathed in ale or he had a secret stash to be able to get this way tonight. His head swayed and the fumes of his breath were enough to make ale out of a babbling brook, as he continued.

-"See, I heard... that you might have gotten that fool Karnaes head but that it was close, almost as if he actually had a chance of killing you. Strange that, seeing how I clearly remember folk saying that you can't be beaten."

Deciding to let the short tempered man reveal his motives, Ulmar didn't say anything, instead grasping his horn and taking a swig of the uninspiring brew.

-"Now I've been thinking. I know that you were born by people here in the hold, good people from what I've heard, not deserving the fate that befell them. I also know that you grew up just like the rest of us and you don't seem to be stopping in age so I reckon that you'll grow old and die just like the rest of us. If you can age you can die, and if you can die, well, then you can die."

Quick but clumsy Vroth was actually mad enough to try to stab Ulmar in the ribs there in the hall of their ancestors, in the presence of the entire clan. Using what he had, Ulmar blocked the crude but lethal iron dagger, letting it slide across the sleek surface of the horn and jamming it stuck into the side of the table. Not stopping a moment to think, Ulmar jabbed the sharp end of the horn into Vroths side feeling the crack of a rib but managing to not actually impale the man. Vroth keeled over in pain hitting his forehead with considerable force against the table. The shocked looks from Hethweg and Herkeld told him that Vroth had taken things too far, further than he had discussed with his compatriots beforehand. Bolbata on the other hand, from what Ulmar could see the only witness outside of himself and the small pack of assailants virtually glowed. Ulmar smiled for show, grabbed Vroth by the hair of his crown and pulled him upright. The man groaned and grimaced at the rough treatment.

-"That was foolish and cowardly. We have no grievance between us and no cause for revenge so what in all the blazing hells do you think you're doing? Would you strike me down at my own table unarmed like a bugbear in the dark?"

Vroth growled at him, not answering, so Ulmar firmed his grip and twisted. He must have understood that things were only going to get worse if he didn't give Ulmar answers so he spoke.

-"You are after my wife. It's no secret that you were intended to be wed and now you aim to make a cuckold out of me by using my wife at your pleasure. She's blinded by lust to you and as long as you draw breath she'll seek your bed."

-"I'm sure murdering me in cold blood will warm her bed to you", Ulmars voice dripped of sarcasm.

-"No, but if you're dead she can only dream."

-"I'm only going to say this once because I'm not likely to forget a blade thrust at me a second time. I have no intentions toward Volda. If she chooses to stay with you that's more than you'll ever deserve but that's her choice. Now get yourself away before you accidentally choke on a crushed throat."

He let go of Vroth who lumbered up with a hand at his side. The man glared and shuffled away, followed by his companions. It might have been that Vroth was jealous, he might also have been insulted enough by the exchange at the small pond to take such underhanded actions or he was just mad. It seemed that violence and blood would follow him around like an incurable pox and he doubted that both he and Vroth would be alive to see the coming of next winter. Ulmar sighed deeply and felt tired of it all. His gaze met Briacs, his uncle was looking straight at him and he couldn't help wonder how long he had been watching. Did he know what had just happened? Why didn't he act to make it stop? And did he have a hand in it? When it came to his uncle it was impossible to tell. The chieftain of the Tuakk nodded inscrutably at him and Ulmar nodded back.

16.

Numbing white sleet ripped into his flowing clothing making it whip and tug in the wild wind while the icy flakes stung his exposed face. Trying to see anything in the bizarre blizzard hurt the eyes, prodding them like icy thumbs. The wind howled with deranged strength pushing out any other sound. Stumbling he tried to keep his guard up only to be forced to his knees which saved him from falling helplessly into the massive storm. Calling upon years of focused training, he forced his hands to sprout flames that nearly drowned in the sleet. Over the deafening wind there was a sound, the only sound, that could drown it out. The bloodcurdling roar of the monstrous thing. Terrified, he slipped and fell landing on his wrist and fizzling the fire he had managed to conjure. His hands immediately felt unbearably cold and wet. Making sure to find his balance despite his instincts were screaming that he should just crawl panicking away, he slowly got up.

He was lost now, both mentally and literally. This had been the first quest that he himself had been responsible for. After years of diligent studies and physical labor he had finally gotten a chance to prove once and for all that he was a worthy liegeman to the Shimmering Tower and everything had been going so well.

His hood was ripped off his head, twisting uselessly around his neck. He stumbled forward, not at all sure if he was heading in the right direction.

There had been seven of them. Six seasoned veterans that had served the Towerlords for more than a decade. He had chosen them with care, trying to match skills and temperament to compliment each other. He had brought two sworn knights clad in thick steel, brave souls of the chivalrous preservation. Their horses had been a hassle but well worth it as soon as combat was joined. They had seemed unstoppable.

His feet were giving way under him, uselessly trying to find grip on the slick ice that covered the ground. He fell dramatically onto his knees but without hurting himself. A rumbling grunt behind him told him that he had to move on.

He had also chosen two honest-to-the-gods rangers. Warriors of the wilderness few would match their cunning knowhow. If they couldn't keep them from running into danger then only fate itself could do better. Their bows had been things of pure art, their mails sturdy and their physique inexhaustible. It was unusual to even find them at the Shimmering Tower much less actually be able to recruit them.

He crept forward on all fours determined not to die easily. He really didn't want to die at all, but especially not this way. He had to push forward and so he did. From the corner of his eye he could see blurry motion before he understood what it was. His instinct told him that the creature had tired of the game and was bounding in for the kill. He was wrong. With a resounding crash that even the storm couldn't quite drown out, the carcass of his horse was only feet from flattening him to the ground. More correctly, it was half his horse. Its' head was buried beneath the broken frame of its body. The light steel harness that he had decided to fit it with, hadn't done much to keep it from being unceremoniously ripped in half. He hadn't gotten to know the beast but he didn't feel that what happened to it was a fate that befitted any creature.

The last two in their party had been stout men-at-arms loyal to the Tower and to their knights. They were a grounding pair with a comforting amount of common sense and general experience in the dealings of the world.

It had been as if fate had meant for him to find them as the knights were moving on after a long service to the Tower and open to the prospect of a noble quest. That very same night he had managed to employ the rare rangers. It had seemed as if fated.

Stumbling forward, using gravity to keep him upright he started running against the wind. Panting, he worked up speed before realizing something that he had observed. The wind had blown away from the creature as if it had been the center of this massive and fully unnatural weather phenomenon. Digging his heels into the ground, he tried stopping only to realise that he couldn't, his heels slipped on the ice and he fell flat on his back. A great hulking shadow loomed up before him, easily ten or fifteen feet high as it moved carefully toward him. He had been moments away from running straight into its huge deadly claws and terrible maw. The shadow took on the mockery of a humanoid shape too large in his mind to be allowed to exist. Fighting off panic, his frozen fingers desperately tried to get hold of his spellbook that he had wisely hung in a chain around his waist. He grabbed the book and opened it, letting several pages risk being torn out by the weather. He might only have this one chance and it was all dependent on which of them he managed to have opened to. Regardless he vowed to cast it whatever it might be.

Mirror Illusion.

It might just work. He had never been very good at illusions, finding them to be a tedious study, better just focus force into a matter and kill whatever you faced. How bitterly entertaining that an illusion now seemed to be literally be the difference between life and death. Grinning a little despite himself he quickly started the incantations and motions of the spell. He was too exhausted to cast it without the help of his book, he was out of options and he hated it. With a snap of his sprained fingers that was so painful that tears flowed into the icy wind he let loose the subtle magic. He was now one of three identical versions of himself, three equally terrified Towermages who were all staring at the oncoming death that was the shadowy form before them. Shaking like leaves they clumsily got up and ran in three completely different directions as fast as his feet would carry him. The beast bellowed in frustration bounding after one of the arcane doppelgangers with murderous intent. He didn't dare look if the thing was after him or not. It had to have chased after one of the others because he was still alive, at least so far. As long as it wasn't toying with him.

They had gotten so far. Traversing the Lumbrian borderlands had been a nightmare. It was an unforgiving chaotic place where everyone seemed to be inflicted with some overbearing lust for killing each other in the most brutal way imaginable. He had led them from one lethal encounter to another, narrowly avoiding death at each turn. It seemed that every conceivable and inconceivable fiend lay in wait around every literal corner of the land in numbers so far undreamt of. They had gotten lost in the endless maze of hills and valleys even when they had the skills of the rangers to rely on. It was no strange thing that the hillmen were immigrating in the thousands within the borders of Valeria, he didn't understand how people chose to emigrate in similar numbers up in these cursed hills.

The flight of snow made a sudden turn now coming from directly behind him. The beast was now after him again. Should he stand tall, turn and face death face to face or should he choose the coward's choice and rabbit scrambling for every breathing moment. The choice wasn't hard, and onward he ran.

The ground under him wasn't as flat and smooth anymore. He realised that he wasn't actually that far off from the entrance to the gully. The walls of it were steep and the entrance was only broad enough to fit two men side by side. There was a faint chance that he could actually get out of here and past the beast, maybe even survive if he only took some moments to prepare and had all the luck of Oranestor at his back. He reached out and felt his remaining mirror illusion out in the valley. Compartmentalizing part of his mind, he hissed an arcane phrase summoning the magic shade to his side. Any beast that used eyes to hunt would have seen a moment's blur as the mirror illusion was summoned and be confused as to which image was the real one. From the corner of his eye he could see a fearful youth bearing his slender features, glass cut jawline, flowing golden hair and stylish goatee running for his life. It was strange to find yourself with a true and live reflection of yourself and seeing the image in such a situation.

With a twirling motion he stopped to face the thing behind him while his image ran on. It was a crazy gambit relying in equal parts on the things hunting instinct and intellect but it was the only hope he had of surviving. The monster was just a handful feet behind him. It charged forward toward him, a hateful wave of bulging muscles that was only a blurry center of this unnatural storm. He forced himself to not flinch as it lumbered on. It's feet were hurtling toward him. He barely had time to panic as they narrowly missed him as the thing chased after the mirror illusion.

It was when he had alienated the rangers that this expedition had been doomed. When the two found out just what his quest truly was, they confronted him, threatening to leave and when he refused them, as he had to, they promptly left. That had only been a couple of hours ago now. He had tried leading them on with an illusion of plausible success as they entered this deadly gully. There had been thick snowfall and a disconcerting wind, but he had imagined that five armed and armored riders would be able to handle whatever was waiting for them. He had been wrong.

When the party had entered the valley the storm had struck them full in the face. Ice and snow in an intensity that he had never known. From that blizzard, a paralysing bellow had scared the poor horses out of their wits just before the monster attacked. The thing rushed in, catching one of the men-at-arms and his steed in a vicious bearhug before any of them had the time to react. The crushing sound of shattering bone and screech of twisting metal would probably follow him into his grave, in whatever short amount of time that was. To his shame he hadn't even seen which warrior the beast had caught in its killing embrace. Then the thing moved on. It ripped, bit, pummeled and crushed. Whatever the group threw at him didn't seem to bother it at all until he had conjured up magical flame at the beast. It had gone berserk. Brave Sir Laderic had stood in its way attempting to hamper the beast with his mighty blade, the result had been that the blade stood out of the things chest while Laderics blood colored the snow. They had all died so fast. The enraged beast had gripped his horse and ripped it in two hurling the front at him.

Now he had a moment to collect himself,he started rummaging through his various bags, spilling several items to the ground. He eventually found it, the only scroll he had left, his last chance. Elated, he started running toward the opening into the valley just realising that he had just placed several hundreds of pounds of monster between himself and where he had to be. Giving in to the self-chastising humor of the situation, he bubbled forth a nervous giggle. The beast was turning after having very intently doing its best to rip the entrails out of his mirror illusion, only to discover that what it intended to maim wasn't even remotely real.

Seizing the moment rather than having it seize him he ran forward as quickly as he could, fighting the cold, fighting the storm, fighting every preserving instinct he still possessed. It turned glaring straight at him, Its eyes slivers of dark inhuman pupils a portal into the alien mind of the thing. The thing seemed to almost smile in expectation of what was to come, if ever a thing as this was smiled. Propelling forward with its burly long arms, it bounded into motion towards him leaving icicles of frozen spittle in its wake. He summoned every ounce of power that hadn't been extinguished in the freezing weather and ignited it into physical flame that leapt from his hands. He forced the flame to leave his outstretched arms and watched as intense red flame hurtled toward the things face. It roared with pain as it made contact, pawing at its face with a clawed hand trying to extinguish the witchfire. It seemed to have broken its momentum but then it leapt blindly at him. Hundreds of horrid pounds of flesh, fur and fat moved toward him. Trying desperately to get out of its way, he dove down feet first trying to slide past along the snowy earth. Something ripped into his side with a bone crushing weight. Despite his best efforts the thing had managed to crash into him, effectively kicking him violently before crashing uncontrollably past him. Straining his lungs for breath, he tried to inhale. There was just a squeezing feeling that deprived him of vital air. He tried again fruitlessly. The third time there were spots dancing in his vision blending in with the icy inferno of the storm. He longed for air. Like lifting a great weight he filled his lungs feeling the life preserving oxygen rush into his body while he gasped. Pushing forward, he strained with breathing. He wasn't even remotely in position but he had no choice. The monster was getting up and he could almost feel it getting close. It was now or never. He cracked the hard wax seal of the scroll, whipped open the parchment and started maniacally reciting the arcane words on the scroll. The air thickened with the feeling of the power of an unleashed storm when with a flick of a hand he released the magic from its binding. The parchment lit up, crumbling away in ashy dust as the ground before him exploded into a cataclysm of roaring fire. A fifteen foot high wall of flame filled the pass into the valley cutting of any entry or exit. Just on the other side of the crackling flame the monster stopped dead in its tracks raising its horrid face to take a last longing look at the prey that seemed to be getting away. For the first time he could see it now. It was a humanoid thing seeming to stand at least twelve feet high. Its arms were a mockery of human form, long and apelike, bulging with muscle, covered with bony or icy protrusions, its massive hands tipped with serrated claws. It may have carried a formidable bulk of fat but it was hard and muscular. Its head was vaguely human in appearance though from its jaws massive tusks sabered outward, and its head was crowned with massive arcing horns. Its' eyes sparked with evil cunning, making him wonder if it would brave the flames to finish its kill. Knowing that even if the magic of the scroll was set by his liege, a true master of the command of the flame it would only burn that long. Shivering and spent he turned and shuffled away as quickly he could.

17.

Even with all the changes that Ulmar had longed for, for
many years he carried a sadness in his heart. The worst
parts of the hills of the True Folk could not be quenched by
his progress. When the feasting was over he had slept
uneasily, keeping an eye open for any would be assassins
emboldened by drink but lacking wisdom. Thrynkattlas
boys were carrying red welts from a savage flogging they
had gotten from Vroth while the warriors had been
meeting with the Marrodar. Most inhabitants of the hold
seemed to find the action perfectly reasonable with even
their own mother ashamed of her children. More goats
were gone and the plotting for death had yet again
commenced. Every inhabitant in the hold gave Ulmar as
much space as he wanted and more, leaving him lonely
and upset. Briac hadn't included him in the planning of the
following day but they seemed to at least be honestly
drawing up plans of dealing with the Redshield Goblins.
And yet, it felt bitter and sour.

Ulmar had retreated to the cold pond mostly trying to get
some peace and quiet from the plotting and bickering. He
sat there on a small boulder as still as a statue, lost in
thought. The birds sang their praise to the coming of
spring living the simple, free life of a beast. Among the
trees they flew from branch to branch caught up in
natures' never ending dance. Watching them lifted a small

part of his melancholy even if they reminded him of how different his own life was. By midday, his behind was stiff from brooding and his stomach growling from neglect. Not that there was much to eat anyway. He wondered if it was time to look over what in the way of leather he could find to boil and try eating. Maybe a bit premature, but, it was only a matter of time.

Something was approaching his little pond. Twigs snapped, feet dragged and sounds like that of metal buckles and clasps made its way back to him. More curious than alarmed, he waited for the approaching maker of sound. It wasn't an ogre or troll, the steps were too light. It wasn't a goblin nor a raider, whatever it was made too much of a racket for that. It wasn't a beast nor the restless dead, so what was it?

Walking into the glade slouching and stumbling was a yellow haired man dressed in long, strange garb of amazing color. He was a thin, kind of pretty man with some impractical quality about him. On his chiseled face he bore a groomed goatee that none of the True Folk would ever bother with. Excluding his sculpted moustache, he was mostly clean shaven about the face in a manner that Ulmar found to be a tribute to the man's impracticality. His hair was the length that Ulmar always attributed to the most useless, when it was too short to hold back with ease and too long to not get in your eyes as you carried out your undertakings. He carried a long, blood-red coat of strange design that was highlighted with bright red leather details and had intricate brass buttons. He carried a number of belts, pouches, bags, straps and a large backpack that seemed to be half full with whatever this strange man had decided would be of use in the wilds. Continuing the bizarre cavalcade, the man was actually carrying a full length sword in a hilt at his side and an actual chainmail under his coat. The two items were beginning to take on the price of a king's ransom in these parts, and few within a week's travel could claim to have seen such intricate novelties for a long time. The man just had to be a Lowlander of some sort, a mad wanderer gripped by some of those broken peoples empty notions. Ulmar gave half a chuckle at the sight, just happy to have come across as strange a fellow as this. As he made his way over the clearing towards Ulmar, the mans' gaze was glassy, unfocused. Seeing him closer now Ulmar could see that he was obviously hurt, blood was fresh on his clothes though no open wounds short of scratches could be seen on his body. Ulmar relaxed his grip on Kharagh and met up with the man, only barely catching him as he slumped down to the ground. He was surprised to hear the clear tones of his voice and even more to hear him utter the phrase "Why must you smell so bad," in flowing Avarossian, one of the tongues of the Lowland people. The man had fainted.

There he was now with a strange lowlander unconscious in his arms. Ulmar had so many questions as he gently lifted up the man and carried him over to the pond. Was this one of the inhabitants of the homestead in the Dell of Turundar? It seemed unlikely that he would have gotten this far alone. Was he from the lowlander village of Penketh? Maybe, it wasn't too far from the Tuakk hold, but the villagers knew better than to venture further up into the hills to Tuakk territory. Briac had for many years held a burning loathing for the newly established village, calling them invaders and a blight upon the sanctity of the land. Maybe this was one of the so-called "adventurers" of the South, people who seemed to be nothing other than trouble seeking graverobbers with a knack for banditry.

Whoever he was, Ulmar had first to make sure that the man was going to survive long enough to answer questions. He loosened the straps of the mans' backpack, laying him out in what at least looked like comfort. He tried his best to examine the man for injuries without having to strip him out of his clothes. He couldn't find any open wounds on his body but when he laid his hands on the mans' left side, he grunted and winced despite his more or less unconscious state. The side was swollen meaning that in the least he was sprained and probably had several broken ribs. He found a water flask among the Lowlanders belongings, tasted it to make sure it was safe and then gave the man a couple of mouthfuls. Ulmar was pleased to see that he swallowed the water, stirring him slightly from his torpor.

-"It'll be here soon." The lowlander muttered hoarsely. "It's after me."

-"There now, stranger. Whatever it is it will not dare to tread into the territory of the Tuakk," Ulmar stated boldly, "Rest a bit so I can figure out how to pull this off."

His Avarossian was rusty so he wasn't sure if the man had fully understood what he said, he had never been an avid study of the language only learning enough to be able to take part in the infrequent trading expeditions with the Lowlanders when the clan needed something special or had something that the Lowlanders deemed especially precious. More often than not the expeditions tended to end with some kind of violence, sometimes even resulting in actual raids on the settlements they were visiting. The Lowlanders' ways were strange and unreliable. He had always appreciated them on the other hand, their ways fascinated Ulmar, his only regret was that the trading trips always seemed to be doomed undertakings.

He wanted to help the man, it was obvious that he needed it, but how was he supposed to bring a Lowlander into the hold without him or both of them getting killed? He knew his people. They would cry out for the mans' blood simply because of what he was, an unknown stranger trespassing in their lands. There would be no mercy for him here, why would there be? He was a stranger and killing him would be a fine opportunity for some of the clan to amass several hard to come by items. The standing attitude among the True Folk was that the Lowlanders were shadows of humanity, in all important aspects non humans and no one would think much of killing even an unarmed and wounded Lowlander.

Briac would most certainly make a point out of murdering him. The Marrodar were infamous for raiding their villages. Whoever the man was, he was far from safe.

Ulmar decided that he had little choice but to wait until the man came-to, so he waited. The birds sang, the trees swayed and the day moved on. He was tempted to open the mans' pack, just to satisfy his own curiosity. The backpack was an artful design of leather and metal fastenings, the likes of which Ulmar had never seen before. It looked practical enough, cunningly designed even. Its contents might be just as interesting.

After a good long while, the man seemed to be getting lucid again to Ulmars great relief.

-"I am Ulmar of the Tuakk stranger. These are the lands of my people. I might be the only that will, but I welcome you. I wasn't sure you would wake up."

-"Tuakk? You're a Lumbrian? A native of these lands?"

-"I am a Loonbriarn, yes." Ulmar had heard the Lowlanders mispronunciation of the phrase "Loon briarn" before, meaning member of the hills of the True Folk. The Lowlanders seemed to have decided to pervert the word into signifying a large territory that included the hills of the True Folk.

-"Are you going to kill me?"

-"Not if I don't have to."

-"I need your help. I'm hurt and there is a monster hot on my heels. It's some kind of big horned ogre who spawns a blizzard from its body. I barely survived my encounter, my companions did not."

-"A horned monster that spawned ice and snow? Did it have two large tusks and bone and ice growing out of its body?"

-"Yes."

-"You survived an encounter with an Ice-King Troll. Very few have."

Hearing the mans' story he realised now what had been the source of the distant roaring that could sometimes be heard at the hold. According to Bolbata, the sound had started to be heard just past Midwinter and he himself had heard the distant sound several times since his return to the hold. This could be dire news if the creature decided to move into Tuakk lands for Ulmar wasn't sure the clan could slay it even with the help of their new Marrodar companions.

-"Please, I'm cold and I'm hungry. If the monster isn't too close I'd like to get a fire going and get something to eat."

The man moved to get up struggling and failing to do so. Ulmar put his hand on the mans' shoulder gently but firmly, keeping the man from trying to get up again.

-"No." Ulmar simply stated.

-"No? Is the monster that close?"

-"No."

-"Then what? Why can't I light a fire?"

Ulmar sighed, not revelling in having to explain the mans' situation.

-"You are a Lowlander on Tuakk lands. If my people find you they will kill you, of that I am certain. Light a fire and you'll draw them here and be cut into shreds before the night."

-"What?" The man looked as shocked as he did groggy. "Why the devils would they kill me? I have done nothing to aggravate them."

-"This is how it is in the hills of the True Folk. Your kind are not welcome. You invade our lands, hinder our cattle with your fences, till our soil, rob our dead and claim that which is not yours. The hills have been ours for countless years. They were here when the first rays of light were born and they will be the last place to freeze during the last winter. They are ours by right. I don't think I agree but to fight the fates on that matter would be madness. Know then that you are an unwelcome wanderer full laden with a hundred things that one of my people would kill for."

The strange man made a small effort getting up, winced and put a hand to his side, apparently a bit too forcefully since he winced some more. Then he just shook his head a little and accepted that he wouldn't be getting up in a while.

-"So you're not going to kill me yet you can't help me from the risk of having me killed. Do you have some kind of plan or are you just taking the chance for some captivating conversation before you leave me here to my fate?"

-"Well it's customary that when you help a stranger in need that he firstly introduces himself."

Ulmar let the question hang there for a while, smiling his lopsided wolf-like grin. The man looked a little abashed before introducing himself.

-"I am Aldred Brynnd Tollemack, Apprentice of the Second Order to the Towerlord Sarsara, the Guardian who rules the Shimmering Tower, Gateway to the North."

Ulmar wasn't sure if he took the dashing man completely seriously or not. Even in his beaten up half unconscious state there was a vivacious tone in the mans' voice.

-"That's a mouthful."

-"Well Ulmar, I hope I can call you Ulmar, I was planning on us being friends so I'll let you call me Awl. I've been known to carry that epithet among my peers. Just remember that if you decide that you're going to kill me you can't call me that."

-"I'll remember that, Aldred."

The Lowlander grimaced at Ulmars comment, Ulmar continued.

-"There just might be a way to help you. Tell me, do you have any food, drink and something that can be given as a gift in that pack of yours?"

Aldred the Lowlander seemed to be struggling to focus before Ulmar realized the man was in truth very openly scrutinizing him.

-"If your people kill people like me on sight, why would you help me?"

-"Because you need it."

-"There's a whole wheel of hard Haffer cheese in there", Aldred spoke carefully, clearly suspicious of the large hillmans intentions, "There's also some thrice burnt mulled wine in there, strong of spirit and sweet as a Summers evening. Gift on the other hand... Will gold do?"

Even if the people in the hills of the True Folk had an appreciation of the worth of gold it wasn't heavily sought after in its own right, the fact being that it had no actual use. Jewelry was a much more accepted form of treasure seeing how it could at least be worn and thereby please the eye of whoever beheld it.

-"Do you have anything a little more... personal?"

-"Probably, maybe, I don't know. What do you consider worthy gifts? I mostly packed what I needed for the road and something tells me that your people, no offense, aren't big readers? So tell me, what is considered a great gift among your people?"

-"Well. Torcs of gold, rings of silver, weapons of steel, a falcon, hunting dogs, a good steed, silken cloth, all manner of spices and furs. The great chieftain of old Waldragh was given a millstone of smooth rock that didn't chip or break while Thrusswerldi Dragonbane was given his dragonbow from the men in the mountain and a mask smithed in black iron from the same. I imagine you Lowlanders would have more or less the same ideas as we in the hills do, yours just might be a little more, impractical."

With a great effort or at least a show of great effort Aldred unbuckled his belt and heaved his longsword over towards Ulmar.

-"Steel. Finely made. I imagine that might do it."

Reverently Ulmar held the weapon in his hand slowly turning it over to study. It was indeed finely made, much more slender than anything the Tuakk or any of the nearest clans could produce. Kharagh was surely a much worthier weapon but this was still a gift worthy of a chieftain.

-"A fine gift but one I can't have you give. I would not send you into the wilds unarmed."

Aldred laughed only to have it turn to coughing or rather a laugh haunted by coughs.

-"Take it my good man, it's more or less for show anyway. If it buys me another day it'll be a worthy trade. For that matter I can also promise you that I'll be far from unarmed without it."

Ulmar nodded his acceptance of the trade. With swift hands he opened the backpack and started looking through it in search of the promised block of cheese and flask of wine. To his surprise the cheese in question was so large it barely fit in his hand. It could probably keep a man from slipping into starvation for at least a week, or three if he rationed the thing. The said wine was kept in a not so insignificant earthenware bottle kept shut with a thick cork. Unused to the material Ulmar pulled the cork stopper out and examined it also smelling the liquid within. It did indeed smell sweet and of strong herbs. He replaced the cork content with the quality of the gifts. No one would be able to fault the stranger for what he brought to the hold. Now he just needed to implement the rest of his plan.

-"Happy?"

-"They will do well."

-"Now what?"

-"Now I need you to stay here and wait quietly until morning is almost upon us."

-You mean to have me lie here freezing in the cold until morning?" There was more bitter acceptance than conflict in the Lowlanders' words. Ulmar didn't envy the strangers' lot in this.

-"I will return during the night and bring you to the hold of the Tuakk. You should be safe here, it's too late in the day for anyone else to come and when I was here they gave me a wide berth. Just see to it that you don't light any fires or make too much sound."

Aldred looked both a bit concerned, and a bit melancholy.

-"I'm not sure how well I'll fare out here in the cold. My tent was lost with my horse and I'm not up to the task of arranging myself in such a manner that I'll keep warm."

-"I'll help you."

Ulmar gathered fresh pine branches and helped make a soft and warm bed for the stranger, half hidden in the edge of the clearing to the pond. It was going to be far from comfortable but he'd probably make it depending on the severity of his injuries. Right now, it was the best he could do. Luckily the man had a change of clothes and a cloak in his pack which Ulmar used to swathe him in like a larva in a cocoon. At his insistence he also managed to dig forth some food for the man from his pack. The rations seemed to be some sort of cake or block of some unknown ingredient pressed together in fat and smelled faintly of berries. Licking the fat from his fingers Ulmar ascertained that it wasn't half bad. He stayed while the man ate in silence and then left the clearing. The man lay there looking snug and content wrapped in the clothes as he was, either that or he was dead already. Either way, Ulmar would find out if he was still alive when he'd return.

18.

The night was at its peak and there was still a frustrating amount of activity in the main hall. Briac and Schilti were deeply invested in telling stories of their ancestors with such passion that few weren't up and about closely following the oral duel or catching up with their comrades. Wasn't anyone going to get any work done the following day, Ulmar pondered to himself. It was only a usual day like any other yet it had a certain festive mood that was taking a hard toll on their already dwindling supplies.

Ulmar sat on the end of the table, a space that had been indirectly given to him and a place where the man felt more home there than anywhere else in the hold. For what felt like an eternity, Ulmar sat and waited. His kinsmen weren't going to sleep as he'd planned. There wasn't anything special happening anymore, no feast nor story, there were just too many of his kin that were lounging about in a restless state, not making any preparations for getting to sleep. All this travel and feasting had skewered their daily rhythm. The wind howled over the hole in the roof that was for the firepit, threatening to blow itself into a mighty storm that would at least push away the heavy cloud cover that hid the moon. A game of dice was being played in one of the more illuminated corners and judging by the level of excitement from the players, or lack thereof, the game had no actual stakes. No one was actively looking in his direction which tempted him to sneak outside to Aldred. He was worried that the man had sustained internal injuries that were slowly lulling him into oblivion or that a Bugbear throatcutter had found him defenseless and fast asleep in his improvised bed. He moved to get up from his seat just as Vroth walked from the dice game over to Greldirs' alcove. Had he been quicker to act on his impulse the man would have seen him and maybe even followed him. Sighing he made himself comfortable and feigned sleep, trying to sneak in some actual rest before he returned to the man by the pond.

Ulmar sneaked between the trees fearing the worst. He wished for a torch to light his way through the inky darkness, knowing full well that he couldn't afford the chance that someone would spot the light and give in to curiosity. There was a nip of frost in the air and the angle of the light against the clouds covering the moon told him that the hour was well past midnight, nearing morning. The Tuakk should have guards posted to keep watch over the valley and there was a slim chance that someone was peering out into the darkness from the top of the great hall, but it was highly unlikely.

He let the sound of the water and his familiarity with the valley guide him. He was getting closer, skipping nimbly across parts of the small stream that flowed from the pond when it filled beyond the brim. Ulmar stopped and listened by a gnarled birch. He heard water running but nothing else.

He got to where he was sure he had hidden away the Lowlander, feeling a wave of relief when his foot touched the bed of now wet branches. Getting more accustomed to the mirk he could see Aldred as a slightly darker smear laying on top of the pile. He couldn't see any movement. Worried Ulmar took hold of the Lowlanders foot while also speaking his name.

-"If you are yet another fever induced raving, I congratulate you on your convincing display." The mans' voice was slurred. Ulmar tugged some more on the mans' foot telling him that he was very much real.

-"It's me, Ulmar. Wake up, Lowlander, we need to move stealthily, and need to move now."

-"Ah, good, Ulmar." The man mumbled with a satisfied tone. "Not that it hasn't been wonderful experiencing freezing to death in your fine countryside, but I think I'm well and truly done with laying around. If you'll just help me up, we can get a move on."

Ulmar helped the man to his feet, one blind man guiding another. They more or less managed without hurting Aldred much more and shuffled off into the trees. It was slow going, more or less dragging the man forward with him breathing hard from pain. He didn't whimper or cry out though Ulmar felt how stiffly the man held on to him sweating like it was the warmest day of summer. They got to the first buildings and were heading up towards the hall. There wasn't much in the form of illumination in the hold so they had to stumble along in the dark not knowing if they'd run into anyone before it was all too late.

Getting to the building properly, the first part of the great hall, the two of them froze. There on the steps of the building was one of Briacs hounds as a dark shape standing right in front of the door. If they took a single step, they could alert the animal to their presence making it bark furiously at the stranger that Ulmar was dragging along. His plan was fully dependent on them getting within the hall itself. If they didn't make it past the threshold there was nothing to stop the Tuakk just cutting the man down, and they might even do the same to Ulmar for good measure. What could he do except stand there? The animal moved a bit along the front of the building sniffing the ground, tracking. In pure desperation Ulmar carried the man toward the only potential ally he had in the hold, towards the shack of the bone woman. Maneuvering between unlit buildings he heard the soft tapping sound of pieces of bone tapping against each other. Collecting his thoughts for a second Ulmar entered her home without knocking on the door.

19.

The odors of the old womans' abode were strong, getting a snorting reaction from Aldred as he was carried over the seers threshold. There was still some glow in the fireplace that gave a faint but distinct illumination to the inside of her shack. The old woman was fast asleep on several furs stacked on a large chest. The woman had no proper bed instead taken to sleeping on the vessel that kept her most precious ingredients. Now she lay there in the dark, a white haired twig-like figure. She looked so unfettered and at peace where she lay sleeping, making Ulmar wonder if he really had the heart of rousing her from her rest to see to a complete stranger in the middle of the night. He could of course just leave Aldred there and come back for him as soon as he had secured access to the hold and made the few preparations that he needed. It felt wrong he concluded, dragging someone into her home and then leaving like a thief in the night. He walked over to the woman and softly put his hand on her shoulder. She didn't flinch or scream but opened her eyes as if she'd been awake all the time.

-"I need you to do something for me Kallabra."

The old woman put her dry wrinkled hand softly on his in a reassuring way.

-"I'll take care of him. Go, put your plan in motion."

Somehow he wasn't surprised that she seemed to know what was going on. Ulmar nodded, rummaged through the Lowlanders pack and pulled out the would-be gifts. He was on his way out when he stopped to turn towards the Bonewoman.

-"How did you know that it wasn't some ill fate that had caught up to you?"

-"It could only be one of two things", the woman stated with what almost sounded like amusement, "And the black wolf does not bite as gently."

Ulmar left for the great hall.

20.

The air was pungent with the stench of soot, filth and all sorts of sharp smells that Aldred connected with the art of alchemy. He realized that he was falling in and out of consciousness, his injuries fighting what the hillman had called "Hrimmkuningaz trötl", an ice-king troll, seemed to be worse than he had feared.

He wasn't really sure what was real and what wasn't. He had been haunted by sounds and memories that were impossible. He was cold, chilled to the bone and feeling miserable about this first real mission he had undertaken. If he'd have done as he should he'd be safe and warm. If he'd been at the tower he could see the Magicus Phronzinn and receive lifesaving care that he doubted existed anywhere north of the gate to the north. Wanting to hold his throbbing head, he couldn't muster the strength to raise his arm to do it.

His mind kept going back to the hillman, Ulmar the barbarian and his dark gaze. There was something so intimidating about his eyes that every time the man had looked at him he had felt a chill run down his spine. He was such a strange individual with the look of bloody doom and the actions of one of the hallowed priestly mothers of

Vanenna. Those eyes, they haunted him, followed him even now though the man was gone.

There seemed to be a Banshee in the room, Aldred concluded dryly. It was a short and gnarled kind of creature that his mind had summoned and he had to congratulate his imagination of being able to conjure forth such a lifelike creature.

Instead of screaming thus rending his soul from his body, it muttered phrases from that Lumbrian tongue that sounded like a hodgepodge mix of Dwarvish, Elvish and perverted Valerian. In all other lands except Valeria, his own language seemed to be known as Avarossian, a mystery that enthralled him as the crooked banshee moved about him.

It touched him. The thing put its hand under his head and lifted him up a bit so it could try forcing some horrible black brew down his throat. You're a genius Aldred, he congratulated himself sarcastically, only someone of great skill and cunning would be able to not only face one of the dreaded Banshees but actually get adopted by one.

She stunk of wet bones and the strange tang of haghead bloom.

-"Drink, drink," she cooed to him, "Drink you outlander fool, so that your strength might grow again."

There was an oily tinge to the bitter metallic brew and on top of that, the almost impossible to describe taste of

131

aetham, the core ingredient found in most restorative potions.

-"Do you skillan my words?"

The womans' expectant owly gaze forced an affirmative answer out of him before he could collect his thoughts. Fever and exhaustion, Aldred concluded swiftly. If he knew what was best for him he should keep his tongue and think before acting, on the other hand he concluded in a moment of self-perception he rarely knew what was best for him.

-"Still of tongue and long of ear", the woman told him in her strange way of speaking Valerian, "for you I have waited. Seen it I have. The Fate of many walk in your shadow and for you is the fate of walking at Ulmar Doomwolfs side. You must keep your tongue when in the hall of Tuakk, no speak from ass."

Aldred was somewhat amused and was going to explain that he very seldomly spoke in any matter from that particular orifice, but was handily cut off by the strange little woman as she peered into him with much the same dark gaze that the hillman called Ulmar did.

-"I have seen what road you walk. I have seen what burns in your heart. What you do is important, this you must understand. Take back what you lost in the hand of Hrimmkuningaz trötl then walk into the shadow of the throne. There you will find your answers."

Aldred blinked vacantly.

-"I take it you are some kind of seer then? A soothsayer?"

-"Bonewoman. I read the bones. Do you skillan what I said?"

-"I understand well enough", Aldred mumbled.

-"Good, now lift shirt and show stomach."

Aldred was tempted to make some kind of joke about her wanting to see his naked flesh but decided against it. Best not anger a healer while said healer has full access to your open wounds. The woman was binding a wet poultice in a tight bandage as Ulmar returned to the small room. Aldred was doing his best to not yelp out in pain while the hillman stood there like a statue of dark foreboding, taking in the scene.

-"Some might still be awake, even if dawn is not far away", Ulmar stated quietly, "I managed to put the gifts in front of Briacs throne without waking him." He let out the detailed description how he had inched forward one foot at a time so slowly that he had worried that dawn would find him halfway to the throne.

Kallabra tilted her head slightly, studying Ulmar intently.

-"What is it?" The woman asked him in the tongue of the free folk.

-"Nothing", Ulmar answered a bit too quickly.

-"We don't keep secrets from one another you and I, something happened to you from when you left for the hold, something that has shaken you deeply. Tell me."

Ulmar couldn't look at the woman, trying to collect his thoughts, trying to tell himself that he had been mistaken.

-"I carried the Lowlander here because one of the hounds was sniffing on the threshold to the hold. I could not have it start barking, rousing the Tuakk and getting that one killed", he said gesturing toward Aldred.

-" When I went back to the hold the beast was still there. I thought I might as well let it in when I entered but then I saw it for what it truly was. No hound but a wolf black as midnight standing at the threshold of our great hall. As I stood there it passed by me and walked into the night. A black wolf Kallabra, or it might even be The Black Wolf. It must be an omen. Does it mean that I am letting in the Black Wolf? Am I bringing death to the Tuakk?"

Kallabra softly stroked the mans' cheek.

-"Tell no one of this."

-"But," Ulmar managed to meekly protest before being cut off by the old woman.

-"Do I tell you how to fight your battles oh great and powerful warrior? Push it from your mind and keep in the now. Help me get your pup on his feet so we can set your plan in motion."

-"You're not coming, old one. Get back to your bed and let me worry about this one."

Kallabra scoffed.

-"I do not like repeating myself, youngling. I go where I will for reasons that are beyond you."

-"Will my plan work?"

The old woman considered it for a moment, hoisting the Lowlander to a sitting position.

-"No. But don't fret, things never turn out as we plan."

Hardly comforting words, Ulmar still accepted them on face value, Kallabras ways were a mystery to him even if you saw past the bones, potions and incantations. He still couldn't help seeing the looming dark figure of the black wolf that had past by him though, he still couldn't help wondering if his actions would doom them all.

Aldred seemed to be getting more and more lucid for every step he took. Like a miracle he found strength in his gait. By the time they were outside the great hall he was walking on his own, sweating profusely but walking on his own.

-"He seems to be getting better." Ulmar wasn't quick to jump to conclusions but this one seemed safe enough until the old woman shook her head.

-"No, I gave him something to shake off the worst of it. He's still in bad shape underneath the potions effects."

Lolling his head a bit to the side Aldred wobbled, when in his mind spinning gracefully toward Kallabra.

-"Dung. Me feel good as rain", he proclaimed in very broken Lumbrian.

-"I didn't know he spoke the tongue of the True Folk."

-"He doesn't", Kallabra sounded somewhat exasperated, "but we can always hope he can bark well enough to keep his head."

She grabbed hold of his chins and pinned his head so he faced her very closely. Aldred was dismayed at the foul breath of the old woman but still kept his focus on her.

-"Long of ear to my words sun hair. You must stand proud in front of Chieftain. On own feet. No fall. When you stand you thank for hospitality. You give gifts to his table and sword to his hand. Do this, do not fail." She stated in broken Avarossian.

Aldred nodded, Kallabra grimaced while letting him go.

-"It's a hard language they speak in the Lowlands. Never thought I'd be needing it again. Now get in Ulmar, and do not open until the third time we knock."

Ulmar stealthily opened the door, snuck to the other side and waited for the said knock. Soft as a pat he heard the first knock. He looked around the hall fearing that even this would be enough to rouse his kin. No one stirred. He heard the second knock only slightly louder, still no more than a scratch at the door. Still no one stirred. The third knock was almost as loud as a creak having the effect of waking one sleeper. The large head of Radi, Briacs prized shaggy red hunting hound was peering at the door. Not wanting to give the beast more than the shortest time to react, Ulmar opened the door letting the others into the great hall of the Tuakk. Aldred stepped in smiling the broad toothy smile of a simpleton as he made his way toward the throne on which Briac had fallen asleep. Radi, amazingly, wasn't barking. The hounds tail wagged and it started quietly making small gruffs, talking to the stranger that had entered its home. Aldred was holding his hands from his side and still smiling like a fool when he reached the table with Briac sleeping on the other side. Some in the hall were stirring. The gifts that Ulmar had picked out for Briac were covered by a cloak that Aldred hadn't noticed the hillman pilfering from his pack. Softly Ulmar pulled the cloak aside and clearly addressed the Tuakk chieftain, the sudden break of silence meant that he could just as well have been screaming.

-"My chieftain Briac", Ulmars uncle flinched from sleep peering about sleepily, "Your guest stands before you with gifts that are worthy of the clan of Tuakk."

The hold was a churning beehive of sudden movement. Radi started barking, waking the other hounds that exploded into wild barks of their own. The clansmen of clan Tuakk had wildly different responses, some only barely reacting, others on their feet with weapons in hand, trying to determine what enemy had beset the hold. Briac, himself, was on his feet with his mace in hand in a mere blink of an eye.

-"Who dares intrude on the hold of the Tuakk, on the ground that has been ours since the dawn of time and paid for with our blood?"

Briac was in no mood for dialog. Ulmar had to act immediately before Briac brought down death on the brittle Lowlander. Without hesitation, Ulmar stepped out in front of the newly woken chieftain, raising his hands in an attempt to placate the man. Briac was halfway into attacking Ulmar before he realised that his nephew was his intended target. Briac took a step to the side which Ulmar mimicked.

-"Stay your hand Chieftain, this is no intruder but a guest in our hall."

-"Guest? This is no guest but a Lowland thief which we can quickly rid ourselves of," Briac attempted to push his way past Ulmar only to be stopped as if he walked into a wall.

-"A guest uncle, bearing tribute to the clan Tuakk, come to us with an open fist and good intentions. He seeks sanctuary from the land in our hall." Ulmar tried to not obviously wrestle the man back, trying his best to shield Aldred by placing himself between him and the chieftain.

-"The Chieftain has not forgotten our ways'", Kallabras voice carried throughout the great hall like a crows caw in a silent forest, "He merely wants us to remind him of the tradition of hospitality so we do not forget. I heard the guest knock thrice, I saw him enter bidden in by a member of the clan Tuakk and I witness the gifts he has brought before you."

Kallabra was a pillar standing amidst a confused uproar all around them. Her words made Briac lose his momentum, halt his attack and take heed of the feel of the clan. Ulmar saw his uncle very methodically avoid looking at Schilti and the Marrodar that were watching the exchange with great interest. There was more going on here than Ulmar had considered, some etiquette that eluded him. He wasn't sure on how the presence of the Bonewoman or the Marrodar chieftain influenced events but they most certainly did. Briac stopped trying to pass Ulmar instead focusing on him.

-"Is this your doing? Have you invited this outlander into our home?" There was spite in the chieftain's voice.

-"He is a guest of clan Tuakk."

Ulmar gestured toward the cheese, the wine and the sword lying on the table with a sweep of his arm. Briac stopped for a while, scrutinizing the intruder from top to toe. His eyes were focused in the way that spoke of him studying something in the corner of the eye, probably Schilti who was smiling wickedly at the chieftain of the Tuakk. Briac stood there a great long while, half an eternity in Ulmars mind, before taking a somewhat less tense stance. Slowly he stepped back towards the throne stopping to study the gifts that were presented to him. Rolling the cheese in his hands he dug out a piece of it and tasted it. He put it down, seemingly pleased by it. He drew out the stopper from the ceramic bottle taking a deep waft of the contents and then a deep sip from said content. He seemed equally pleased with the wine. Then he studied the sword. He picked it up, weighed it in his hands and then drew it halfway to study the metal.

-"You bring us a gift of steel", Briac announced smiling, "This is a worthy gift. Introduce me to our guest, Doomwolf, and never shall it be said that the Tuakk do not honor hospitality to those that have passed our threshold."

-"This is Aldred Tollemack, warrior of the Shimmering Tower."

-"Apprentice." Aldred managed to squeeze in before being silenced by a stern look from Ulmar.

-"You, Aldred Tollemack, stand before the chieftain Briac of clan Tuakk, the one true ruler of these lands," Ulmar stated, with a certain amount of ritual.

-"I grant the stranger Aldred Tollemack sanctuary under my roof, let it be known that he is under the protection of clan Tuakk while he travels our lands. It is sad that our guest will only keep to our lands the next few days for soon the warriors of the Tuakk and of Marrodar will march under the goat together."

Aldred bowed flamboyantly, only realising half way through the bow just how much bending his bruised abdomen would pain him. He bit his tongue, finishing the bow and pretty deftly hiding his discomfort.

-"I thank chieftain Briac, very many thank." The crudeness of the mans' grasp of the tongue of the True Folk was a stark contrast to the elegance of his dress. Or, it might be the perfect illustration of the difference between their two peoples, Ulmar considered.

Briac lifted the sword high, showing it to all in the hall, taking extra time to display it for the gathered Marrodar. With a swift movement he pulled the blade from its scabbard and swung it in wide arcs around him. There was a murmur of approval from the Tuakk at the sight of the exclusive weapon. Aldred was swaying a little sweating so profusely that he seemed to be dipped in oil. Briac crashed his hand on the Lowlanders shoulder with enough force that the younger man almost swooned then and there.

-"Tonight you sit at our table. Rest until then." Then addressing the spectators of the hall, "Now get up the lot of you, dawn is upon us and there is much to do."

With a collective groan of disapproval, the Tuakk started getting ready for the day ahead. Briac walked out the hall shouldering Ulmar so forcefully that he took two steps backward from pure force. Ulmar understood that he would pay but wasn't that concerned with the price, mostly tired of having to placate his uncles' whims.

21.

They watched as Aldred slept in Ulmars alcove. The two of
them would be left well enough alone, one being a feared
crone and the other a cursed bloodletter. The hall was
soon more or less empty barring the Marrodar guests, and
those that were ill. Kallabra was constantly walking to and
from her shack, fetching one potion or another and all
sorts of ointments, powders, talismans and inscrutable
things. Ulmar kept asking about Aldreds condition till the
old woman threatened to sell her patient to the hags under
the hills for some peace and quiet. So he stopped
pestering her with words and instead watched the strange
man sleep. At last, Aldred opened his eyes and proclaimed
that he was feeling better even if all he could smell was
pinecone. The first thing he attempted to do was study
from the clasped tome that he wore chained to his side
before Kallabra stopped him with a touch from her hand.
With a whisper she explained in broken Avarossian that it
was hard enough to keep a warrior from losing his head.
There was no reason to rush into the fire. Aldred resealed
the clasp and left the book well enough alone.

It wasn't long before the people of the hold were starting
to prepare the evening meal. The small assembly of
nominated chefs were bringing in sacks filled with newly
harvested grass, bark and moss and were hard at work
diluting the current stock of foodstuffs with these new

ingredients. Some of the children had managed to scavenge up some dandelions and spring thistles that were an apparently welcome addition to the coming meal. The scene was more than Aldred could bear.

-"What are they doing?"

Ulmar and Kallabra gave him such wondering expressions so he was swift to add.

-"Do you eat that?" He demanded, riled up in outrage.

-"I don't see you bringing anything to the table. The wolves have been merciless this year and this is what we have. Don't worry, you'll be fed." Ulmar didn't mean to sound as annoyed as he did, however, the situation, life, just dug into his heart making him boil over.

-"I'm sorry", Aldred looked ashamed, "it's just that this isn't food. There is food aplenty in this world and no one should have to live like this. You shouldn't have to mill bark into your bread or eat grass. It's just terrible."

-"Don't worry, there'll be much more to eat. There might even be goat cheese." Ulmar patted Aldred on the back and smiled.

When it was time for dinner Aldred was placed on the other side of the table from Ulmar next to an apple-chinned woman by the name of Bolbata. She seemed like decent company, excluding the way that she seemed to have a devil's glimmer in the corner of her eye as soon as she spoke to Aldred. At first he mistook it as lust but soon came to realise that it was something darker. At least she spoke good Valerian.

-"How did you learn Valerian?" He leaned toward her with one of the Hillmens drinking-horns in hand. He was still very much cracked and torn but felt more out of his mind drunk than anything else. Whatever the Bonewoman had given him had left him quite numb because the ale he was sipping was barely any better than water. At his comment she shook her head.

-"Avarossian. I don't understand why you people always call it Valerian. People spoke Avarossian for ages before you people claimed the land to the South."

Aldred had heard it several times before but didn't buy the strange twist that according to everyone except themselves Valerians spoke Avarossian, only with an odd accent. There was no point in arguing with the woman, instead he returned to getting information about the people and land from her. She was more than willing to gossip with him.

-It's not that we want to kill all the Lowlanders, it's just that you're not people, not really. You're shadows, not real," Bolbata made a quick gesture in front of her face. "It doesn't matter if we kill you or let you live. It's when your people change the lands and defile our home that we have to march under the goat against you.

Utilizing a bit of sleight of hand Aldred pulled out another wrapped honey sweet apparently from nothing. Bolbata snatched the thing hungrily.

-"What does that even mean, "march under the goat"? Are we talking about a real goat?"

-"The goat of war!" Bolbata exclaimed exuberantly. "When we march to war we give offerings and plead to the goat-headed demon of the hills, the war demon, to bring us victory. We sacrifice a goat and fasten it to our standard to march under its favor."

-"Don't you mean God of war?" Aldred tried correcting.

-"No. Demon. The Gods fell long ago. The only things that remain are great demons like the goat of war and the black and white wolves. If you still have Gods you should feel lucky. Ours are long dead."'

Aldred shuddered at the thought of Gods dying. He wasn't a faithful worshipper of the deities of the Valerian pantheon but he was comforted by the knowledge that they were there. But to worship actual demons? It was a reckless move that was doomed to bring pain and misery to whoever was that stupid. No wonder the whole region was literally cursed, a churning pit of never ending conflict. A small boy with a twisted back and blotchy hair served them their food. It was a little better than Aldred expected but not a lot. There was no hiding the boiled grass and the fibery taste of wood. There was a sad excuse for a piece of meat on his plate that he was fairly certain was goat, an animal that he had never developed a taste for.

Aldred was placed only three seats from the chieftain Briac of the Tuakk, and only two from the chieftain Schilti of the Marrodar, something he felt was a clear sign of honor from his reluctant hosts. He didn't know who the other two persons were, a dark blonde woman and some large bearded man, but according to the ranking of seating arrangements they clearly were important people. Aldred was uncertain if the Barbarians of the hills kept to the same seating practices that were a part of Valerian formal society but from his observations they were a highly hierarchical people so he couldn't see why not.

Apart from being very smelly, dirty and prone to bursts of violence, Aldred was starting to appreciate the Lumbrians. They were of course quite crude as well and lacked finesse but there was something refreshing with the absence of social machinations and formal bureaucracy that was his life in the Shimmering Tower. A dizzying cluttered mess, but still refreshing.

-"So how did you learn Avarossian?" Aldred wanted nothing more than to steer the discussion away from demon worship and killing of Lowlanders, though to be honest he was very curious about that fact himself.

Bolbata smiled for the first time, honest and open. She was a striking woman, with brown hair that was almost red at the tips, set up in an intricate assembly of braids. Under the grime and layers of pent up aggression she could have been someone whose company Aldred would have sought. He intended to keep her in this mood if possible.

-"I am the daughter of Hylvingur, son of Horolda, daughter of Mereth who is the direct descendent of Thryggvi Nameseeker, the first of the Malskillanji. In your tongue that would be something in the line of the master of tongues. As the world crumbled and the great throne of old was cast down by the ancient enemy, great heroes of the True Folk wandered what was left of the world performing great deeds. She, the great mother of my fathers, looked upon the ruined world and saw that the words of men and allies had broken into many tongues, like a great river forced to divide into smaller rivers, then streams then small brooks. The words of the world were her calling and she intended on mastering them to better master the world itself. Chasing the wind she learnt the tongue of the Feyborn undying ones, from deep within the mountain she stole the words of the bearded men within. But however she travelled, and whatever she did, she could not master all the words of men. Their tongues changed and shifted like the sea ebbs and tides and to know them all is to have power over all the world."

Lost in her story, the woman's eyes glittered and she drank deeply from watery ale.

-"Scaling the mountain that has always been swathed in mists, Thryggvi sought out the giant Ritvaldur who called the peak of the world his home. It was known far and wide that the ancient giant gazed upon the world through the blood of the first God which he kept in a deep golden bowl. There was nothing that Ritvaldur could not see using the bowl, no sounds were hidden from its depths. As Ritvaldur peered across the world the giant muttered what it saw and heard into the bowl trapping the secret of tongues and many other things within the blood. It was this power that my ancestor sought and bravely asked for from the giant in its own hall.

I will give you the power of the tongues of man it claimed, for it is infused in the blood, but only if you beat me in a game of trials, the giant proclaimed. Each would best a trial set by the other and if Thryggi won she would be given a taste of the blood.

A trial, the giant tasked the woman to catch a beam of the midday sun and keep it for him until midnight. As soon as the giant tasked her to, Thryggvi shaped a piece of clear ice so it caught the light in a sharp sliver and started a small fire which she kept till midnight. Upon his return the giant claimed that he saw fire but no sunlight and refused to acknowledge the woman's victory. But in the air of fair play, he would perform her trial and then maybe he would grant her the power of the tongues of man. Thryggvi lifted a golden ring for him to view and told him that her task was to lift the gold over his head.He would best her challenge. The giant agreed and as soon as he did she cast the ring in a hot brazier which she fanned with wind and breath until the gold melted. She then poured it into a crack in the mountaintop and asked him to begin. Furious, he protested that this was no longer a ring to which she answered that she had asked him to lift the gold.

Feeling cheated, the giant refused to acknowledge her victory so Thryggvi splashed her hand in the blood and ran swiftly for her life. She licked the blood and felt the power of the first God fill her with the secrets of the tongues. Seeing that he would not catch her, Rimvaldur cursed Thryggvi that never shall a descendant of the blood-thief be blessed with more than one child and as soon as the child is born the parents' own parents would die. That was the price my ancestor paid and because of this the secrets of tongues shall be known to every child of that line.

-"So you know all the languages of man then?" Aldred asked her, amused and entertained.

-"No. With every generation there is less of the Gods blood in our blood and the curse does not bite as sharply. My grandmother lived a full week after my birth before finding the black wolf in her bed. I can't know if it was because of me, but it doesn't matter much. I myself speak five tongues of man and five of other things. Avarossian and Brejch are good for trade, the tongue of the Undying is for when my soul soars and Giant is good for swearing. There are other Malskillanji, every tribe of repute has one, but most of those are folk that have a talent for words. Some claim to be of the blood, but both you and me understand why it cannot be so."

-"Because of the curse. I try my best to stay away from things like that, curses are best avoided if you ask me."

Bolbatas eyes went wide for a moment, before she was overtaken by a massive fit of hearty laughter. Aldred tried calming the woman, confused what he could have said that was so wonderfully amusing. He laughed a little awkwardly and kept repeating what, what, what. Having her fill of fun and getting several stares from the people of the hall she pressed next to Aldred, put her hand on his forearm and started whispering in his ear.

-"You say you avoid curses and yet you walk in the heels of the worst one that ever passed the land of the Tuakk since Irogar burned the vales."

Bolbata put her head cheek to cheek to his, focusing his gaze on Ulmar who sat in the shadows on the farthest end of the table. His savior was highlighted by those shadows, his already dark gaze now something terrifying. The man might be thinner than he used to be if one saw to the skin, but he was still a tall muscular brutish nightmare to behold. Black of beard and long of hair Aldred hoped he would never cross his ire.

-"That one was born in curse and brought death with him. His father and mother were Lathrik and Aina, proud members of the Tuakk destined to lead the hold onto greatness. They were bound together during the dead of Winter as the white wolf howled his triumph over the world. It is an ill thing to be bound by love under the gaze of the wolven brothers but the rash couple insisted that their love could not be contained till the melting. So the Tuakk celebrated and feasted for seven days. The frost was mild as soon as the first mead was poured and the black wolf found no shadows in which to hide. All things the Tuakk did were met with success and we felt like newborn gods in the hills. It was quickly apparent that Aina was blessed with a child and it would be born at reaping. At this time the Tuakk reared a mighty flock of longhaired cattle that had to be herded through the bellowmark so most of the clan was away on that errand. Lathrik and Aina were left to lord over the hold, those left were mostly the old, those too young to travel and a handful of others. As the week of reaping was upon the Tuakk there was a mighty storm that hailed from the direction of the hold. Heralding its coming flocks of ravens sang doom as they flew by and as the storm engulfed the land, the sky was clothed in black and crimson in a way that no man had ever seen before. The old chief Raedulf, Lathriks father, hasted back with a sizable contingent and at every turn ill omens haunted them. In the midst of night as lightning cleaved the air, they came back to the hold. No guard hailed their arrival, no hound ran up to meet them. Except for the anger of the storm nothing stirred, nothing moved. Opening the door the Tuakk were met with death. No fires were lit to show the fallen but all that had stayed had died. It was as if they had lain down and simply stopped breathing. All except one. In a crib at the cold firepit a newborn childs' cry was competing with the storm in its screaming. There was Ulmar with his fathers axe Kharagh placed beside him as healthy and strong as any parent could wish for. Chieftain Raedulf lifted him up to examine the child and found that the childs' right hand was as black as soot and his left as white as snow, marks of both of the wolf brothers.

Raedulf was heartbroken. His clan was cursed for his childs' folly and their doing had let the wolves in through the door. He decided that the child had to be cast from childs' rock, like any newborn that was found to be unworthy, before it would be the death of them all. The Bonewoman Kallabra, old even then, argued that the Chieftain was a fool to anger whatever power that had a finger in these doings by harming the child. He did not listen and instead headed up the hill to the cliff. When he came near he was met with a sight that haunted him till the day he died. None of the others had the heart of seeing another young child meet its fate so they only heard their chieftains' wild howls. He returned in fear and told his people that at the cliff the black wolf and white wolf had blocked his path. The demons were larger than horses with glowing eyes and drooling maws. He ran howling back and was herded into the hall babe in his arms. Kallabra took the child and explained to them that with every curse there was rhyme and reason and this one had to run its course if they didn't want to bring it upon themselves.

Raedulf had no choice but to allow the child to live, in fear of what would happen if he didn't. For one year, there was a lingering evil over the clan. All children that were born during that year were stillborn, even with every trick and talisman the Bonewoman tried. It was not long before Raedulf was dying from a broken heart, just another victim of the Doomwolfs' curse. He chose to support Lathriks younger brother Briac to replace him when he was gone. And it is said that he told Briac of dreams of wolves surrounding Ulmar and tasked his brother to protect Ulmar for the good of the clan.

Ulmar grew strong and tall and it was obvious that some power guided him. He was quick to grasp what it was to be a warrior, leading the clan through battles undefeated to this day. Death follows in his shadow, spreading around among all who are close to him. Most here have reason to thank him and a reason to kill him. Even his cousin has an outspoken blood oath to kill him, so one day she needs to try or die in the attempt. So, now you know what curse you chase by the tail, it is only right to know of the doom that would befall one."

Aldred was no stranger to tall tales and occult happenings. He had, after all, lived in the Shimmering Tower since the tender age of seven and been subjected to the madness of the Lumbrian borderlands first hand.

The first and only task of the Towerlords, the great wizards that held fiefdoms on the borders of the Kingdom of

Valeria, was to guard those borders against whatever horror was beyond. At the Shimmering Tower, that mostly meant trying to keep the Lumbrians that were immigrating, and the fools that were emigrating, doing so in an organized peaceful fashion and keeping the worst rabble from becoming a later problem for the realm. Sometimes though it meant scouting and sometimes it even meant dealing with threats that were massing in the borderlands. He had personally been on sorties where they found horrible mystical occurrences like stones bleeding, rain falling back into the sky and an entire village that aged a year for every day. He had faced trolls, ogres, goblins and raiders. So looking at the striking figure it was far from impossible that the man was indeed carrying some kind of massive curse. To be fair, everything in the borderlands seemed to be cursed. Ulmar met his gaze and Aldred couldn't help feeling a chill run down his spine. Ulmar nodded toward him and Aldred reciprocated in kind. Maybe he was letting this Bolbata woman steer him wrong. Hadn't Ulmar saved him from certain death? Yet a small voice deep within him reminded him that the Hillman could still be cursed and lead him to his messy doom.

His thoughts were interrupted by the redbearded chieftain by the name of Briac that was loudly making some declaration. Bolbata listened intently, then turned toward Aldred.

-"My chieftain, the mighty and triumphant Briac, son of Raedulf, wishes to know what it is that you seek within our lands." She added softly, "I advise you to show some of that southern silver tongued wit if you know what's good for you. I will translate"

"My Lord Briac", Aldred tentatively began, wondering how to explain himself to satisfaction in a room full of axe wielding Barbarians. "I am on a quest for my Lord, the powerful Sarsara the guardian, to gain knowledge of a hidden enemy that threatens my liege. There have been many signs of a danger on the rise and I must travel further into your lands to find this threat for her. I humbly ask your permission and hope you'll aid me by letting me traverse through your lands."

Briac, who had been listening intently to Bolbatas' translation while stroking his voluminous beard, did not look amused. Frowning, he fed scraps from the table to his hounds.

-"This is the way of the Lowlanders and I have no love for it. I ask you, you talk and yet you tell me nothing. I expected nothing less than you'd try to hide your intentions, but I warn you that I expect to understand your true motives before I let you take a single step further on Tuakk land."

Aldred took in the view of the great hall around him. The magnificent woodwork of a structure he'd have sworn was well beyond anything anyone in the region could accomplish, filled with dirty and rugged barbarians each brandishing some crude but deadly weapon. He'd be better off trying to trade with Hobgoblins he thought to himself, if there were any left.

-"My Lord, please. I meant no offense. I simply didn't want to test your patience with rambling on about the trifling details of my quest. I seek passage through your lands to follow the omens that were set before me. I seek passage to the mountain you call the throne."

When she came to the name of the mountain Bolbata lost her rhythm almost as if she hesitated translating the word at all. When she did, the gathered Tuakk broke out into murmurs of disbelief. Briac waved his hand dismissively while shaking his head.

-"No. You cannot go there. It is forbidden that any of the True Folk travel to the mountain."

-"But my Lord Briac, I'm not of the True Folk. Which means it can hardly be forbidden for me. I have no intention of bringing any misfortune to you, I just need to get to the throne."

Briac stroked his beard deep in thought. He picked up the sword that Aldred had given him, then seemed to come to some conclusion.

-"You are correct in that you are not of the True Folk but going to the throne is forbidden for a reason. None climb the mountain for all know that evil holds that peak. If I would let you go your foolishness would fall back to us, curse us, when you meet your doom."

-"Then I will travel back another way. I have no intention of letting any curse fall back onto you. I must get there."

-"You are persistent like a fallen boulder, Aldred Tollemack of the Shimmering Tower. You make promises to avoid something you have no control over. I still say that walking up that mountain will only bring you ruin but I will not stop you there. Do you even know anything of the throne? How do you intend to contend with the maneater tribes that claim the lands at the foot of the mountain? They are a fierce and wicked brood, who carry the blood of ogres in their veins. They would be pleased to get their hands on such tender meat as yourself I reckon,"

The clan sniggered at Aldred, much to his annoyance. His answer was therefore a little more defensive then he had intended.

-"They would come to see that there is much more gristle in me then they'd thought. Your concern is appreciated, but I promise you Lord Briac, I have a plan to get past the maneater tribes."

The chieftain raised an eyebrow.

-"I see. Do you even know how to get to the mountain?"

Aldred had hoped that he wouldn't be confronted with that question. Truth be told, he only knew that it was

Northward from the Shimmering Tower, and had an approximate area based on a map that he had studied, which was far from reliable in its accuracy.

-"Then I beg of you, let me hire one of your people as a guide. They don't even have to come with me up on the mountain, just get me close enough that I can find my own way. You will find that I can more than pay for the bother."

The chieftain leered at the stranger in his hall. Aldred knew that the chances of finding the help that he needed were slim at the hands of Briac.

-"I am a generous chieftain and I sympathize with your situation", Bolbata translated, but the tone and posture the chieftain had spoke of anything but those qualities. "I'll tell you what, if you find anyone who is willing to guide you, they can do so with my blessing, but they need to do so out of their own free will."

Aldred looked around the hall. The gathered Tuakk and their Marrodar guests avoided his gaze. None was willing to go against their chieftain or face the curse of the mountain. Aldred got up, calling out that surely one of them would be willing to accompany him. He wondered if he should offer to pay whoever would be willing but decided against it. Then he saw Ulmar. The man very deliberately put down his drinking horn and got to his feet. The other Tuakk seemed to be in awe of Ulmar, looking at him in amazement as he proclaimed.

-"I will do it."

Briac ignored his clansman, then seemed to come to some sort of conclusion once again.

-"Stay your stride, Ulmar son of Lathrik, your clan will need you when we join the campaign against the Redshield Goblins. I'll not have our strongest warrior out on a fools' errand when there is war to be waged. No, let someone else take your place, if anyone will."

 Ulmar didn't back down. Aldred felt an appreciation of the immovable presence of the man. He was like a dark tower, standing unbreakable in the shadowy hall.

-"I am the one who brought this man into our midst. It is my responsibility to see to it that our guests are safe. I fear no curse, for what will it do? Impart a second curse on me? You know it to be the true course of action. Let me do it."

Briac took his time to think the proposal through. He took in the mixed responses of his clan, some torn between what they themselves thought of the decision.

-"It is not my part to keep you from your destiny. I said I would allow any who would go the option to go and I will stand by my word. I would still advise against it, we need your power in the upcoming battle that you yourself were stubborn to see fought."

-"It's a matter of clan honor Uncle. It must be this way. Two clans of the True Folk will be more than enough to root out the goblins from their hole. I know Hild has many ideas about how to do it, use those and you will surely crush them swiftly."

The two men seemed to have reached an accord and the hall of the Tuakk was settling to the reasoning behind that course of action. As they did, the lanky man that Aldred had come to understand was the chieftain of the clan Marrodar stood up and in a hoarse voice uttered his protest.

-"Have you gone mad? We will need the Doomwolf if this is to be done. You yourself made it clear that he would be leading the warriors into battle. I'll not chase after some woman when it comes to war."

Briac tensed up. He shifted his attention to his guest, though his words were for the entire hall to hear.

-"Ulmar the Doomwolf will contribute to the battle as much as Karnae will. We will fight and win without them. The Marrodar will follow my orders as the clans' Warchief and if I say that Hild of the Tuakk will be leading the attack then she will. This is not up for discussion."

The finality of his words had Schilti of the Marrodar slowly sitting down in his seat. The expression on the man's face though, said that this was far from over. Aldred wasn't sure what kind of bond the two clans had to each other but he foresaw bloody trouble on the horizon. The chieftain Schilti hardly seemed to be the kind of man to forgive and forget.

The hall slipped into conversation again. Aldred felt relief and a pang of trepidation at what had just happened here. His quest could continue which seemed to be, at best, a fever dream from when he had gone up against the Ice-King Troll and ever since. It was all he needed, a chance to press on and make something of this mess. Four people were dead, his superiors at the Tower must be screaming for his head by now, but he still felt that his mission was just that pressing. Whatever evil was festering in this part of the world was growing from the throne, it had to be. Now he just needed to somehow explain to the Hillman that the first thing they needed to do was to regain the strange ancient artifact that had been lost to him in the nearby valley. They needed to face the murderous Ice-King Troll.

22.

The warriors left on a twisting path that would take them high into the nearby hills, hopefully circumventing most of the goblin tribes' defenses. Ulmar and Aldred watched them go as they stood in the bottom of their gulch. Aldred wasn't very clear on how much time had passed or what had happened during those days. Keeping on his feet until the end of that so-called feast had drained him of what reserves he had. He knew that the strange old crone Kallabra had kept treating him night and day with the vigor of an undying dancer. He suspected that the woman had sneaked in more than a fair bit of magic to the mix since most of his fever was gone and he felt remarkably much better in a more or less uncanny way. His side was still swollen and sore, keeping their pace to a slow crawl.

Ulmar on the other hand knew every detail of what had passed while the Lowlander slept wracked in fever and pain. There had been much too much interest in the sleeping man and really not the innocent kind. He had hardly slept these last few days fully expecting some hateful fool like Vroth to dishonor the clan by trying to murder Aldred. His ploy had worked though, they were away from the hold on some strange adventure just like the heroes of old. He hoped that the foundation they had laid with the Marrodar would be enough to steer his kinsmen from blood-feud for a while longer. He breathed in the fresh air and blessed the sun rays that warmed his bones. He was away from the Hold, and pleased to be so. If the Lowlander was to be trusted in the matter of directions he knew well what valley the Ice-King Troll had claimed as its own. It was very tight in its openings with steep walls and several caves. It was a perfect den for something like a great bear or in this case a troll monstrosity. They could probably easily make it to the valley by midday, but he had no intention of charging into the valley without some sort of plan. He also liked the idea of facing the thing during the brighter hours of the morning when the sun had a chance to batter down some of the monster's white wolf given powers. So, Ulmar led them across the valley floor in a slow winding trudge which gave him ample time to forage the few edible things that could be found in the nearby valleys.

Aldred seemed a bit confused after a while, looking up towards the sun and scanning the surroundings. When they stopped at a cold brook that ran from the shaded ice of the valley he broke the silence they had held for several hours.

-"I'm sure the valley was pretty close by. I managed to get to yours half dead after all. So why is it taking such time getting there now?"

Ulmar shrugged offering the Lowlander some petals of fallchogh berry flowers. They were sweet and could keep you going for a while but poisonous if eaten for more than a few days at a time. Aldred refused his offer, instead pulling out a small pouch and pouring some of the contents into the palm of his hand. He then tossed over the pouch to Ulmar who, to his delight, discovered it to be full of raisins. He poured a generous helping for himself, taking the time to savor the sweet sustenance before answering.

-"Are you in a hurry to tackle the troll? You can barely get to the valley, much less take it on."

-"So are you leading us away from it?"

Ulmar smiled at Aldred, diffusing much of the other man's irritation.

-"Don't worry Lowlander, we'll get there. I plan on having us camp where it's safe and then take the troll on when the sun is high in the sky. An Ice-King Troll may not be much like any other troll but it still shares the same heritage. It'll be sluggish and slow then and believe me, we'll need any advantage we can get."

Apparently remembering his battle with the monster, a dark look crept over Aldred. He shuddered.

-"I see your point." Aldred smiled again. Tired and miserable yet smiling. Ulmar couldn't help wondering if the man constantly smiled when he was among his own. It was infectious, making the oh so feared Doomwolf grin like a fool. He found that he enjoyed it.

They made a small camp next to a small clump of trees and the brook. They were close to the valley of the Troll, even here one could hear the whisper of wild winds and feel a constant cool breeze sweep into their valley. They could be called fools camping so brazenly next to danger, any number of things could set upon them in their exposed position. Ulmar, though, was counting on them having more than enough warning as ice and snow would herald the monsters coming. Ulmar even afforded them the luxury of a small fire that he tended with tender care.

-"So those things are dangerous then, I take it," Aldered seemed to regret his phrasing quickly adding, "I mean, even to you and your clan."

-"If it would attack the hold it might slaughter every living thing in it and still suffer no lasting damage from all of our warriors. It is madness to fight it."

Aldred reminisced of the large and terrible thing. How easily it had butchered man and beast even when they were clad in armor.

-"If your entire clan can't take it on, how are we supposed to?"

Ulmar chuckled.

-"I thought that this was your idea, was it not, to take on the thing again."

-"I know, I know, I just don't know much about the thing", Aldred stated while absently poking the fire. "It would be so much easier if we knew just how tough it is, just know more of it. My master always reminds us that knowledge is power."

He flicked some embers that careened into the brook where they extinguished with a hiss.

-"I know it doesn't like fire, that's the only reason I'm still alive."

-"You fought it off with a torch?"

The Hillman didn't know of course the true measure of power that Aldred possessed. He was tempted to explain to him in more detail just what he could do, but wasn't thrilled by the idea of what his words would lure in the way of reactions.

-"Not quite. A bit more powerful than that."

-"Well except for moving in when it's most likely to be resting and sneaking in then I'm not sure."

A particularly strong breeze fanned the flames into a tall fiery tongue that licked the sky for a moment. Aldred closed his coat tightly around himself thinking he should pull out his blanket for warmth before he realised that Ulmar didn't have any cloak or pack other than a small shoulder-bag filled with what little supplies were left and of course his massive and mysterious waraxe. The Lumbrians he found to be dressed in warm and practical clothes mostly made of wool, leather and furs. It confounded him that the veteran outdoorsman that the hillman seemed to be wasn't wearing more or carried more. Aldred pulled out his cloak and blanket and handed Ulmar the blanket. Ulmar gratefully accepted it.

-"Ulmar", Aldred began tentatively, "do you fear the Bone-Woman's powers?"

The larger man shrugged.

-"Less than most. She wields secrets that weren't given to man, which threaten to consume her any moment she uses them. Personally, I wouldn't say that no good can come of delving into the unknown like many of my people claim, she's proof of how much one can accomplish with the power. Magic always seems to come with a price though and almost always that price is all too high. I still do not feel comfortable around them but I don't know if I'd say I fear them."

Aldred was surprised that there was a glimmer of true insight in the barbarians' words. Magic always came at a steep price and he could personally confirm how dangerous it could be to cut corners or embrace power when it came to those powers.

-"I need to show you something. Just take the time and know that I'm still me and I have no intention of hurting you."

Aldred tried to move slowly and held his arms out in a gesture that he hoped was nonthreatening. Ulmar was clearly suspicious as Aldred wondered if this was a good idea. A little bit too swiftly the apprentice murmured his incantation and let fire engulf his hands. It was too sudden and too much he realised, his inner showman had gotten hold of him. Ulmar watched the smaller man stand up, mutter and then a shining red flame breached out from his palms and spread across the mans' hands. Actual flames. Fire. Ulmar understood how feral he must look and was barely aware of the sizable rock before it had left his hand and was hurtling toward the Lowlanders head. Conflicted between feeling that he might have overreacted and outraged at the obvious display of magic he had no time to resolve his feelings before the rock brutally impacted the blond man's skull. With a painful smack of impact Aldred tumbled backwards, the fire going out as he fell heavily to the ground.

Ulmar wondered if he had killed the man. He lay there still on his back making no sound and no movement. He covered the distance between them in a half dozen swift strides and stopped over the lifeless man. With a resounding wailing of pain Aldred put his hands on his forehead where the stone had hit him. The outdrawn "ouch" ended in the apprentice laying laughing on the ground.

-"What's wrong with you? Why the blazes would you do that?"

Relieved, Ulmar laughed with the man sheepishly, quick to help him up to a sitting position. They sat there laughing together a while, Ulmar not knowing what to say or if he even wanted to apologise. There had been fire, *actual fire* in the mans' hands. Or rather, coming from the mans' hands.

-"You can summon fire to your bidding?"

Ulmar examined Aldreds soft hands for any sign of scorching but found none. Aldred looked dumbfounded for a moment before he answered Ulmar.

-"Why yes, I suppose I do. It's rather more complicated than that but pretty much the truth."

-"Did it hurt?"

-"No, not..."

-"What more can you do?"

Aldred chuckled still with a hand pressed against his forehead. Ulmar quickly pulled out some of the bitter brew that Kallabra had given them to strengthen Aldred on the road. Aldred looked at it and made a face of disgust showing just what he thought of his medicine. Ulmar mercilessly poured up some of the brew in a guksi then quick as an adder forced it down Aldreds throat. Aldred pushed away the guksi and started talking in what seemed to be an attempt to dissuade Ulmar from administering more medicine.

-"All sorts of things I suppose, most things are possible but every spell is carefully researched and designed. Magic is the will forming the world around you through intellect and discipline. It's an inadequately rough description but I hope it'll give you an idea of what it is. My magic comes from study and understanding, through which I can manipulate the universe to change the world around me. But I can only cast those spells that I have gained understanding of and mastered. The more complicated things I need to weave spells to perform and once I call upon them, the power of the magic tends to rip part of them from my mind, so I brush up on them to regain the power. Some things I can call upon more or less at will and even shape them to a degree. Personally I have an affinity for fire."

-"Does fire burn you?"

-"Yes it can, but the flames I call are under my control. Mostly. Fire is after all a wild force."

-"And this is how you fought off the Ice-King Troll? You called fire from your hands and burned him?"

-"Yes. I threw fire at him. It worked to a degree, but it was all too little."

Ulmar sat down next to Aldred considering what he had learnt. He wondered if Kallabra had known that the Lowlander was some sort of fire summoning witch. Probably, she had lived long and seen much, not to speak of she had strange and mystical powers of her own. He imagined that if someone delved into the dark arts they would be able to know a fellow practitioner if they came over them. Had Briac and the rest of the Tuakk known ,none would have even suggested that they did anything other than kill the man in some outrageous manner, if they didn't fear that his power was too great that is. He was glad that the lowlander had the wisdom to keep his dealings to himself when they were back in the hold. Ulmar should be more mortified and even fearful but couldn't help being intrigued by Aldred and his mystical ways. There wasn't ill will and darkness in his eyes as he would expect from a demon summoner, there was curiosity and laughter.

-"Summoning fire", Ulmar smiled and smacked Aldred on the back and immediately regretted his forceful gesture as Aldred more or less fell over, "that, we can use."

-"We go tomorrow."

Aldreds statement might have been meant as a strong and unwavering one but came across almost like a question.

-"Only if you wish death upon us both. I don't wish it upon you, and certainly don't want it for myself."

-"We need to get going as soon as possible. I need to get back the item, and then we need to go. The longer we wait, the more dangerous whatever power is growing from the throne gets. Besides", Aldred very clearly looked over

Ulmars gear, "if we wait much longer we'll starve. I only have about four days' rations left all in all, after that we need to get to a village for supplies. Unless your bags are deeper than they seem."

-"Then we stay for three days. Press on quicker than that and we only run to our graves. You need rest and the health that Kallabras' potion brings you. That gives us a day to get to a village if we survive and I know of one nearby where you can trade with other lowlanders for more food. Try to get to the troll before that and I'll return to the hold and let the thing pick its teeth with your bones. Three days, so empty your sacks of whatever edible you are carrying and we'll see how far we'll get."

The two benched their discussion and piled their foodstuffs on a large slab of rock that sat on the edge of their campsite. There was much more than Ulmar had been led to believe. The Lowlander was carrying four blocks of travel rations that were a compact mix of dried fruit, dried meat, spices and animal fat. He called them westland rations and it seemed one could eat them as was or stir them into porridge or soup if one could only find a vessel that was large enough to hold them. Even one of these would be enough to keep a man going for several days Ulmar thought for himself. It was clear that the Lowlander was unused to starving. Excluding these, they still had half a pouch of raisins, three actual apples (Ulmar had no idea how the man could keep apples in an edible shape till now.), a pouch with dried chanterelles and a compact sausage of some kind. Ulmar, on the other hand had managed to procure a slice of goat cheese, some mostly edible bread, a blacksalt root and luxurious slice of womcalf which was a kind of sausage made from ground gristle, leftover meat and innards including tripe all served stuffed in any stomach or intestine one could get hold of and spiced with salt and onion. Considering Ulmars diet the last several months it made him happy considering all that had to do for only four days. Aldred would probably feel some effects of hunger and seeing how he was wounded Ulmar decided to let him have the lion's share of food, there was still more than enough to go around.

23.

They camped in the cold valley for those three days, just as
Ulmar had insisted, making a makeshift shelter from the
wind from braiding pine branches into a bush wood frame.
Sometimes during their stay they could hear the
bloodcurdling roar of the creature, reminding them that
this temporary reprieve was just a wait until they could face
the thing in the valley.

They tried making a plan of how to deal with the thing, but
couldn't come up with anything better than trying to sneak
in, and if that failed, fling fire at it before Ulmar charged in.
Instead they got to know each other some more. Ulmar
told Aldred of his Winter, with his stay in the small
neighboring valley to the hold and the relative peace and
quiet he had enjoyed there even if he narrowly avoided
death. Aldred on the other hand told Ulmar of his own
Winter in the fortress that was dubbed the Shimmering
Tower. According to Aldred, the name was literal, as the
high stone tower shimmered with a soft golden glow that
could be seen for miles during the dark Winter nights. He
had been housed in his master's lodgings, a series of
rooms that was high in the tower itself. This was the first
time that Aldred had spoken of his master Lya
Stormwhistle, a fully fledged wizard that served under the
Tower Lord Sarsara. Ulmar realised that Aldred was holding
something back as he told him of the falling out that he

and Lya had during the dark times. Aldred professed to have made contact with a network of like-minded defenders of the realm that had spread warnings of incoming doom from the great mountain that was shaped as a throne. Lya, who was talented in the scrying and soothsaying ways, had refused to acknowledge the threat stating that the oncoming destruction was a war of clans among the true folk and no business of the Valerians. So Aldred claimed that he had organized the expedition himself, mustered funds and folk to wander out as soon as the weather allowed it. Owing to a young white dragon setting up its lair near the border of the towerlords domain, Winter seemed unwilling to retreat to the North. Ulmar had heard of the terrifying beasts but had never faced one himself. He was amazed how matter of factly the Lowlander spoke of it, a member of one of the most terrifying and powerful beings in the world. It sounded like the dragon was similar to the Ice-King Troll in that it spread the breath of the White Wolf around it enforcing Winter. Still there was something missing from the young apprentice tale, something that might be important or might just be that Aldred didn't find important. Ulmar didn't press the matter, more interested that Aldred regained his strength. Kallabras medicine worked wonders getting Aldred in better shape every day so when the third day finally came he was mostly stiff and sore but nothing worse than that.

There was no more avoiding the matter. They needed to get moving to regain whatever magical trinket that Aldred was prepared to die for, and the Ice-King Troll would be waiting for any who were foolish enough to enter its valley. In silence they collected their gear and left for the valley soon after the first morning rays found them. Aldred had spent all day yesterday with his nose in that strange book he wore on a chain on his hip so apparently he was now ready as he'd ever be to face the beast.

They reached the entrance to the small valley soon enough. Aldred recognized it due to it having the skeleton of a great big buck scattered about, a sign if anything, that there was danger ahead, but on the other hand there seemed to be danger all round the lands beyond the Valerian border. They strode ahead, getting the first clear image of the area. The valley was shaped like a crooked ship along which sides there were a multitude of entrances to caves of unknown depths. There was still a fair amount of snow in the valley as if it had been exempted from the coming of spring making it a white wound in the surrounding hills. Ulmar could easily spot a handful of snowy mounds that couldn't be anything other than the remains of beasts and men. He noticed how determined Aldred was to push on, despite the anguish he must feel at the sight. Not speaking, they made their way into the valley and towards the snowy mounds. Only a few flakes fell down on them as they neared the remains. The massive troll wasn't anywhere to be seen at least, good news if ever there was. Aldred stopped at one of the mounds, it was roughly the shape of the frontal parts of a large steed and even the snow couldn't hide the frame of the dead creatures' steel barding.

-"This is, was, Prevalence. A fine steed if ever there was one. It seems my naming was more than a little premature."

Aldred started looking around for the rest of the beast.

-"I imagine that Trolls are fond of the taste of horse-meat. You can still see the drag marks."

It was clear as the sky to Ulmar, the grooves and marks that the heavy horse had cut into the ground, even covered in snow as it was. He realised that Aldred, who seemed to come from a world very much different than his own, might not see them. To try and be helpful, Ulmar indicated how the marks headed straight for one of the cave entrances. Ulmar brushed flakes from the increasing snow from his hair and walked over to Aldred who was crouching by his dead steed.

-"It was in my saddlebag.", Aldred whispered, his voice sounding drained. "How are we supposed to get hold of it, if it was in my damnable saddlebag. I can't find anything in all of this and it could be anywhere from here all the way to the bottom of the world for all we know. For every moment we tarry will just make it that more difficult to find now that it's snowing."

-"It might be snowing more, but we'll find it I promise you. I've found harder prey in little time."

Aldred got to his feet and helped Ulmar canvas the ground as they started searching the ground from the horse carcass toward the cave mouth.

-"Does it ever stop snowing in this, and you'll have to excuse me for calling it thus, damnable part of the world?"

Ulmar shoved over a rock that for a moment seemed to be a leather pouch.

-"It won't snow much now, watch the sky, it's almost clear. When melting takes hold it almost never snows. The only reason it's snowing now is how close we are to the Hrimmkuningaz trötl. You see some things like white dragons, Hrimmkuningaz trötl, or the white wolf himself spread frost about them wherever they are."

The snow was getting thicker. The sky was still quite clear, the sun was high in the sky spreading warmth and light over the world. Yet there was an ever increasing thickness to the snowflakes that danced across the valley. Cold seemed to be seeping from the rock itself around the cave mouth they were heading for. The two of them grew restless as the realisation started to seep on them.

-"Is that?" Aldred managed to sputter out.

-"Hurry!" Ulmar hissed in answer.

The Troll was on its way. They started searching with much greater intensity which neared frenzy. They were half way up to the cave entrance without even a hint of anything even faintly resembling a bag. Aldred crept down on all fours shuffling aside the snow from anything that was large enough to be the bag while Ulmar used Kharagh to poke at any mound he came over. The only thing giving them cover from where they stood and the cave opening was a single round boulder, other than that the ground was smooth mostly made up of gravel and rocks making Ulmar wonder if it was for better or for worse that the side of the valley was covered in deceptive ice. The snow was practically forming a sheet that covered the sky making it increasingly difficult to see anything at all let alone find the saddlebags. Still there wasn't much of a choice, if they didn't find the thing they couldn't get to whatever Aldred was seeking at the throne.

Cold wind whipped the clothes around Ulmars body, numbing him and making his exposed skin sting painfully. He shivered as his breath puffed out in great big misty clouds. He had to force his eyes open, keep scouring the ground around him. He almost slipped on a sheet of ice that he would normally have seen easily, but keeping his gaze constantly searching at this pace made it difficult to keep track of the ground at one's feet.

There. It had to be it. Ulmar more or less leapt forward, jabbing Kharagh at the small mound. The snow initially gave way softly before the axe clanged against something hard that could only be metal. As the axe did so Ulmar could feel a sharp warm pain shoot up his arm and spread out through his body. He wasn't sure what had happened and had no time to consider it further. He grabbed at the snow covered leather and pulled it up. The bag wasn't more than halfway full so he could only hope that whatever they were risking their life for was in it.

-"Here!" Ulmar lifted the bag and tossed it over to Aldred as soon as he saw that he had gotten the Lowlanders attention. Aldred caught it and visibly brightened as he held it.

-"Now run! Run before we serve as the Ice-Kings next meal!"

Aldred was heading back toward the opening to the valley before Ulmar was finished shouting. They started running and had gotten a dozen yards before a massive beastial roar annonced the arrival of the feared Hrimmkuningaz Trötl. Ulmar slowed down, heavy-heartedly reconciling with his fate.

-"Run!" He bellowed to Aldred. "Run back to where we made camp and if you feel the snow follow just keep on running!"

Aldred nodded and kept going into the snowy valley. Ulmar was pleased that at least the lowlander would make it out, that he wouldn't share Ulmars gruesome fate. He flexed his muscles warming up for the struggle ahead casually strolling back into the wind and back to the boulder. He was now standing in the full force of an unnatural blizzard that threatened to chill him to the bone. He could see a great shape sauntering toward him. He knew it for what it was not so much seeing but imagining the long, thick arms that ended in claws and the humanoid head with its thorny crown. It was death and it was coming for him.

-"You waste my time Troll!" Ulmar threw his spite filled words at the thing. "If I am to walk into the shadow of the wolves then let it be done with!"

Ulmar was careful to put the mass of the boulder between him and the monster as he took on a brazen battle-stance.

-"I am Ulmar the Doomwolf of the Tuakk, son of Lathrik and Aina, descendant of Trimboldumn, born of the True Folk and slayer of countless vile things. I hold Kharagh, it, and I will break your teeth and bleed pain from your flesh!"

Ulmar could feel his blood pounding in his temples, his body shaking from the scent of the upcoming combat. A massive rumbling burst out from the shadowy figure of the Troll. He realised it was laughing at him, a long, terrible hearty laugh. The figure stepped closer to the boulder and the snow seemed to open up so he could get a clear look at the monster. It was indeed as he had heard it described, a huge manlike or ogre-like thing with long massive arms that ended in sharp claws. It carried compacted fat layered around its bulk much like a fat man but it seemed hard, like a natural armor of sorts. From its body, dark, icy protrusions grew, being either bone or ice, they definitely seemed deadly. Its head was a mockery of human visage in shape and in its mouth two massive tusks grew. On its head several sharp spikes grew toward the sky, much resembling a crown. Its eyes were not those of a savage beast, instead there was a glimmer of intelligence, of calculation that told Ulmar that it had understood what he had told it.

-"King meat!" Its rumbling voice was hard to make out but it had really spoken to him in his own tongue. Ulmar had heard that some Trolls could speak but none of them were said to be more intelligent than the slowest man. He got the impression that when it came to this particular Troll that fact might be mistaken.

-"Then choke on my bones!" Ulmar snarled, as he grabbed a rock and threw it straight at the monster's head.

The rolling laugh turned into a guttural roar as the rock impacted with the monster's brow. The space between the monster and himself was now full of raging snow-filled wind making said monster only stand out like a dark pillar in front of Ulmar. He could hear great thudding steps as the Troll accelerated at a frightening rate straight toward the boulder between them. What hope Ulmar had put in the object being a barrier between them was rudely doused as the monster slammed into the rock which hurtled toward him as a deadly ball. If the boulder hadn't been spinning sideways Ulmar would probably have been summarily crushed but instead he managed to clamber hold off the thing, a moment before being thrown to the side. He landed heavily on his side while being more or less buried in snow. As he came to a stop he felt the scratches of what felt like a hundred sharp frozen rocks as they scratched him bloody. As quickly as he could, but all too slowly, he got to his feet only to be face to face with the monster as it hurtled its fist toward him in an attempt to crush him. Without hesitation, Ulmar threw himself heedlessly to the side, rolling and quickly finding his feet. As he did, he pushed upwards, landing a blow after he spun the axe full circle. The brutal impact of the ever sharp Kharagh cut through skin, fat, muscle, tendon and bone as Ulmar chopped through half of the troll's throat and chin. The axe kept momentum which Ulmar used to spin into a fierce backhand swing that lodged the axe deep in the center of the things belly. The Troll spun, roiling in pain making it possible for Ulmar to put all his weight on the hilt and rip his weapon free. Dancing away from the aimless blows of the troll he got out of the reach of its claws to find where he could land the killing blow. The troll choked and sputtered then came to a stop facing Ulmar. It spewed black blood in an attempt to roar at the insolent human. Ulmars heart dropped as he saw the massive monster smile as the horrible wounds he had inflicted started to close before his very eyes. The troll shook and what blood had been spilt was mostly on Kharagh and on the ground. The Hrimmkuningaz Trötl bounded toward him with a deadly menace, meaning to squash him into a pulp. Ulmar did the only thing he could think of, he charged the monster back. Hammering his feet to the ground he built up speed, roaring at his enemy. The troll jumped with raised arms intending to land with pulverizing force and would have succeeded if Ulmar had been slower. Instead Ulmar ducked under the crushing monstrosity viciously cutting upward between the thing's legs. The troll buckled and Ulmar smashed a second blow into its back, then a third and a fourth. Black blood colored the ground around them as the raging Hillman kept his massive axe in constant motion. He ducked under the troll's wild swing and heaved a blow into the things' armpit. Any other weapon would probably have snagged a rib or gotten caught in bone but Kharagh cut with the anger of its wielder. Ulmar felt the fury and joyous exaltation of the berserker build with every blow, and knew that soon there would only be glorious destruction. It was the call of the berserker that he had fought all his life but during this last battle, he intended to give in to it. Then the troll met his axe with an outstretched hand, getting it cleaved in two, but instead of pulling the appendage back the thing closed its mangled hand around the axe and even Ulmars arms and simply threw the man as far away from it as it could. Kharagh slipped out of Ulmars grasp, sailing through the air and lodging into a large rock.

Ulmars rage was broken. His elbows ached from being pushed to the brink of bending backwards and he was tired. He sat there panting waiting for death. There was no way he could get to the axe before the monster caught him. Its wounds were all closing, only small lines that could have been scars remained. But he knew he had hurt it. It was almost as furious as he was, and he prayed to whatever power might be watching to give him the strength to resist it some more, hurt it some more and make his death into a good one.

The thing loomed over him with unrestrained anger. It spread its arms to grab the broken man. Then a red blaze of fire the size of a mans' head sizzled into the mouth of the troll. The Hrimmkuningaz Trötl faced the underwhelming stature of Aldred, who stood speaking and gesturing in the strong wind with hands that were swathed in fire. Ulmar both felt sincere gratitude towards the man for coming back to help him, and heavy disappointment that he would share Ulmars doom. He couldn't help but be impressed by the sight of the dashing man, how much he looked the part of a hero as he flung another blaze straight at the monster.

There was hope to keep the struggle going now, Ulmar pushed toward the axe, helped by the wind, gaining speed much quicker because of it. He grabbed hold of the hilt of Kharagh and turned only to face the much greater force of an increasing blizzard. He couldn't see the troll any longer but knew that it stood in the heart of the unnatural wind. Ulmar imagined the force of the wind snuffing out the fire from Aldreds hands and the troll savagely biting the Lowlander to death. A new funnel of white hot rage burned in Ulmars heart. He forced himself forward when he should not be able, pushing for every step keeping the monster in mind, determined to aid his new found friend. He could hear his voice run out into the wind, hear how he was roaring out his defiance with words that he felt but did not understand. He met the Troll head on, it faced him as he pushed his will into a white ball of righteous fury as he raised his axe once more. Ulmar was barely conscious, barely able to see and heard only the howling of wolves in his ear. The Trolls' eyes widened as Kharaghs blade shone intensely white and flashed into a blinding explosion of light. The last image Ulmar saw of the Troll was how it was turning in horror with an eye and chunks of its face turned to stone. The blizzard raged on but lessened as the monster fled as fast it could from the Doomwolf.

Ulmar sagged on the ground, beaten, cold and confused. Not that far from him Aldred had sunken down on his knees and cradled his left hand. As the snow ebbed to a persistent sheet Ulmar made his way over to the lowlander. He wanted to ask him if he was ok, if he was hurt but Ulmar was too tired to speak instead he just put his hand on the man's shoulder.

-"The damn thing burned me. It actually burned me. Just look."

Aldred showed Ulmar his palm. It was as if someone had branded him. There was a large part of a circular pattern and in it there was a complicated arrangement of runes, decorative patterns and arcane markings.

-"I felt something was happening so I reached for the seal and it burned me. Why did it do that?"

Ulmar had no idea, no idea why magic acted like it did or even what Aldred was talking about but he knew that they hadn't killed the Troll, only driven it off.

-"We need to get away before it returns."

Ulmar helped Aldred to his feet, and together they hastened out of the valley only stopping to pick up a mangled backpack they happened upon on the way.

24.

It was near dark as they shuffled to a halt by a creek in an unknown valley. Ulmar should have known better than to wander around blindly in the lethal lands of the True Folk but there was no helping it, he was all too exhausted. They were barely able to scrape together a fire for the night, ending up with a smoldering pile of birchwood. Aldred was much more present than Ulmar, though he cradled his scorched hand like a wounded bird. Ulmar mostly felt drained as he stared at the Lowlander. As they sat there Ulmar broke out in a hearty laugh which drew a confused look from Aldred.

-"We are alive, Lowlander. Do you know how lucky we are after going up against a Hrimmkuningaz Trötl? Even among the heroes of old, few survived an encounter."

Aldred shook his head though he looked a little more lighthearted.

-"Let's see this thing of legend that we've risked our lives for."

Taking out the saddlebag Aldred was slow in his movements, hesitating as he came to the point where he would have to pull out the item from within. With his burned hand he cautiously tested the thing with dabs of his fingers just like you would with something that was scolding hot. After a handful of testing touches he finally pulled an object from within. He tossed it over to Ulmar who caught it easily. It was a flat, round disk made of brass, bronze or even gold. It reminded him of a large coin of some sort minted by a metalworking giant. The object felt heavy in his hand, yet not overly so as it rightly should, being slightly broader than you could fit in your hand. Inscribed into the metal were an intricate design of arcane symbols, runes and decorations that perfectly resembled those in Aldreds palm.

-"What is it?"

-"No one knows," Aldred responded. "They are known as Saedr Seals, and I know that they are very old and steeped in strong magic. I've heard of several others, maybe half a dozen at the most. That one seems bound to the mountain that's called the throne and with it I will find my way past the mountains hardships and discover what it is that threatens the land."

Ulmar reflected the light from the fire in the seal, studying the intricate metalwork. Whatever it was, he admired its intricate decorations, how when he followed one he discovered a completely new facet of patterns. If it was that old it should really be grimier, less smooth and shiny. The discs' features reminded him of Kharagh spawning all sorts of ideas in his mind. It was pretty but he didn't understand how it would help them.

-"How do you know that?"

-"It was told to me by a Seer."

Ulmar nodded, accepting the explanation at face value. If the Bonewoman had told him something similar he would have done as she wished from trust alone.

-"Then we will make it out as we get there."

Aldred relaxed after Ulmar had given the seal back to him and he had put it away. The lowlander leaned back and smiled just enjoying drawing breath at the moment. Yet curiosity lured him to action.

-"Your axe. I've understood that it was given to you when you were a newborn? Where does it come from?"

-"Kharagh is older than the tales of my people, some say it was one of the first weapons to be forged by the fallen gods when the world was in its crib. I say those stories are just that, stories. Kharagh is a thing from another time, when our people ruled the world. It is no more and no less. Why do you ask?"

Ulmar held the weapon casually in one hand. It caught the red light of the flames, its reflections dancing along the metal of the menacing head.

-"I have never seen anything like it. If I had to guess I'd say that it's made from next to pure darksteel, mined from the roots of the mountain and inlaid with moonsilver, the combination is impossible. Only a handful of master smiths among the Dwarves have ever been known to be able to work darksteel. The secret of forging moonsilver is an art that the Elves have guarded since the dawn of their race. To see them forged together is like seeing midnight marry the noonday sun. Those runes that you see cleverly hidden in the artwork are also dwarven, but they are interwoven by elven runes and stranger still are those symbols tying them together, they look very much like Archoterroran mystic symbols, used by ancient human spellcasters. The artwork in itself is unknown to me. What you hold in your hand is a paradox, a mad daydream, yet it's there. It doesn't read as magical, I hope you'll excuse me but I've already checked, yet there is something that whispers that it is more than what it seems."

-"I'm not surprised. The heroes of old mastered the world in a way we will never do again. It is said that Trimboldumns grandsire lived in a great city that never grew dark; instead it was lit by conjured starlight. In their time there was no need for hunger and all men knew the art of carving runes into parchment. During that age, great and powerful artifacts were crafted and only a handful have survived the ages to this day. I believe that it was then that Kharagh was forged. It is true that this was before the fall of the Gods so some might have had a hand in its creation, but I doubt that it is older than that.

For me this is, and will always be, a hand on my shoulder from my father and mother and from them a path into the past to my ancestors. It is a mighty weapon indeed that scores of warriors envy me for, but to me it's much more."

Ulmar wasn't sure why he was this comfortable opening up to Aldred, who in all honesty was a complete stranger. There was just something so open and honest about the man, he spread an air of life and hope around him. He also felt deeply that he was on the right path following him on his quest. Being a little self conscious at that moment he steered the conversation slightly away from himself.

-"That "Saedr Disc" as you call it, it looks a lot like Kharagh. Do you think that it could have been forged by my ancestors?"

-"Possibly. I couldn't help observing and thinking the same. I know it's old, so it's far from impossible. As I've come to understand it, it was found deep within some ancient ruin from long ago by a band of roving adventurers. But where they were at the time I'm unsure of."

-"Well I am in your debt for the spell you cast that drove off the Ice-King Troll", Ulmar said remembering the terrifying form of the great monster, "If you hadn't I would surely have been dead by now. That white blast came at the best possible moment"

Aldred tilted his head to the side.

-"What do you mean? I didn't cast any such spell."

-"Of course you did. The shining white light that swathed around the blade of Kharagh made it shine brilliantly as the sun. If it hadn't been for that we would not have been able to drive off the Troll."

-"That's the thing, I didn't cast any such spell. I have no idea what kind of magic it was but it can't have come from anything other than from Kharagh itself. The thing is not imbued with any magic so I'm uncertain how it happened, but it wasn't me."

-"The disc then. You said that it burned you. Could it have been from that?"

Aldred stroked the ruined saddlebag affectionately.

-"That's the most likely source really. As you charged the Troll I felt something pulse from the disc, some kind of wave in the air. It's why I pulled it out. As I did there was a white flash from it as your axe shone like a star. Well, that settles it, that has to be the source of the magic, there's no other alternative."

-"Let's go through the spoils of our battle then."

Ulmar pulled forth the backpack he had managed to grab when they were on their way out of the valley. Aldred came over to him and they sat down to examine what they could salvage from it. The leather was badly savaged by three ragged claw marks that ran the length of the pack. It was a small miracle that the piece of equipment had managed to hold together as long as it had. From it they pulled a set of dark green traveling clothes that would need some serious attention with needle and thread if they were to be of any use again. There was a handful of usable camp gear as well, including a fully functioning tinderbox at which Aldred scoffed. He explained that the day that he couldn't produce such an insignificant flame that could light a fire, he would be beyond the use of said fire and had no use of it. Ulmar, on the other hand, put the box aside among the salvageable gear. Securely fastened in a pocket they drew out a coin purse that contained no less than fifty gold in mixed coins. According to Aldred the sum was enough to secure equipment and lodgings in any civilized settlement for as long as their quest would take. The True Folk had little use for coins as such, so Ulmar took Aldreds word for it. Ulmar was much more content finding a small salted pork and a stout bottle of wine wrapped in a mostly undamaged cloak. He was unsure how long ago it was since he had the pleasure of wrapping himself up in a cloak so he was quick to take it as his own.

They also found a beautiful leather bound book among a small stack of scribbled missives. Aldred picked it up and just held it. The mans' happy face bore lines of woe that Ulmar felt very misplaced on the lowlanders dashing features.

-"This is, *was*, Ardews. He used to read from it when we camped for the night. He was a squire you see, a very dutiful one at that. He had convinced his master that it would do him well to know of the poetry of Eadenheart if he was to find a noble-born wife. So he'd read aloud for us by the light of the campfire with a passion worthy of any bard. I suspect there were other motives afoot though. You see, Ardews was shrewd beyond his years and a surprisingly gentle soul for a mercenary. I suspect that his master couldn't read. When I signed them on, Sir Elefter signed clumsily and let Ardew read the document for him. I suspect that Ardew was trying to show Sir Elefter that there was more to life than the sword, the cup and the saddle in his own way. And now thanks to me, he never will."

Ulmar felt for Aldred. He had wrestled with the same kind of feelings when his own kin had followed him into battle and never returned home. He hadn't himself found a way to reconcile himself with his feelings and suspected that it was something men had to carry to their graves.

-"We cannot decide when death finds us. Would they have chosen another path, they could have died years ago or lived till they were a hundred, we cannot know. They chose to follow you and you did all you could to keep them safe, you cannot change what happened but you can choose to honor them by fulfilling your mission. Maybe their deaths will mean that countless others might live."

Aldred smiled at him and mumbled out a "I'm sure you're right" but Ulmar could see that the weight of the fate of those he had led to his doom still burdened him. He decided to leave it be and focus on the future.

-"What now? We have your magical disc that you needed, what do you intend to do now?"

-"We need to get to the Throne but first we need to get provisions. What I've understood is that we are at least a week or two from the mountain. Do you know of any villages that we might find provisions in? Any lowlander settlements?"

-"Penkath. We should head to Penkath."

25.

The village of Penkath was a rugged homestead of Lowland frontiersmen built within the borders of ancestral Tuakk and Marrodar lands. It was mainly constructed around the non existent road that theoretically connected the settlement to two other newly constructed villages. To one of its sides the village had a small river which provided it with more than enough fresh water and also powered the village mill. Penkath was a collection of maybe fifty timber houses, none larger than three stories, among these the village inn and hall being the largest. As of yet there wasn't a single stone or brick building but the village had the vibrant feel of a settlement in growth so it was only a matter of time before hardier materials would be used in the construction of more permanent buildings. The village was not far from the dell of Turundar whose inhabitants most assuredly had come from Penkath.

Ulmar hesitated as they got their first glimpse of the village. As a Tuakk, he couldn't imagine that he'd be a welcome sight in the Lowlander settlement. Stopping suddenly to do so, he wrapped Kharagh in his new cloak and fastened leather straps to keep the package fastened in the cloth. At least this way he might be safer from thieves and not overtly display any aggression toward the people who invaded his land.

-"Won't that leave you a bit naked?" Aldred queried.

-"The day Kharagh can't cut through cloth is the day the mountains turn to dust."

With that they kept on into the village.

There was no defensive perimeter, only a low fence meant to keep the livestock in check. As they walked the gravel road it became more and more obvious that there was precious little in the way of preparation for the inevitable raids that were the way of life up here in the hills of the True Folk. Ulmar wondered how it was that the place hadn't been burned to the ground long ago if it was as open as it seemed. Certainly, the doors of the houses were thick and bound by iron bands, but in no way impregnable. Maybe the people here believed that locks and bars would keep raiders away.

They started to see and pass villagers who were on their way on daily errands, milling along the street in a strange combination of purpose and haphazardness. Many seemed to be the resident settlers, farmers clad in strange designs, all dressed in a veritable rainbow of colors in Ulmars eyes. The majority of these courteously tipped their hats at the sign of the two travellers but none stopped to introduce themselves. Ulmar noticed just how at ease Aldred flowed through the crowd and couldn't help but wonder how he himself would have fared if he'd have to traverse the village alone.

There were also rugged outdoorsmen, trappers and travellers that had a much more suspicious air around them than the farmers of the village. They were the sort that the Tuakk most often happened upon, they looked much more like Ulmar and his people but were despised for their honorless ways. Still, another handful were hanging about the street armed to the teeth and armored for battle. These were probably some of the famed Valerian "adventurers" that even Ulmars people had heard of. They seemed to be gangs of rootless, would-be heroes that were hard to distinguish from petty highwaymen and graverobbers, if any such distinction existed. A gang of five such questionable individuals followed Ulmars' movement with overt hostility as they neared the middle of the village. They were wise enough to keep their distance but openly followed the pair as Aldred steered toward one of the two three story buildings in the village. The house smelled of food and had a large wooden sign with fruit and meat painted on it.

-"Right, let me do the talking if you'd be so kind," Aldred stated as he pulled open the door.

Entering it was clear that the house was an inn of some kind. The first floor was organised in an open way with a large dining or tap room dominating most of the floor and a door to what was probably the kitchen in the back. There was a large brick fireplace, which was an alien sight to Ulmar who was accustomed to firepits, and a counter near the kitchen that seemed to serve as a bar. Though not overtly full the room was far from empty, most of the patrons having the look of either travellers or fighters.

Their entrance was more or less anonymous thanks to two short and stocky men with intricate beards that were openly shouting at each other. Ulmars heart jumped as they very much fit into the description of the elusive men from within the mountain.

-"Well at least I can rely on the knowledge of my father and his father before him instead of sticking my arsewoddled thumb in the air and just guessing at it."

The speaker, bald on top and wearing a wide assortment of tools hanging from his outfit sneered at his opponent.

-"Oh that again. Do ya not have anything new to contribute but your incessant jabbering about the long dead and departed? Just 'cause your daddy knew his way around a hammer don't mean that you have an inkling about any of it. It doesn't just seep in from the air ya know, ya actually have'ta work for it. But, only work I've seen you doing is heave your fat belly around and talk ill of your betters."

The speaker, a blond fellow with a beard that seemed completely unable to keep from curling in on itself, was red in the face as he spat out his retort at the first.

Sliding into a chair a short way into the room Aldred maneuvered them from prying eyes and the risk of being in the immediate line of fire. As he did slide down he also gestured to a young woman nearby who had answered his summon before Ulmar had fully sat down.

-"Don't you mind these two, at it more often than a dog catches fleas. What can I get you luvs?"

Falling into the custom of his people, Ulmar started to introduce himself.

-"I am", was all that he managed to pronounce before Aldred blatantly interrupted him.

-"Thirsty. So he'll be having a large ale andli'll have whatever red that most passes for civilized, we'll both be having whatever's quick and warm and we'll also be taking two rooms. To be clear I'll be paying upfront for the next three days."

With a dazzling display of sleight of hand Aldred pulled out several golden coins and let them dance along his fingers. The woman smiled most ingratiatingly as she quickly plucked the coins from Aldreds hand.

-"Gracious me, my lord, I'll be straight over with your drinks before you know it. Don't mind the two of them, they'll be punching it out in a few blinks of an eye and then they'll be locked in at the marshalls, it's just one of them weekly occurrences."

With that the woman was away towards the kitchen. The two stout individuals were still at it, if anything all the more heated now. People around the argueing two seemed excited over the prospect of what was to come openly passing coins in wager. A stout woman at the bar was by now shouting at the two "not in my bar you don't" over and over again to no avail.

-"Well your *Khrungztaftr* bleats into a weak *Hrangztathr* so instead of *vorstakkacht zalk dvergi* I'll just let you burp your Valerian."

-"*Throkk tuuvan beandi!*"

Whatever the phrase had been it marked the opening of hostilities between the two of them. Recklessly the two men from within the mountain threw themselves upon each other, fists flying while spewing what had to be insults in their native tongue. In their fury, they kicked over chairs and even managed to overturn one of the smaller tables as they ended up rolling on the floor. Ulmar was waiting to see if any of the gathered people would step in and stop the combatants but even Aldred was leaning back to watch the fight, like some sort of entertainment. The woman at the bar on the other hand was still furiously shouting at the two stepping around the counter with a bucket which she summarily overturned over the two. Ulmar wasn't enjoying the unworthy display. If this was indeed the hall of the woman with the bucket the two men from within the mountain were bringing shame to themselves and all around them by acting thus under the roof of another. Purposefully putting down Kharagh on the table Ulmar got up and stepped into the fray. He heard Aldreds protest behind him but didn't care. With a great pull Ulmar lifted the two from the floor and with a great heave he tugged them off each other. The combatants were much heavier than Ulmar had counted on, compact, but they were pulled from each other all the same.

The surprise of the arrival of an outside force was written in their faces as they with slack jawed faces stared at Ulmar for a moment. That moment passed quickly enough as they ferociously charged at each other again. Reacting Ulmar bludgeoned the balding man with a savage punch in one fluent motion pulling his body back into an equally savage elbow that cracked into the blond mans' forehead.

-"Enough!"

The shout was probably not strictly needed as the two lay on the floor dazed and moaning. There was a disappointed murmur from the patrons who had been betting on the combatants, none doing much other than returning to their drinks. The thick door was heaved open as a trio of determined people stepped into the inn. Leading the trio was a tall and lean woman with the build of a mountain lion. She wore long flowing garb that was securely bound around the waist and arms so as not to get in the way of her movements. Ulmar determined that this had to be some sort of Lowland warrior, as she wore a slender breastplate and had a multitude of gold coins sewn onto her outfit while carrying a wicked leatherbound baton. Her hair flowed like a slender black waterfall, much finer than any of the True Tolks hair. Her two rugged companions were quick to flank Ulmar and the combatants grasping their batons as a deterrent to any more trouble.

Ulmar was pondering how to tackle the oncoming misunderstanding as the woman who's hall this was marched up to the warrior and started proclaiming her appreciation of Ulmars assistance.

-"These two were at it again as usual, see, wrecking the place, kicking and screaming. Then this one clocks them down, just one punch a dwarf. Quick and fine as you like. Pull these grimy louts' out of here and lock 'em up but I'd be much obliged if you weren't to harsh on my guest."

By now Aldred was at Ulmars side bowing elegantly to the tall warrior.

-"I assure you my lady that the dear proprietor of this establishment speaks true, my friend had no other intention than to come to the aid of a business owner with a problem and deployed only enough force so as to neutralize the disruption. I beg my ladies mercy in this matter."

The warrior raised her hand in a manner that spoke that she was accustomed to be instantly obeyed.

-"Yet our village smith lies unconscious on the floor. You still want to put your good name behind the actions of this barbarian Dovie?"

-"Certainly will", the proprietor acknowledged.

-"Very well. Merle, Nola, lock these two in the pit,", the warrior proclaimed, indicating the two men from within the mountain. "You two, follow me."

There was no room for protests to the womans' order. Ulmar and Aldred followed her out into the street. As they left Ulmar heard the owner of the inn, the woman named Dovie, encourage them by stating "Don't you worry, she's a fair one, our marshall."

The woman led them to the gap between two buildings so they had a certain amount of privacy before speaking further with the two companions.

-"I know your kind. You are far from the first or last hillman to wander into Penkath. What do you seek here hillman?"

-"Nothing but supplies and rest before we'll be on our way," Aldred interposed on Ulmars behalf.

-"The hillman will speak for himself, Dance Wildfire, or we will address the issue of you abandoning your post at the Shimmering Tower."

Aldred looked startled at the warrior's statement, completely dropping his swathe demeanor. He looked much younger when taken aback, making Ulmar wonder just how old Aldred was.

-"We pride ourselves with keeping ourselves apprised of the Towers' doings. It helps of course when the Tower posts a bounty upon the safe return of one of its own."

The warrior focused her attention yet again upon Ulmar.

-"So, what is your purpose upon visiting Penkath?"

-"I am Ulmar of the Tuakk, known as the Doomwolf. Son of Lathrik and Aina, descendant of Trimboldumn, born of the True Folk. I swear that I have no sinister purpose upon your hold, I simply seek rest from our travels and supplies for the road ahead."

With the slow delicate movements of getting out of the range of an asp the woman took a step back. Under her cool facade she seemed almost frightened or at least careful, Ulmar noted. She had reacted to his cursed title so there was no telling what she would do next. She seemed to be crossing off points from an inner list which meant that it was likely that she wasn't going to act rashly. Whatever the outcome was, Ulmar intended to see it through. A Greysock might have had the time to fly over the entire village before she at last spoke.

-"I am Anahea Novamahe born under the spring stars at the shore of the neverending seas, daughter of Teeuila Novamahe daughter of Weylarei Novamahe. My blood is that of the Ohoka who are blessed by the great windspirit Nanane. I am the Marshall of this village, mine is the charge to keep it safe from all who would do it ill. I give my name freely but ask you not to repeat it to anyone. I welcome you, Ulmar Blackaxe, the one who walks in the shadows of Wolves as soon as I have your oath that you will not bring death upon this village."

At last Ulmar had met someone who knew the art of introduction. Whoever this Anahea was, he decided to trust her to act honorably.

-"You have my word. As long as I walk the land of this hold, I will treat any who dwell here as my own blood."

-"Brave words among this lot. I accept your oath and I hold you responsible, Dance for fitting him into our society", Anahea said, aiming the last part toward Aldred. "I would also like to give some friendly advice, don't give anyone else your name."

With those words she parted with the two companions.

-"Elyds mount! Life with you is never dull. Come on, let's get indoors before she changes her mind."

-"She seemed different than other Lowlanders 've met," Ulmar stated while they were crossing the street and heading toward the inn.

-"Can't imagine there are many fine haired, olive skinned nobles in the Lumbrian Borderlands. That my friend was an honest to God's Nannoian manslayer, if the stories about Nannoian society are true. She's a noble warrior, a Chieftain of sorts that owes allegiance to another chieftain is the best way I can think of explaining it."

-"So she is a chieftain in the service of a king?" Ulmar opened the door to the inn noting Aldreds grimace at his attempt to reconcile Aldreds explanation.

-"Close enough. What she's doing here is anyone's guess though."

Their conversation was broken off as Dovie met them at the door swiftly herding them back to their table.

-"Thank Gyrd that you are back. I've been keeping an eye on your things while you were gone. Not to speak ill of my own guests but it's best not to leave things out in the open unguarded if you can help it. Here come and have a sit down, foods ready so just dig in."

There was a feast waiting for them as they sat down at the table. There was a tray of hot sausages, a tray full of turnips, two circular loaves of rye bread, butter and a whole pot of soup just for them. Ulmar was overjoyed at the sight of all the food digging in with wanton abandon. The food was hearty and well rounded, so Ulmar was quick to sample the stein of ale, finding it strong and filling. It was a sad thing that this seemingly insignificant lowlander village could serve a feast so much better than the Tuakk could when they pulled all their resources together. Aldred on the other hand sighed a little and muttered, "soup and sausage, i guess it's better than nothing." Ulmar had a hard time understanding what could be better than having a large helping of hearty food and good drink. He decided not to challenge him on the matter.

They ate their fill, Ulmar doing the lion's share of the eating and quenched their thirst, Aldred doing the majority of drinking. Ulmar quickly grew accustomed to the buzz of the other patrons finding the sound of their voices soothing. He closed his eyes and digested his plentiful meal feeling more content than he had in a long while. Aldred left the table and returned with an iron key.

-"When you're ready, our room awaits. Good thing is that we're sharing a room, which means there's a much smaller chance of the villagers slitting our throats in the night."

Ulmar opened his eyes astounded and much less at peace.

-"Is that what they do in the Lowlands? Invite people into their holds and kill their guests?"

Aldred laughed, a charming beautiful sound.

-"First off, if we're to travel in civilized lands you need to understand that we might be guests here we're paying for the privilege with coins. It's how these people earn their living. Anyone with enough coins can stay here if there's room for them.

Ulmar grunted disapprovingly.

-"And you call us uncivilized", he muttered.

-"Secondly", Aldred continued without paying heed to Ulmars statement, "it might not happen often that guests frequenting inns are murdered but it has happened on occasion. We don't actually know anything about these people, they could be wonderful or villainous, probably they're somewhere in between and both at the same time.

We'd be much safer within the borders of Valeria but we aren't. These are the Lumbrian Borderlands, the people and their settlements are just as dangerous as any beast or plague that roam the hills. Keep your eyes open and stay close and we'll be fine."

The people who ran the inn seemed to be good people in Ulmars eyes. Looking over the establishment he counted Dovie, the barmaid that had met them when they entered, a cook he barely got a glimpse of and a young boy who seemed to be tasked to keep the fire going and carrying messages to and from the others. He tried imagining the child with his big ears creeping into their room with a dirk between his teeth or the barmaid standing behind the door with a club over her head but failed. He just couldn't make them out as bad people even if he was well aware of the treacherous nature of lowlanders.

The armed band that had followed them around was another thing entirely. They were still close by, no longer focused on Ulmar anymore but still very close. They had an air of trouble and moved like they were used to causing it. He had no difficulty imagining them creeping into their room and brutally stabbing them to death as they slept. The five seemed to be led by a short bald man with scars all across his face. He was dressed in simple traveling gear under which he had leather armor with brigandine parts. The others were heavier in their armor but still paid the short man heed, like wicked dogs to a cruel master.

While looking at them he realised that several in the room carried traces of being true folk. He saw the scalp tattoo of a Marrodar, the beard braid of a Rannvelger and the ceremonial cheek scars of an Orveigh. They might have adopted the Lowlander ways but kept some mannerisms that spoke truly of their heritage. Ulmar was unsure how he felt about them, they were most certainly rogues and renegades cast out of the tribes for crimes against the True Folk or they could just have been seduced by the promise of endless food. Some of them were beginning to get a bit fat, he reflected.

-"Are all men from within the mountain as those that we happened upon?" Ulmar couldn't conceal his disappointment at the encounter they had earlier with the mythic figures.

-"The Dwarves? No, they're very much like people in general. Some are good and some are bad, most are somewhere in between. There are a lot of them in Valeria, they came in with us on the ships and in almost every regard, they're just people. That being said, I've always found that there is some kind of lingering bitterness and restlessness in them. They're never content, never truly happy. No idea why. They're famed craftsmen and make excellent guards. I guess you were unlucky to meet some of the less savory ones."

-"The one with all the hammers hanging from his garb had the stench of a hundred empty kegs of old ale about him, just stronger."Aldred nodded sagely.

-"They also make excellent drunks."

Ulmar and Aldred spent a fair amount of time in the taproom just lounging about like the rest of the thinning herd of patrons engaged in bouts of small-talk and otherwise just sitting in silence. When they both had grown tired they sauntered up the stairs to their room on the second floor. There were two modest sized beds spaced in opposite corners and a small table in between. The door was sturdy with an actual iron lock making Ulmar a little bit more comfortable at the prospect of letting his guard down in this place where they might or might not be murdered in their sleep. Ulmar curiously touched the blanket on his bed only to discover that it was smooth and thick. When he happily commented on it Aldred mostly smiled courteously but this time not claiming that it wasn't up to par. With a content sigh Ulmar collapsed into the bed, drew the still wrapped Kharagh close and summarily fell asleep.

26.

The next day was, to a large extent, spent trying to hunt down those precious provisions that they would need on their travel to the throne. With some help from Dovie, they learnt that there were no less than three individual provisioners in the village all specializing in different goods but mostly in competition with each other. Claiming to not want to waste money, Aldred dragged Ulmar with him as they went from provisioner to provisioner in negotiation, actively playing them against each other. Ulmar had the suspicion that Aldred was mostly enjoying himself, not needing to haggle deals but wanted the man to make the most of their time in the village before they were yet again in the lethal wilderness of the hills. eeing to the provisioners, there was one that was a surly kind of sort that first seemed to be a miserly sort until you realised that it was actually just how the man looked and spoke. The man named Freghert had an impressive moustache and apparently hailed from a distant land called Addarik. Ulmar wondered how far spread the lands of men were upon the world to have such an abundance of people.

The second one was the first ones' opposite. Haeda had a pleasant way about her but was hard to press into giving up a single coin of her asking price, somehow managing to almost make you forget that she wasn't negotiating at all.

The third, a close mouthed matronly woman called Blue had the most different wares of the three but was slow to adapt to the negotiation.

The nearest reference Ulmar could think of was that it was a verbal wrestling match over the coins, a strange but entertaining thing, at least when Aldred was doing the negotiation. That first days bartering ended with a standstill between the merchants and Aldred, but had put him in a good position for the next days' negotiation.

-"I've made a decision that I've put a lot of thought into. I, and most certainly you, my grimy friend, need to bathe. For every time we put our necks on the line we have earned ourselves the right to a good bath."

-"Why?"

Aldred laughed heartily at Ulmars' query.

-"Because if you don't take a bath soon the mere smell of you will raise your slain enemies. Because I could hardly sleep for the smell of you. Because it's glorious with a relaxing hot bath."

Ulmar chose to not respond to the friendly insults.

-"A warm bath? What's the point? Bathing might get you sick in this weather. It seems like some kind of Lowlander madness."

Aldred scrunched his nose at Ulmar and made a big show of moving upwind of him.

-"Lowland madness? Surely you bathe sometimes?"

-"We do, when it's required but only if the weather will allow it."

-"Believe me, it's required."

After some inquiry they found out that one of the buildings nearest the inn was in fact furnished as a small bathhouse with three single seated tubs. The house was run as a side business by Gyned, the barmaid they had met the day before. They found her waiting upon the tables of the inn and it didn't take much convincing from Aldred to have her accommodate them.

-"If you pardon me for saying so", she stated not knowing if she should look at Ulmar or away, "it seems more than your days due if you know what I mean." On their way to the bathhouse they passed the two dwarves that gave Ulmar a grudging nod of recognition.

-"Seems like city life agrees with you my friend", Aldred chirped, "just look at you, making friends, taking baths."

Ulmar smiled sheepishly not knowing what to expect from the would-be legendary experience of cleaning himself in warm water.

The bathhouse was a small three room house, the largest of these dominated by three copper bathtubs that were kept from each others' line of sight by large screens. By the tubs stood small tables laden with bowls and boxes full of alluring smells. It was somewhat cramped but not overtly so. The walls of the house had all first been painted white then had depictions of forest scenes full of flowery vines, game animals and youthful people at play.

-"Thank all that is holy, at last some sort of vestige of the civilized world."

Gyned was hastening past carrying two heavily laden buckets of steaming hot water.

-"It'll be ready in a jiffy. The sirs can pick a tub and I'll get them nice and warm. Thank you my lord for your appreciation, there's generally not much call for the place but there's been a noble or two who's had errands in these parts that have frequented our establishment. Like we had an honest to Gods Lord the other month, who had himself a nice proper soak. Then there's the lady Anahea of course, our good Marshall. If it weren't for her I imagine we'd have to close the place up between patrons but she's very particular about how things are done and a right nightmare to service. But don't you be telling her that now."

Aldred swooped up to a tub gracefully making a half bow to Gyned.

-"Wouldn't dream of it", he tested the water with his pinky only to withdraw it gingerly, "Now, Ulmar, get yourself to a tub and get in when it's ready."

The scene was pretty enough so Ulmar shrugged and figured that he should get it over with. He walked over to the tub furthest to the left, leaned the disguised Kharagh against the tub and started undressing. His clothes were certainly dusty and grimy from the winter so he had to concede a point to Aldred that he might be getting a bit too dirty even compared to the season. Lines of filth were in the groves of his skin and every place where the clothes let in material from the outside world. He moved his body to shake off the worst of the stiffness and thoroughly enjoyed the breeze upon his naked skin.

He heard Gyned come back into the room carrying two fresh heavy buckets. As soon as she entered he heard her in a giggling voice proclaim a ceaseless stream of "Oh dear". Expecting the woman to need some assistance Ulmar turned to face her, finding a red faced blushing barmaid trying her very best not to look at the very naked hillman. Curious about what was going on Aldred popped his head forth from behind the screens, let out a spontaneous laugh before he stifled it.

-"Ah, you are naked. Very, very openly naked. How about you grab that towel over there and do our host a favor and wrap it around yourself. Hmm?"

Feeling that he was missing some fine point of so called civilized society he wrapped the towel around his waist and looked questioningly at Aldred.

-"It's not considered proper to be naked in public."

-"But we aren't in public, we're in her house", Ulmar helpfully explained.

-"Still, towel. Just trust me. As soon as she's gone you can slip it off and slip into the water naked as you want but until then; towel."

So Ulmar waited. Gyned smiled embarrassed at him as she passed but still glanced at him, hungrily looking him over. While she was topping off the bath, he discovered an almost full length mirror that he suspected to be polished steel standing in the corner. It was a strange thing to see oneself as others did. He realised just how scarred he had become, every scar a different story of a painful wound he had survived. As he stared at himself, he felt old. How many more winters could he keep himself from the maws of the wolves at his heels? Maybe he should have bonded himself to a mate and raised a child but the thought of maybe passing on the curse that had haunted him through his entire life felt cruel. Aldred on the other hand hadn't had many scars at all from what he had seen. He hoped that his life had been better than his own.

 Gyned finished up and was halfway through the door when she popped her head back in.

-"Now if you need me sirs just ring the dong, I mean just give the bell a dong. No! I mean just ring and I'll be here in a shake."

Gyned fled the house laughing leaving Aldred in stitches. Ulmar just sighed and decided that this had to be another one of those lowlander mannerisms that was just beyond him. He was satisfied that the two of them had found joy in the situation and made a mental note of keeping some parts of himself shrouded in the company of lowlanders from now on.

Another satisfaction was the deep sigh that Aldred let loose on the other side of the screen.

-"Get in, it's perfect."

Ulmar tested the water, found it to be hot but not dangerously so and then stepped into the tub. It was like finding a warm summer day in this bleak spring weather in a single second. His first impulse was that it was much too warm much too fast but he pushed the impulse aside as he was inclined to truly test the experience. He realised now just how cold his body had been and wondered how long it had to carry the weight of the cold weather he no longer felt with his waking mind. Soaked in water he felt the alleviating effect the water had on his joints and quickly got an appreciation for the practice of warm baths, even if he was still convinced that he'd probably pay for the pleasure with his life. Maybe it was a good end to a hard life, he had eaten well, slept long and was now bathing.

Like a goat that was to be sacrificed, maybe the moments before his death could be the best he experienced. As he lay there Aldred started calling out instructions to try the contents of one box or bowl or the other, and how to use said contents. Some of the stuff was far beyond his taste, sickly sweet or numbingly fragrant yet there was enough on the table for him to find personal favorites among. The water was quickly turning into a brownish mess making Ulmar wonder how much of the dirt that Aldred seemed to worry so much about just ended up clinging on to him again in the end. As if the Lowlander read his thoughts, he rang the bell to summon Gyned and asked her to draw another bath for Ulmar in the third tub, he'd of course pay for the bother. Said and done, Ulmar moved to the second tub and resumed his cleansing soak. Aldred took the opportunity to shave, or so he explained to Ulmar, making him curious on how the Lowlander kept his grooming outside the confines of his Tower. It seemed that the man had packed a very sharp knife, a straight razor, and a small mirror and was re-establishing his high upkeep look.

Bathed, one of them newly shaved, the two went to the inn to fill their bellies and quench their thirst. Ulmar could really get used to civilization.

27.

As the two strangers entered the villagers resumed their conversation, if in somewhat hushed voices. They had been gossiping over the weather, this year's harvest, over the surly troublemaker dwarves, their burgomeister, the marshall and life in general. As they often did when they had exhausted the topics of their day to day lives, their stories diverted to the local legends of the Lumbrian borderlands. As the case often was, Trynt the eldest of the group was set on talking sense into Wessick, the youngest in the group. If it was that there was a certain amount of entertainment that captured the others' attention then so be it.

-"I tell you, that one has the dark gaze that reminds me of the Blackaxe. There's the same kind of foul feel to the man. Eyes that could pin a bear to the ground by looking at it."

Trynt tried to in a clumsy half hidden way, avert evil that might have followed his words with a small gesture.

-"Bulldung", Rorig, the groups sceptic exclaimed, "there's no way in a pixies backside that you ever laid eyes on Ulmar the Blackaxe."

-"I have to agree with my friend Rorig here, there's no way at that." Wessick jumped at the chance of being in the right for a change.

-"Listen, listen. I have seen him with my own eyes I tell you, seen him as clearly as I see that one sitting over there. His eyes were dark just as his, dark with the gaze of a demon. That's what he is you know, a demon. When he was born the demons of the land saw their chance and offered his people to fill the boy with power if they just sacrificed a hundred souls to their demon queen. The Hillmen gladly agreed so that night a swarm of demons carried off the souls of those that were too slow to get away till they had collected a hundred, then they snapped hold of the newborn's soul from within its mouth and dragged it out kicking and screaming. What was left was just a husk into which a demon lord stepped using the body like a garb. That's why the Blackaxe can break a man with a look, he aint human you see.

I saw him as I was making a trip to Mekket, just north of the Shimmering Tower and there he was just standing and looking at me through his demon eyes. There were wolves all around him licking blood from his fingers and I tell you that if there hadn't been a gulch between me and him I would have been caught and gutted."

A collective shiver went through the gathered farmers as they looked at the stranger whose gaze reminded them of the infamous Barbarian warrior called the Blackaxe.

-"I don't know about that", Wessick began warily, "but I've heard that he is in fact a wolf himself, a werewolf. The only reason he takes on the shape of men is to gorge on the blood of the enemies of Clan Tuakk. They bound the wolf to their side by witchcraft you see so that they might reclaim the Clan's glory days. The only thing that might hurt him is blessed silver, try anything else and it'll just bounce off him."

-"That actually might be true", Rorig was stirring his ale deep in thought, "I heard that when he faced the Marrodar a few years back he took an arrow to the chest. It fell to the ground without leaving a mark. He wasn't wearing no armor, neither. As bare chested as the day he was born, he was. The iron just didn't want to bite."

Trynt looked like he was about to object but seeing the odds stacked against him he leaned in conspiratorially.

-"Have you heard about the time that he defended Willems gorge against Northern raiders for three full days until help arrived? Seems it was a caravan travelling between two tribes and it was full of women and children when they were jumped by marauding raiders. The villains thought they'd found an easy target, but then with an earth shattering howl, old Blackaxe gets up on this huge boulder and just stares the brutes down Three Hundred bloodthirsty Barbarians screaming for blood and he keeps them at bay with a look. So he gives the caravan orders to run for home and get help while he fights. So he swings his axe through shield and bone, killing half of them or more before his clansmen arrive. Those marauders are so scared of facing him that they scarper off as quickly as their feet can take them. He's not human, I tell you."

Warding off the images of the unnaturally strong and terrifying man charging into battle the men drank deeply from their mugs. Being everything but discreet the men glanced at the Lumbrian traveller imagining how much more terrible the Blackaxe must be when this one was more than intimidating in his own right.

-"One says demons the other werewolves but what do you reckon about him being in league with witches to enhance his powers? I've heard that he made the hags under the hill a blood promise that he would reap three hundred and thirty three souls in their name every year and they gave him his black axe for it. With it there is no shield that can stand against it and no armor to protect against it."

Lifting his head from the table where he had happily been snoring the balding dwarf put in his opinion on the matter making the villagers jump in their seats. The dwarf was being loud, frighteningly so.

-"Yar stories are filled with ghosts and goblins that one might think you lot are a flock of woolly sheep. I'd not give a rotten copper for your stories *breghkar* but I'll tell you all this. There's no way anyone other than a dwarf has forged that axe of his. Sounds to me that it's made of darksteel and only MY people have ever been able to do anything with that."

The villagers hushed the dwarf profusely knowing full well that their little story session was a nuisance that any of the powers that be would be more than a little annoyed at. The dwarf gave them a look of disgust, waved them off and promptly fell back into unconsciousness. Feeling that the interruption was a sign the group disbanded each going his own way. Aldred pushed Ulmars arm playfully as he said.

-"I didn't know that you were a demon in disguise", he stroked his beard and looked up into the ceiling in mock deliberation as he added, "Although, that would explain your love of filth and interesting table manners. Or are you a werewolf, come to bring death on the lesser people?"

Ulmar refused to acknowledge the man's taunt as long as he could, bursting into a quiet laughter when he could no longer contain himself.

-"Blocking arrows with your chest that has to be a neat trick, you'll have to tell me how."

Ulmar raised his stein and raised an eyebrow.

-"That one is actually true. A Marrodar shot me from fifty yards straight in the chest. No idea why nothing happened, I guess the Marrodar just make bad arrows. It hurt though!"

-"And fighting off three hundred marauders?"

-"They were thirty. I only killed three, I think. Wounded a lot of them and had to hold the pass for one and a half days before Briac and the other warriors arrived. I was on my way back from egg hunting with Kallabra and many of the elder ones, like old man Hod. They left for the Hold while I stayed. I didn't think I would make it though, that was never the plan. Wasn't alone either. The Bogvale boy stayed with me the whole time. He couldn't fight but he kept watch as I rested."

-"Amazing." Aldred raised his goblet in a toast in an overly dramatic fashion. "I propose a toast. To my friend, the arrow-proof marauder-slaying demon-puppet werewolf, may he never be late with his quota of mortal souls."

In just as much mock seriousness Ulmar raised his stein in toast and drank deeply. For the first time in many years he could just be himself, instead of living up to the grandeur of his own legend. There would always be stories but this way he could experience a moment of reprieve. He was looking forward to his soft bed that only hurt his back a little.

-"How long do you think we'll stay here then?"

-"About two more days will do it. Until then just rest and eat. I don't think I've ever seen anyone eat with such passion as you do, almost makes me hungry every time you do it."

28.

The next day Ulmar spent time getting to know the village of Penkath. In the morning he ate his fill, brought a knapsack filled with a hearty lunch and strolled around. The place was truly a strange spectacle. Most of the people seemed very busy though not at all looking at the chores he had expected. It seemed that a steady stream of food and drink gave them the opportunity to live like craftsmen and merchant kings on the fruit of the labors of the farmers. It wasn't unheard of among the True Folk that some were excepted from the chores of the acquisition of food, so to Ulmar it was a novelty.

Wandering around the fields and close to the cattle, Ulmar found the farmers of the village to be hospitable, their initial fears of his intentions dismissed after he lended a hand to several heavy chores. He came to like them and their strange honest optimism. Many of them had set forth from lands far from the coasts of Valeria for the promise of land that they could work without the suffocating masters that had lorded over them Others were Valerians that had some starry eyed notion of taming the lands north of their kingdom out of some sense of adventure.

He helped repair the fences, driving new poles into the earth and then hammering them into place with heavy sledgehammers. Their work progressing faster than planned, allowed them to spend time just speaking with the stranger. Wary of disclosing his true identity he claimed to be named Dughall, a pet name Hild had given him during their childhood. He hoped that they wouldn't put much weight into the meaning of the name as in the tongue of the Free Folk Doogh-ghall meant "dark stranger". He still found it quite appropriate.

The farmers told him of the great city in the south that they claimed was so large that a man might enter it on one side in the morning and not reach the other end until nightfall. A city full of free people to which every wonder from all the corners of the world were brought, and traded with anyone who had the fortune to procure whatever they wished. It was the city of the old King, from which the Kingdom of Valeria was ruled by the Regents council. To Ulmar it sounded like a wide eyed fairy tale that he one day hoped to explore.

During the afternoon he visited every shop and establishment much to the horror of several of the owners. He visited the tailor with his shop that was covered in bolts of cloth, the carpenter who was too busy working on a decorated chest, to even acknowledge his presence and of course, the village smith.

The tantalizing sound of hammer working the anvil drew him in like a bear to honey. The smithy was a ramshackle building in the middle of the village that was covered in all sorts of ironwork projects in different states of completion. As he had hoped, he found the smith to be one of the men from within the mountain, the balding one, that was in quick fashion producing a sea of iron nails. The muscular smith seemed tired or bored as he worked seemingly flinching at every beat of the hammer. Ulmar approached slowly not knowing what he wanted.

-"I've not got anything for you. Better leave hillman, we have enough of your kind in the village as it is."

Undeterred, Ulmar watched the smith heat the metal, pound it into rods and with experienced moves hammer the rods to needle sharp points. To see metal heated orange and as pliable as clay was a sight to be seen indeed. The smith sighed deeply and lay down the hammer.

-"I don't know what you want, Hillman, so say your piece and be done with it. It's too damn warm to work on a dry throat anyway."

-"My people still tell tales of your people. Of your honor and your skill, that no craftsman ever was or ever will be can measure up to the skill of the men within the mountain. To see even one would be a tale to tell but to see two then my people would say I'm lying."

The smith poured the nails he had made so far into a rough wooden box swaying a bit where he stood.

-"You've only met one, Hillman and that would be me. And a sorry excuse for a drunk at that. That other one, i'm not sure how to put it but he's not a true "man from within the mountain" as you put it. He came with those other humans down south, creeping off boats like vermin. He's a good enough fella but not a *Dvergur*. He has no roots, no mountain and no ancestors. That's a bad thing for a *Dverg*. He hates me for it but I can't unmake things, fate has been forged and that's the end of it."

-"That's almost what we say about the Lowlanders. My people call them shadows, claim they aren't real and we shouldn't bother with them. I guess that is the same."

The dwarf swayed past Ulmar, spitting in a bucket near Ulmars feet. The dwarf stunk of stale beer and coal, the tools that hung from his clothes clattering as he moved.

-"I guess it is. That explains a lot. You lot seem to have a lust for killing each other, especially you, broken."

-"What did you call me?" Ulmar had a couple of times heard the epithet being used to describe him and his kin, but was unsure if those using the phrasing had meant him, the Tuakk or the true folk in general. He had just always assumed it was due to his curse. Could the Dverg have figured out his true identity?

-"Oh relax, it's not like I called you mudmen like many true *Dvergar* would have," the smith had taken to walking around the workshop overturning cups and steins until he found one that still held liquid. With happy grunt, he swigged the contents brushing away what had missed his mouth with the back of his hand.

-"So are you going to be all angry and frothing like so many of your people at the truth, cause I'll tell you right now I'm in no mood for fightin'."

This close to the Dverg, Ulmar could see his bloodshot eyes and crumbled dirty clothes. Among the Tuakk it wouldn't have mattered much but he could imagine that the people of Penkath would be much more picky about it.

-"Did you say you are a drunk?"

The dwarf scoffed, pushing himself past Ulmar in what almost felt like a deliberate means to push the offending human in his workshop more than just to get him out of his way.

-"Drunk, yes. Wasteral, yes. Good for nothin layabout, yes. A *Dvergur* this far from the Kingdom of my ancestors you have to realise that there is a reason for it. If Ruthgrim just would have been born a true *Dvergur* he would have the run of the smithing in the village, but that's not how the fates were forged. He's not got the training nor ancestry to be *Mrastrai* and all his wailing and moaning will only get him a solid wallop for his troubles. So that's said, now what do you want?"

Ulmar was still pondering the question, not sure he had a satisfactory answer.

-"Nothing," he conceded, "I just wanted to see you work. My village lost the riddle of steel a long time ago and now there isn't even anyone who knows the mastery of iron."

The dwarf raised his eyebrows in disbelief underlining his words with a hammer as he spoke.

-"You want me to teach you the *Mrastrum* of metal? *Krakktrilm* hillman, you are even madder than you look! I'll not have you pick up a thought and call yourself smith. If I'd have taught anyone I'd have begun at the roots, no use trying otherwise. You're a decade or two too old and a *Dverg* short of having that. Not get out of my workshop, get."

Goaded out of the smithy by a stubborn Dverg, Ulmar stepped out into the street. That meeting had been much more than what he had expected from a *Dvergur* or was it *Dverg*, even if had more or less thrown him out of the workshop. It was intriguing to consider that the men from within the mountain in such regards mirrored the life of the hills of the True Folk. Maybe all the Valerian Lowlanders were shadows of human and Dverg alike. He wondered if the meeting had gone better if he hadn't knocked the smith to the floor during their previous encounter. He had spent a total of maybe a hundred heartbeats on the street before Aldred found him. The apprentice beamed as he approached him, grabbed his shoulders and exclaimed;

-"There you are. You have to put your finest gear, we have an audience with the burgomeister this evening. On second thought, we might just have to pick something up for you to wear, you look like whatever lives under the roots of trees."

-"There's nothing wrong with my clothes", Ulmar protested a bit defensively.

As if to mark a point, Aldred lifted a finger taking on a very serious face. He then slapped his hand on Ulmars chest which set off a small cloud of dust from his body. Making a face as if the point was moot now, Aldred patted Ulmars shoulder, setting off more dust into the air and dragged Ulmar to the tailor.

29.

The honorable Mistress Febe van Vjanten ruled over her sizable house just as she ruled as Burgomeister of Penkath. Aldred later explained that Febe hailed from the people of Vannhem, which was the only kingdom to share land with Valeria. Apparently the kingdom was positioned seven days riding on a good horse west of Valeria. The burgomeister was old, almost as old as Kallabra or old man Hod, or so Ulmar believed. But her age had not dulled the mind within merely sharpened it with a bitter touch. Ulmar wasn't sure why they were invited to her home for dinner but assumed that it was akin to feasting with a chieftain of the True Folk. He was sorely mistaken.

Arriving at the old woman's house when sunset was beginning to make itself known, the two of them had to wait a small eternity before a servant of the burgomeister finally arrived at the door. Ulmar had taken the opportunity to fidget in his new attire, not at all comfortable with the outfit Aldred had insisted was the best they could do in Penkath with such short forewarning. The rebellious tunic was a deep brownish red color that reminded him of rust and was extensively embroidered with patterns that looked very much like the imagery of the True Folk which ran around his neck and cuffs. He had at least been able to keep his own boots with the argument that he impossibly had time to break in a pair of boots in a matter of an hour or two. The servant that opened the door seemed to very much look down on the pair of them, making Ulmar wonder if this was part of what the people from beyond the great seas had to put up with from the households of nobles on a daily basis. If that was the case he could see the appeal of moving to the hills of the True Folk. Aldred introduced them both to the fellow and had to more or less convince the man to gain them entry to the Burgomeisters home before they were at last let in.

After spending some time in a small, cramped room-like open area at the bottom of the stairs the servant fetched them with a sneering "if you'll follow me the burgomeister is waiting for you." Ulmar had to bite his tongue not to challenge the claim by informing the man that the only reason she had was because he had kept them waiting in some indoor corral like cattle but refrained from doing so when Aldred gave him a disarming smile.

The wrinkly woman was sitting in a comfortable looking armchair by a small round table nursing a small mug. She didn't even look up as the servant announced them.

-"Introducing the honorable apprentice Aldred Brynnd Tollemack, aspiring wizard to the Shimmering Tower and master Ulmar of Clan Tuakk."

Taking her sweet time stirring the contents of her mug, the burgomeister of Penkath placed the mug on a small cloth, aligning it with meticulous precision.

-"You are late."

The absurdity of the statement made Ulmar grunt. Aldred on the other hand put on a brimming facade smile that he saved for desperate occasions, bowed elegantly and addressed the lady of the house.

-"My dear mistress van Vjanten I do sincerely apologize for the inconvenience. Would we have known that you would grace us with your invitation earlier we would of course realigned our schedule to your convenience."

The old woman, who in Ulmars mind was nothing like Kallabra frowned.

-"Well there's nothing to be done about it now. We shall dine before our meal grows cold."

The three moved over to the table, two of them making idle small talk as they awaited to be served. It was becoming painfully apparent that the burgomeister was very purposefully excluding Ulmar from the conversation. He had tried to make casual small talk, a skill which he did not feel comfortable with but ended up sitting silent. The servant entered carrying a stout earthenware pitcher. The thought of some good ale lightened Ulmars mood considerably, he waited patiently as the servant made the round, pouring up liquid in the simple goblets, naturally he got to Ulmar last. Expecting ale he was surprised to find what the man had poured was in fact water, plain and simple. Ulmar held the goblet staring at the contents while considering the implications.

-"You disapprove of drinking water?"

She held onto every word, savoring them. Ulmar was beginning to see the woman's intentions.

-"Why would I? This is the clear good water of the lands of my ancestors. I would have nothing else."

To make a point Ulmar emptied his goblet in a single motion, the burgomeister mostly looked a little miffed. The servant now returned with a heavy tray laden with hot food. They were served a helping of hot stew and presented with bread and butter. Considering the water Ulmar fully expected this meal to be part of some test or attempt to rouse his temper. They quickly started eating upon which the old woman challenged him again.

-"No beast has given its life for your meal, Barbarian."

Ulmar raised his bowl and smelled the contents. The stew was thick and filling and smelled of vegetables that Ulmar had never tasted. The old woman might mean to find a bridge to launch an assault over but Ulmar was not going to bite.

-"No need for it. Your food smells good and nourishing. I thank the Burgomeister for this meal."

The old woman frowned, yet again ignoring his comment and led the gathered diners on a stretch of silent eating. Aldred and Febe engaged in casual small talk that had a definitive cold undercurrent. The dialog seemed to be purposefully kept in areas where Ulmar was ignorant, making him a bit bored. Determined not to let her ruin an otherwise good day, he focused on enjoying the meal. The other two seemed to not be making any effort in eating till what was on the table was done so Ulmar filled his plate once more. That seemed to be a mistake.

-"I've always seen overeating as a bad habit born of an undisciplined mind."

The comment was laid very casually, but was undoubtedly a jab in Ulmars direction. Without thinking of it he responded to the old woman's barb.

-"Then you have never had to be very, very hungry."

Ulmars tone was cheery, so it was jarring to meet the anger of the old womans' response.

-"And why should I? I lead a people that are strong and diligent. Why should we be met with the hardship of starvation, when we work a bountiful land that will feed any who have the will to work it? That is kept for the crude and Godless."

Ulmar put down his spoon slowly to collect himself. If she would have been of the True Folk he would have challenged her on her assaults, she was not though. He had hoped that Aldred would be more diligent in working the social niceties on his behalf. He realized the Lowlanders predicament, the burgomeister seemed hell bent on antagonizing Ulmar. He thought of the farmers and decided that he wouldn't let the chieftains and kings of the lowlands reflect upon the people as a whole.

-"Then you don't know these lands. Maybe you have been that lucky that the wolves have circled you instead of clipping your hamstrings. But sooner or later the white wolf will share hunger and frost while the black brings pestilence and death. That day you will regret how lightly you weighed these lands."

Ulmar expected the burgomeister to lash out, become angry, instead she merely smiled contently. Whatever her motives, Ulmar realised that she had stepped into her trap.

-"There we have it," her voice cool and cruel. "There is the true face of the Lumbrian oppressor. There is the brute that raids our herds and pillages our farms. So just because we settle what you have not managed to tame for centuries you feel that you can claim these empty lands and punish us in jealousy?"

-"These are not your lands, these are the lands of the Tuakk and they have been so for longer than any of your nations have stood. You encroach on our hold without the slightest understanding of the dangers that you face."

-"Your lands?" Febe sneered in disgust. "I see no roads, cities or documents to prove your claim. Half of your people are still wandering vagabonds migrating all year long. We have no need for your boasts and brutality in this village, Hillman. You have eaten your fill and can leave as soon as your belly will allow it."

Seeing a way out, Ulmar simply got up, patted Aldreds shoulder and left for the inn. He was feeling tired anyway, rather looking forward to his big fluffy bed.

Aldred was left alone with the old shark. Ulmar might not have understood the intricacies of their errand here but he did. He had wondered earlier if he should have warned the Hillman about the burgomeister from Vannhem and her ruthless ways but decided that it might be better that he didn't know. Lumbrian Hillmen were never very welcome in the free villages of the Borderlands and Penkath was no exception from that. He had heard stories of other true born Lumbrians that had mysteriously disappeared overnight, their gear sold only days later in Blues tradinghouse. Febe was known to have an aversion for the barbarians holding them responsible for countless acts of violence perpetrated against the settlers in the hill-lands. Ulmar had managed himself quite well; all things included, there had after all been a slight chance that Febe would have had them both murdered. By the look of the annoyed leader of Penkath there still might be a chance that they still could be.

-"The company one keeps could be seen as a direct indication of ones' character," thankfully the burgomeister seemed to be calming down.

-"I've found that a diversity among friends can only brighten your life. To experience others ways of life is to gain direct insight into other ways of thinking which of course can only bring wisdom."

Febe was in no way like the nobles of Valeria or even worse, the old kingdoms of the world. She was much more blunt, preferring to act. That still didn't mean that she in any way was helpless in the art of subtlety and manipulation, only that she was more likely to get bored and act rashly. From what he had understood she was from low birth herself, ironically hating the nobles for their haughty and oppressive ways. If the rumors were true, she was born the daughter of a sausage maker.

-"To stray down the roads of thoughts of heretics, murderers and thieves will only disillusion you to what is right and what is wrong. Play the wolf long enough and you will become the wolf regardless of your intentions."

Febes reference to wolves made Aldreds heart jump a bit. He sincerely hoped that she hadn't found out the mans' true identity. In that case he would sleep lightly until they left the village. The burgomeister's seneschal reentered the

241

room with a tray full of small cakes. From here Aldred could spot red velvet sponge, devil-dades and ladylace, his mouth watered at the expectation of the glorious sweet treats. Maybe he could risk his neck a little while longer if he could just get a plateful of the desserts. As the servant put down the tray Aldred had with a daring display of sleight of hand pilfered a thick slice of red velvet sponge-cake and was thoroughly enjoying the bocquet before chomping a big gulp out of it. The sharp sweetness of the cake gave him goosebumps. How anyone could manage treats like these in a backwards outback like this was far beyond him.

The seneschal had to no extent been procrastinating in his duties, two cups of steaming hot tea with a dab of honey and a splash of milk were already poured and placed in front of the diners. Feeling an odd combination of giddiness and frustration Aldred attempted to sway the old ruler of Penkath.

-"We seem to have gotten off on the wrong foot, let us drop any pretences and be honest and straightforward."

-"I sincerely doubt that."

-"My most honored Burgomeister please, I have in no way meant any offense."

-"No offense? You have brought the chief madman of all the barbarian wretches to my door and expect clemency? From where I sit you haven't done anything except spread lies from the sad moment you entered my village. How can you sit there in smug idiocy and claim that no offense was meant?"

Aldred knew that he should be more careful, perhaps not scarf down possibly poisoned cake and tea with reckless abandon even if it was cake to die for.

-"Uhm, now whatever do you mean?"

-"Ulmar the Blackaxe. Ulmar the Doomwolf. The murderous bastard with demons at his heel. Where that man walks death always follows and you brought him to us, to me. He is one of those that slaughter the good folk of the land for no better reason than he can and believe you me, you reap what you sow."

Aldred gestured with his cake annoying Febe intensely while she waited for him to swallow.

"Ah, so you know him?"

Aldreds charm fell flat at the woman's feet.

-"Well I give you my word that he's none of the things that you heard. You should really get to know him, terrific fellow."

-"I would rather be set adrift by Garrahandran pirates, than take the word of a forked tongued witch." Febes words might have been brimming with anger but her voice was cold as the faraway mountains. She leaned in towards Aldred like she was sharing an intimate secret with him.

-"Do you know what they do to witches where I come from? In Vannhem we see them for what they are, wandering blasphemies that pervert the world around them, rotting all that they touch. We seek them out, we drag them into the light and we put them to trial. We do not condone pacting with evil like they do where you come from. So let me make it absolutely clear that I harbor no good intentions toward you. I loathe you and your kind."

-"Yet you haven't," Aldred stated pleasantly as he helped himself to some mouthwatering ladylace. Febe glared at him as he swiftly stuffed his mouth in an attempt to get the most out of their meeting.

-"You haven't put me to trial, you haven't made arrangements to have Ulmar killed and you won't lift a finger harm us and here's why." He lifted his cup and half emptied it before he continued. He hoped that he wouldn't overplay his hand or upset the old woman to her grave. "You're scared, terrified even, that you have the most notorious hillman in all the Lumbrian Borderlands staying in your village accompanied by a witch no less. But here's the thing, trying to murder Ulmar might not be the best of ideas. Can you imagine what would happen to your village if the man that to this day is undefeated would survive? If even half of the Blackaxe stories are true, or even a tenth, then none within fifty leagues from here has the slightest chance of even wounding the man, let alone killing him. Now take into account that I am a fully fledged fire flinging fiend fighting in the name of my honored Lord Sarsara of the Shimmering Tower. Even if you managed to gut us both in our sleep will you risk the wrath of a small army of rather vicious militant wizards? I think not. So let's dispense with the not so veiled threats and calculations, and just let me speak my peace."

Febes' mouth bore the bitter creases of someone who had had to deal with countless setbacks and disappointments through her lifetime. It probably wasn't as noticeable usually but he knew that he had gotten to her.

-"Speak then."

Aldred made a half bow where he sat and snatched another piece of red velvet sponge cake before Febe managed to wave the servant away, taking his tray with him. Aldred watched in disappointment as the delicacies were denied him.

-"Yes, thank you. As you have hopefully found out by now I am on a mission from my master that is of the utmost importance to the Shimmering Tower." As Aldred reached the end of his sentence he was quick to interrupt the Burgomeisters protest before she managed to utter it. "Yes I know that you know that my quest might not be completely backed everybody back at the tower but I promise you that they are well aware of it. At least the most important individuals do. But then you know that we'll only be here a short while before moving on. We are in no way interested in your village, it's people, it's riches and its workings. Leave us be and we'll manage our business and move along. We'll be that much richer in supplies and your people will be that much richer in, well, you know, gold."

-"How long then?" Annoyance was in her voice.

.-"Three days tops. After that we'll be gone."

-"Three days. After that I leave no guarantees."

Pleased with the outcome, Aldred drew out a cookie he had pilfered earlier and made a show of eating it. He got up and swaggered out of the house of the less than impressed Burgomeister.

30.

Ulmar couldn't sleep. Village life, for all its convenience, was still a little too chaotic for him that evening. People were about, there was loud singing in the inn but foremost he was still annoyed at the arrogant ruler of the village. He had intended to just push through and force sleep upon himself but the night was clean and brisk and the winds smelled of adventure. Walking out to the edge of the village, he was cheerfully greeted by some of the stragglers that tended the fields. They did not know him and yet they accepted him after such a small thing as helping them during the day. Walking around one of the sturdy storage buildings he wondered if life could be so easy always, if it shouldn't be. Someday soon the simple people of the village would come to regret their foolishness and discover the true face of the hills of the True Folk, the face of death.

The upset cackle of the village geese told him that that day was much sooner than anyone had planned. The agitated birds were cackling, hissing and flapping their wings running around the village streets. Ulmars senses sharpened at his surroundings. He started paying meticulous attention to every splatter and creak around him. Something was wrong. He could hear the horses whinnying in their stable. Then he got a whiff of wet iron. Blood.

Following his nose more than his eyes in the mirk, he sneaked down a short alley between two storage buildings finding what he was looking for. There was a dark outline of a human body face down in the mud with a thin long shaft sticking out of it. Ulmar grabbed Kharagh from his back imagining he could feel attackers all around him in the periphery of the buildings. Might be goblins or bugbears, either way the village was most definitely being attacked. He jogged silently between the buildings wishing that he could shout after Aldred. He felt a pang of anxiety at the thought of the young man with a goblin arrow in his throat bleeding out in the dark. Was this retribution for the united Tuakk and Marrodar raid against the Redshield Goblins? The thought seemed plausible.

Walking obliviously along the street, he saw one of the farmers stagger along inebriated. He ran all the faster hoping to warn the woman of the danger ahead of her in the dark, and to get her to safety. With the horrible crudeness of battle the shaft of an arrow seemed to appear out of thin air piercing her ribcage. Before Ulmar could move three steps further, two more arrows pierced her abdomen, silencing the poor farmer before she could even scream out in pain. Ulmar screamed violently in his mind, devastated at the haphazard murder that was committed before his very eyes. He was too slow. The attackers were spread out around the village and already set upon brutally. Judging what the most tempting target was nearest him, Ulmar raced toward the largest storage building, instantly rewarded by the dark shapes of several raiders that were breaking into it.

Ulmar could not be contained any longer. With a roaring bellow that easily matched the roar of the Hrimmkuningaz Trötl, he charged the raiders. Bringing his great axe to bear he swung Kharagh so low that the blade scraped the naked ground and then arched the blow straight at his enemy. The dark shape lifted a weapon in a vain attempt to parry not knowing that even the strongest steel would melt away like snowflakes in summer against the might of Kharagh. The axe barely slowed when it sliced metal in twain, then the blade whisked through muscle, bone and tendon like it was made of air. His hastily produced cover for Kharagh was now folded over his hands, the cloth never being anything other than a trick to hide it and never a hindrance for the axe. The companions of the cut shadow retreated hastily as they met with unplanned resistance. All around the village, he could hear screams of battle, screams of warning, screams of fear.

Bent on finding the Lowlander apprentice, Ulmar stepped out into the street in mid raid. Fire was quickly lit, torches ignited then flung upon the rooftops of nearby houses. There was always fire in the shadows of a raid. The light they spread gave the first glimpses of the attackers, human, as they moved around with brutal efficiency. From the village hall could be heard the metal banging of a warning bell that did little other than restate the obvious. Surrounded by the din of battle there was a stirring deep inside Ulmar, the lust for combat reared its ugly head bringing a feeling of anticipation of the fight ahead. There should be more fire, more death. But it seemed that the sturdy buildings of the Lowlanders were proving to be more of an obstacle than the raiders had counted on. He sped along the street bent on getting to the last place where he had seen Aldred, the Burgomeisters house. Only feet from him one of the attackers pounced out toward one of the so called adventurers, dagger in hand, murder in his eyes. Reacting, Ulmar thrust his axe like a spear into the mans' ribs and caught the attackers raised hand in a smooth motion. With a wicked tug he disarmed the now screaming man and kicked him to the ground. In front of him lay the crumpled form of a warrior with very easily identifiable hair and temple tattoos. Eloch of the Marrodar.

Ulmars head reeled at the implication of the not long ago ally of clan Tuakk raiding the village. He tried to understand what treachery was afoot. What were they doing here? How had they betrayed his kin? Hesitating at murder Ulmar lowered Kharagh and shoved the adventurer away from the incapacitated warrior on the ground.

With high-pitched hissing, fire flew across the street in an unnatural way that could only be produced by Aldreds magic. Abandoning any thought of the Marrodar, Ulmar made towards Aldred. The Lowlander shone like a bright beacon in the night, red furious flames licked across his body as he with fluent motions seemed to dance along the street. There was no trace of fear or anger in the man, only excitement that reckless battle could bring. In that moment, the apprentice was truly a thing of beauty.

Shaking off his distraction Ulmar approached Aldred trying to stay clearly in the light so he wouldn't misconstrue his intentions and launch a deadly volley at him. He was tempted to ask if he was wounded, but opted on just focusing on the moment.

-"We need to get control of this or we'll lose the village."

Aldred acknowledged him with a simple nod, creased his brow and looked around the scene. He pointed down the street, fire still dancing all around his hand. Ulmar followed to where he was pointing, seeing a small knot of resistance. The two men from within the mountain were standing back to back in the street, earlier squabbling but now seamless brothers in arms. Their earlier tools of the trade, now in use as deadly weapons. Further still down the street the village marshall Anaea with a breastplate hastily pulled over nightdress weaved her way between adversaries, her spear keeping threats at bay. The two of them ran up toward the fighters barely avoiding a rogue arrow shot from the dark. A warrior stepped half into the light raising the wicked outline of a bow. Death wasn't aimed at him, instead the arrow hurtled toward the villager that he recognized as the eldest of those that had spun stories about him in the Inn. Knowing that it was a chance at best Ulmar lunged out after the deadly projectile, clasped his hand around the shaft only paying for his overconfidence with a thin scrape along his arm. The arrow stopped its trajectory only a thumb's length from the villagers eye. With a disgusted twist Ulmar flung the arrow to the ground. Another projectile was already whistling through the air heading straight for the villager. Raising the axe in time Ulmar blocked the arrow with the flat of the axe blunting the deadly point. Grabbing the villager by the collar he shoved him out of the way of more arrows, giving Ulmar the opportunity to face his foe.

There standing defiantly in the light of a nearby fire stood the towering outline of Hild.

Ulmar stopped, utterly confounded. The raiders were the Tuakk and Marrodar warriors that had left to deal with the Redshield Goblins. He was fighting his own kin.

There was no going back from this. He had taken up arms against the clan in general, marking himself as a traitor. He might be able to redeem himself if he immediately switched sides and joined the Tuakk. He couldn't though. Anger boiled inside him at the sight of this meaningless violence. How could they be slaughtering these people who were mostly trying to make a living in the hard lands of the true folk? What right had they to bring death upon them? Stepping two steps along the fifty yards between him and Hild Ulmar roared at her and all his kin.

-"Stop this madness! Pull back and cease these murders!"

Reacting to Ulmars proclamation, a Marrodar he didn't know by name lunged at him. He swiftly sidestepped the jab and summarily broke the warriors' nose with a single quick jab. Taking a threatening step toward the bleeding Marrodar, the man fell back, very conscious of the fact that Ulmar could easily have just cut him down where he stood.

Ulmar stood fully between the raiders that were his blood and the people of the village, flexing and furious he was a terrifying sight to behold.

From the dark the howling of his kin could be heard. A bloodcurdling sound that was intended to spread fear in those of weak hearts so the clan could fall back. There would not be more violence this night. Ulmar could now focus on helping the villagers extinguish the fires set by the raiders. Still crumpled in fear, the villagers that had told stories of the life of the Blackaxe lay in the mud by the road. The man was petrified with fear and it took Ulmar a while to realise what he was staring at. Kharagh, the fabled black axe of his ancestors.

Ulmar offered the man his hand which he tremblingly accepted. The man slouched, crept together as if he was expecting a savage beating. Ulmar considered if he should try to explain to the man that he had nothing to fear from him, he didn't wish to inflict any harm on anyone but decided that it was a futile project. Instead he squeezed his shoulder in a comforting manner and left him there staring at his axe. He wasn't the only one who did. All around him people stared at the black silhouette of Kharagh as it reflected back the red light of fire back at them.

-"We need to help them put out the fires."

Aldred was slow to react, waking from a distracted torpor. He considered Ulmars words, mulling them over to understand them. Then he smiled.

"I don't think you've been paying attention my scary friend, I make fires, but I'm not much use putting them out."Aldred scanned the darkness, looking for more attackers. Ulmar stepped in front of him, blocking his line of sight.

-"They won't be back tonight. We need to prepare. We need to put out the fires."

Grudgingly, Aldred acquiesced to the Hillmans wishes, doing his best to help handle the chaotic blazes that were greedily consuming several buildings. At every step the people openly stared at Ulmar but none moved against him. Even the so-called adventurers did little except keep their distance.

With a ripping rumble, the wall of a house dislodged from the frame and crashed into its neighbor. The flat surface was like a massive torch put against the building spreading fire to the yet unscathed building. With horrified howls the owner of the house wailed his dismay frantically trying to get someone to help him save his dying house. In desperation, the man tried pushing the burning wall back at the building from which it had ripped. No one would help him though. Villagers, travellers and adventurers stood there in dismayed silence watching a lost cause unfurl before their eyes. It was foolish, a sure way to be pinned between the collapsing inferno and the yet almost unscathed home, the best one could hope for was to be horribly burned. Ulmar would not have it though. Violent death had pounced upon this village like any other place in the hills of the True Folk proving to him that his homeland indeed was cursed beyond salvation. Yet a part of him refused to give in to darkness and death, refused to believe that it was the way of these lands that those who could prey upon each other. Determined, he stepped toward the inferno ignoring Aldreds questioning call. The wood was hot, almost on fire. He took a sturdy hold on the warm wall and started heaving. The wall refused to budge as he felt his muscles push to their extreme. He pushed hard enough that the soil began to give way behind him and he mostly managed to push himself from the wall. Looking back at the spectators he glared at them, challenging them to help him. Most looked away. Three of the armed travellers seemed to startle into activity under his dark gaze, running up to the wall to help. Aldred was there as well, side by side with Ulmar. Emboldened by the help that had arrived, he put all his strength into pushing back the wall. They roared in their effort as the wall inch by inch started to give way, moving ever so slow back toward the building from which it had detached. In an exuberant moment the pivot point was passed and the wall tumbled back, connecting with its origin with a ripping crash. The wall managed to raise large parts of the by now raging bonfire that was formerly building, casting a cloud of soot and ash into the air. A spontaneous cheer erupted from the onlooking crowd that was slowly being churned into motion. The homeowner professed his thanks over and over to Ulmar who brought him and the rest of the small party that had worked on moving the wall to the now forming line of people passing along buckets of water from the nearby river. They toiled by the river for what seemed ages as the villagers fought to save those buildings that had been ignited. Ulmars arms were sore from passing the heavy buckets and his back was strained but he could have gone on for a day and a night if it was needed, determination winning over his body's restriction.

31.

During the night he could hear the clear voice of Anahea passing orders in the village proper. Ulmar was confident that the efforts of the villagers were now in good hands, feeling no further need to take initiative in the post battle efforts. Dawn was steadily approaching as the villagers' gusto was waning. Soon there would be little in the way of energy for anything other than the more basic efforts among those that had fought through the night. The Tuakk and Marrodar on the other hand would be rested and ready for battle by dawn.

Convinced that he was the one who best understood what dangers these people faced, if not the only one, Ulmar detached from the bucket brigade as soon as he could. Misinterpreting Ulmars intentions, Aldred sleepily yawned and stated.

-"No one ever said that travelling the Lumbrian Borderlands would be boring. Now that things are faring a little better I'm heading toward my soft, safe bed."

Ulmar shook off some of the fatigue marching with determined steps toward the Burgomeisters' house. Aldred caught up to him with a short jog.

-"What are you up to Ulmar? I don't like the look in your eyes."

Ulmar stopped to face him looking more angry than determined though his feelings might have been the other way around.

-"I need to speak to Anahea or Febe. This is only the beginning and these people don't have the slightest idea of what is to come. If I don't speak with them now the ground will be soaked with blood until it cannot drink anymore."

Feeling that he had made himself more than clear he started off again.

-"What do you mean that this is only the beginning? What do you know that you're not telling me?" When the hillman didn't answer him Aldred continued. "Look I understand if you feel responsible in some part for what happened here but is this really your fight?"

-"It has always been my fight."

Seeing that there was no deterring Ulmar from getting involved, Aldred took on a more chipper demeanor.

-"Well I guess we'll have to find them then. Please try to rein in your most Lumbrian impulses and if you feel that you might be on your way to lop off someone's head just give me a signal and I'll take over. After all, putting out fires might not be one of my finer skills but talking most certainly might be."

Ulmar appreciated that Aldred was onboard with what had to be done. He had been dreading butting heads with the stubborn people of the south and really appreciated having Aldreds skills in negotiation at his disposal.

32.

They found Anahea and Febe in the improvised
headquarters of the work efforts that had been set up
outside the Burgomeisters' house. They stood around a
table with a handful of other prominent villagers
coordinating their efforts. People were milling about
around them, interrupting, arguing and questioning in loud
voices creating a confused chaos. By the looks of things
the marshall and the burgomeister were not seeing eye to
eye on the priorities of the day. No one challenged as
Ulmar and Aldred walked up to the table, only then
spotted by the burgomeister. The old womans' eyes
widened in outrage as Ulmar approached.

-"You. You! I'll have your head for the part you played in
this, barbarian," she attempted to rally what support she
could at the table leading to a hesitant reaction from the
villagers. "Don't just gawk, tie him up or get me his head."

The order that the Burgomeister had just given remained
unfulfilled. Some of the villagers made some action to
move slightly toward Ulmar, one even being so bold as to
draw a short sword, but none got closer than five paces
from him. Ulmar glared at them as they neared fully
expecting to have to defend himself from the assault of a
confused and wounded village.

-"Most esteemed Burgomeister", Aldred stepped forward, bowing quickly and putting himself between the villager that was most likely to act and Ulmar, "surely you can see that my companion was quick to offer his blade in the service of the village thus having nothing to do with this terrible attack?"

The Burgomeister sneered at Aldred with all the venom of someone discovering a snake in their bed.

-"It can't be a coincidence that just after the Blackaxe arrives that the Barbarians are at our door."

-"I can swear that the Blackaxe fought the invaders." Anaheas comment blew in like a fresh wind. The Marshall stood there with her arms crossed ready to argue Ulmars case.

-"No matter. We can't take any chances."

The Burgomeisters' comment that was so carelessly uttered in the open spread like a bad feeling through the crowd around the improvised headquarters. Ulmar thought he saw a shimmer of regret pass over the burgomeister but she hold fast, probably too stubborn back down. Anahea walked over to her, getting close enough to speak in relative privacy with her. Febe ardently shook her head at Anaheas words while the marshall seemed to be trying her best not to raise her voice.

-"I understand that you have little love for me or my people, I'm not here to change your mind on that. Hate me if you will but listen to me. This is only the beginning."

The chaotic atmosphere gave way to fear as the villagers stopped to hear the terrifying Barbarians' words. The tired people milled about starting to whisper among themselves and lament their oncoming doom. Ulmar could hear the marshall tell the burgomeister "we should not be speaking about this out here", mostly resulting in Febe waving the marshall off.

-"And why not? Why should we not decide what happens as a community? Why shouldn't we all hold this brute of a man accountable?"

Both Ulmar and Aldred had been in similar situations where mobs quickly became lynch mobs but this time there seemed to be a timid consensus that the stranger shouldn't pay for what had happened during the night. Rather several villagers voiced their support for the stranger. "I saw him fight the raiders", said one, "He saved Trynt", said another. Not getting the effect that she had wished, Febe conceded.

-"Fine, let's speak of this inside."

Febe led Anahea, Aldred and Ulmar inside her abode to the agitated demands of the villagers that were congregating quickly by the improvised headquarters. No sooner had the burgomeister gotten up the stairs before she was voicing her discontent.

-"Those fools might not be able to see a snake in the grass but I will not be fooled by the spy in our midst. They may say that you raised your weapon against your own kind yet I see no proof of actual battle. Tell me Barbarian, what wounds did you suffer in defense of our home?"

Passing her pointing finger Ulmar fought some primal part of himself that just wanted to reach out and break it. He was starting to nurture a burning dislike of the old woman even if he realised that people like Aldred would have faced worse in the hands of the true folk.

-"A warrior struck is a warrior fallen. You should know that," Anahea declared in a way that reminded of citing a saying. "Enough of this. There might be rhyme to your reason but at least give him the opportunity to speak before you scream for his blood."

She nodded at Ulmar who took the opportunity to speak before Febe had rallied her defenses.

"When the True Folk enter battle, their intentions can be as different as flakes of snow in a storm. The clans have shattered, taking on many ways, some even speaking other tongues than others. Yet some things stay the same. These warriors did not gain enough plunder to satisfy a raid nor did they kill enough of your people to satisfy bloodlust if that was their intention.

They will be back. You should see to your defenses and await the clans intentions that will be delivered by the light of morning. Then we will see if your lives might be spared."

-"If the clans are so shattered and have such different ways how do you know this?" Anaheas' question cut to the point of something that Ulmar was wrestling with if he should disclose or not. He made his decision and sighed.

"They are the Marrodar, a clan that shares your borders and revels in pillaging the lowlanders and they are the Tuakk, my kin."

Febe exploded in a tirade of accusations, Anahea looked shocked and Aldred mostly looked resigned. Deciding that enough was enough Ulmar slammed Kharagh down on the table with a stunning slam.

-"Enough! Screaming your hatred will do nothing for your people, save hasten their demise. Let me help you instead, there has to be a way to end these killings without the extermination of your people or mine. Let me stand before my kin and hear their demands, let us find a way to live side by side."

-"Do you offer the knowledge of how to defend against your own blood?" It was hard deciding just what the marshall was feeling, what her attitude was regarding Ulmars words. She might have been disgusted at Ulmars betrayal, surprised by his willingness or something else entirely.

-"If that will keep us all alive then yes. If it would mean that I could avoid the spilling of more blood I would willingly let any nighttime demon flay the skin from my body. I will not let my kin slaughter any more of you, neither shall I let you end my kin. This I swear."

With a quick move Ulmar cut a thin red line across his forearm and let the blood soak into his hand that he then clenched.

-"My friend", Aldred said patting his companions back, "I have to admire the way you move mountains. To try is to give way to utter folly but damn it if I don't believe that you can."

-"We need every arm that can hold a weapon if it is truly two Hillman clans that are standing against us. Think about it, would it really be such an advantage to send him as a spy? Would the plotters of such a scheme not realise that with all probability this would be his reception? A spy would use guile and trickery, not this. If this is the way the Lumbrians spy on their enemies it's a useless way to do it."

Febe lumbered over to one of the comfortable armchairs looking tired and wrinkly. They gathered around the table that went with it pondering Anaheas words.

-"I still say it's a trick." The Burgomeister massaged her brow.

-"Then you are a fool. If you doubt my interests then send someone to the storehouse at the end of the village that smells of fat and wool. You will find the remains of a raider there. The blow that felled him could not be made by anything other than Kharagh. By killing him I have broken my allegiance to my chieftain."

Febe cocked her head and gave a bitter frown.

-"It all depends on how far you are willing to go."

Feeling the frustration of discussing with this tree stump of a woman Ulmar growled.

-"If that were true why haven't I killed you now? I have the advantage on the village chieftain and the village warlord. I'm armed and there is nothing you could do to stop me."

Ulmar half expected that the marshall would tense up at such a hostile statement. She did not, instead remaining as cool and relaxed as ever in his company.

-"If... if there is such a body Anahea will follow you to it and confirm it. If there is, we shall decide your fate later."

-"No. You will need me. I will be speaking with Briac of the Tuakk come morning."

-"If there really is a body, then I might let you stay."

-"I will speak to Briac. I will stay and I will keep away useless slaughter."

33.

With a heavy heart Ulmar was accompanied by Aldred and
Anahea as they walked back to the alley to check for a
body. During the walk over, he imagined what blood
relative lay there mangled in the mud, cut in half by the
great axe that was supposed to defend the Tuakk. Guilt
haunted him, he was supposed to be the great warrior and
protector of his kin. The great Doomwolf that was
supposed to honor and keep the Tuakk, keeping them
from the cold embrace of oblivion. Now chances were
great that he had yet again been forced to spill the blood
of his kin. He'd have rather spilled his own.

They were back at the alley. Ulmar took a moment to
collect himself and brace for what waited for him in the
dark. He took comfort in Aldreds vitalizing presence, the
strange man a reminder that life could be better than it
was in the hills of the True Folk. He indicated that he was
ready and started into the alleyway. The darkness was
forced away as Aldred called an open flame which he held
in his palm, creating a magical torch.

The horror of finding a man mutilated by battle is an
ordeal in its own right, finding a friend or relative is a thing
that cuts scars into the soul. This was yet another cut in the
fabric that was Ulmars inner being. Sitting, as if resting with
his head slumped against his chest was a long haired and
bearded man. Even now Ulmar thought that he recognized

the fallen warrior choosing to push the thought aside to keep from drawing hasty conclusions.

The fallen warrior was cut through his forearm and split across the chest exposing parts that never should be so rudely seen. His blood had poured out all around him leaving a dark pool and giving the fallen skin pale as snow. This was Ulmars doing. Just a moment of violence put an end to an entire lifetime. This man should have lived a long life filled with love and joy but instead he sat there and would never rise again.

Moving as delicately as he could he lifted the warrior's head and confirmed that he had murdered Eldrig.

Ulmar had never gotten to know him very well, even if they had grown up and lived in proximity to each other. Eldrig had been one of those that had rightly avoided Ulmar like a black wolf plague, keeping as far away from him as possible. He knew that Eldrig was a father of the twins Ule and Alve, strong siblings that promised to make his parents proud. He also left Talava without the love of her life.

-"His name was Eldrig. He dreamt of the times when our people were strong and united. I remember when he sat at his loves side for days at a time when she was near to giving birth to their children. He was a quiet man that was skilled with his hands. He must have come here to find food for his family."

Working in relative silence, they made preparations to carry the man over to the small village shrine where the other casualties had been gathered. During the skirmishes a total of four villagers and two raiders had been killed, according to the local priest of Gyrd. Entering the small shrine the villagers had been arranged on gurneys side by side before the altar. There was no sign of the raider though. Confronting the priest, Ulmar found out that the dead had been unceremoniously dumped on one of the garbage heaps on the outskirts of the village. Seeing the hillmans growing hostility the priest professed to have managed to dissuade the villagers from at least defiling the body. Little comfort as it was, Ulmar couldn't ask for much more, knowing full well the horrors of war. Moving quickly Ulmar got the fallen raider, who turned out to be an unnamed Marrodar and moved him back to lie outside the shrine side by side with Eldrig. Then he gave the priest strict instructions to keep them safe from the vengeance of the villagers.

34.

-"He spoke truely. By helping us he became a kinslayer."

Febe frowned per usual sitting in her armchair, seeming less than thrilled at Anahea who brought her the news.

-"To me it mostly tells of a man that would kill his own kind."

-"We will lose this war", Anahea grimly predicted.

Aldred coughed, giving himself the opportunity to steal a hard cookie under the eye rolling gaze of the Burgomeister.

-"Certainly this isn't a war per se, my dear Marshall?"

-"But it is. This is a war that started the day the first settler staked their claim to this land. It's a war that will continue till only one people remains, and this disorganised rambling will lose us that war." She then focused her attention on the Burgomeister, "You gave me the responsibility of dispensing justice on those that would break the law and keep safe all those that would dwell here. Then let me loose from this chain which hampers me. Give me charge of the defense of the village. Let me be the one voice that guides us through this time. I have known war, I know what we face and I can tell you that without a clear leader we will fall."

Febe drummed her finger against the table considering the Marshalls words. Ulmar and Aldred stood back, holding their breath so not to get in the way of what they thought of as delicate negotiations.

-"Penkath already has a leader. Me. I was one of the original settlers and I've molded our community pulling it through hardship and toil and I'll be damned if I give up control at the first sign of trouble. You have my blessing as the militant arm of the village, but all decisions go through me. Swear it will be so."

Anahea stood with a straight back in front of the Burgomeister.

-"I will not."With those words, Anahea left the house of the Burgomeister with Ulmar and Aldred in tow leaving an old woman in stunned passivity.

35.

Morning was on the horizon. Anahea, Aldred and Ulmar
had found a small but sharp knoll on which they had a
slight advantage in elevation over the immediate terrain,
and a clear view of that area. The wind was kind, only
providing a fresh breeze which revitalized the tired
warriors. They hadn't gotten any sleep during the night,
which meant that the Tuakk and Marrodar would be well
rested while they were not.

Ulmar had spent the time between their dramatic exit from
the burgomeister with wrapping his fallen kinsman and the
Marrodar raider. It had been hard to find enough fine cloth
to wrap them in but the result had turned out well. The two
bodies now lay on that same knoll resting near Ulmars feet.

-"What can we expect?"

Ulmar weighed Aldred and Anaheas' mood. Both seemed
calm enough and the tone of Aldreds voice was steady. He
considered sharing how uncertain he was of their next
actions The true folk were a people steeped in tradition
taking ritual very seriously but Ulmar could just as easily
imagine Briac or the Marrodar just deciding that since the
lowlanders weren't people they could just commence
slaughtering them.

-"We stand under the banner of the goat..."

-"Tell me why?" Anahea asked while eying the goatskin they had fastened on a long pole with open scepticism.

-"Because the goat of war is the War demon of our people. The cloven hoof goat-headed demon of the dark hills that craves battle and blood. By raising the goat we show our intentions of waging war. If Briac intends war and marches under the goat he must meet with us to discuss terms. They will be here by dawn."

The small group waited, shifting slightly but not speaking. Words had escaped them as words would only create uncertainty and focus their attention on details they would rather ignore. Anahea had donned a strange suit of armor unlike any that Ulmar had seen. The breastplate was the same as she had worn during the night, an assembly of iron or steel plates riveted on a leather back. Yet it had several black sleek polished rocks fastened on it and the designwork was foreign to him. The armor had several sections that were joined with intricate knotworks and several of the armor plates seemed to be made of wood. In actuality there was more wood, fabric and stone in the armor than metal or leather. Anaheas long spear was also of alien design, the spearpoint being of the same sleek black stone as the stone on her armor. Ulmar and Aldred, not having much in the way of change or armor, were clad in the same attire as before.

Ulmar committed the scene to memory. Despite the serious nature of their errand, despite the fatigue and the uncertainty of what was to come he was enjoying the moment. The view of this small snippet of the hills of the true folk was beautiful with the rugged trees climbing the hillside overlooking the wild river. The wind caressed them with its cool touch while the clouds danced far overhead. It was a good moment to be alive, one of those rare moments that he loved the land that he had been born in.

They were creeping in from the hillside. He could feel them more than see them but they were clearly there. The others seemed to feel it too, fidgeting with their gear. Ulmar played several scenarios of how this would go in his mind, most turning into a total bloody mess. He had taken what precautions that he could, raising the banner of the goat and placing the wrapped dead in front of them so they wouldn't be flanked if his people decided to attack.

From the concealing undergrowth of the edge of the trees, a wicked banner topped with the skin of a goat, its head crowning the pole, was raised as the forest exploded with the roars of hidden warriors. The war banner swayed to and fro as the Tuakk and Marrodar chanted ancient battle hymns that graphically described the fate that awaited those foolish enough to face the wrath of the true folk. There was no answer from the hill, Aldred mostly changing his grip on their banner.

The chanting of the warriors went on sparking activity in the village. People ran to and fro between the buildings behind the little group on the hill. Upset voices debated action and after a while several armed villagers started nearing the knoll. Annoyed, Anahea spun round and motioned the villagers to back off.

After what felt like an eternity a group broke off from the edge of the forest making their way to the knoll. Even from this distance Ulmar recognized the silhouettes of Briac, Hild and Schilti.

With determined steps the trio made it to the base of the knoll and started climbing. At Ulmars side he heard Aldred mutter "here goes nothing." Briac, Hild and Schilti stopped about twenty feet from them. The trio was battered and bruised though stood proud, it was evident that they had seen battle not long ago and by the look of things they had fared well. Ulmar took a tally of weapons, Briacs massive mace, Hilds cruel longbow and to Ulmars surprise Schilti was equipped with Aldreds old sword that had been given to Briac as a gift. Ulmar also noticed that briac had mounted a golden torc as a belt buckle and that Hild had at least a partial chainmail under her fur attire. Always ready to do social battle, Briac let the head of the large mace drop to the ground with a heavy thud and then leaned casually against the handle in a very relaxed way.

-"Why if it isn't my own nephew, out on his adventure", he began in a mockingly playful sort of way, "Out to save the broken little bird of a man that flapped under his nose. I was certain that I heard your Lowland flea mumble that you two were on your way to the throne to walk on ground, upon which no mortal man should walk. Instead I find you here, breaking every law, and throwing in your lot defending things less than people. When Hild told me that the unbeatable Doomwolf was doing just that, I told her that no, that would be an impossibility. My own blood would never sully his hands by taking up arms against his own people for less than nothing. You must be mistaken, said I. Still here you stand mocking our ways and cursing your name as you use our traditions to insult us. You should be relieved that it was only us and not the goat of war itself that answered this insult, you see, we will only flay you alive and burn your corpse. What the demon may yet still do to you is much, much worse."

-"Uncle. You left for the Redshield Goblins, why have you abandoned your mission to rid the hills from them?"

Both chieftains of the true folk grinned wolves grins at him.

-"Ah, but you see, you were right to speak up for your cousin Hild. We have a budding Warlord right here," Briac gestured toward Hild, Hild only focusing a cold unblinking stare at Ulmar. "Her plan and leadership not only beat the goblins in their own den, it broke them. Our long hated enemies had no time to rally and nowhere to run, their vile corpses now food for crows. I guess that in this way we owe you our acknowledgment, we would never have seen her if you hadn't persisted. It took only hours to crush them but the thing with goblins is that they leave precious little in loot. There are no usable stores of food to be had and after our battle we are hungry."

-"Knowing of fat little lambs a wolf will feast," Schilti interjected, his raspy voice sounding more wild beast than human.

-"You will not find plunder here, only the tip of a spear", Anahea answered in a heavily broken but fully understandable tongue of the true folk.

-"The Lowlander woman can understand our speech but lacks the wit to know our words", Schilti scoffed. "To see a Tuakk woman match the skill in battle that men possess is strange as it is, know that she is the exception while you are nothing more than a temporary distraction at best. Dress your women however you will, it will not aid you."

The Marrodar were one of those clans that did not fight alongside their women, having in Ulmars opinion, a very low view of womankind in general. It had not always been so but for several generations their ways had changed. Ulmar was pleased to see that Anahea did not act rashly even if such action might have been justified. All he wanted to do at the moment was to find a way to avert bloodshed.

-"You will not find spoils here. These people are more than willing to defend what they have just as is the right of anyone to do. Pull back the clans so we might come to an agreement."

-"Agreement?" Briac lost his cool facade for rage. "There can be no agreement with these less than men. These are vermin that have infested our ancestral lands. They will be driven out or killed, it doesn't matter which to us."

-"Don't do this uncle. We can find a way to resolve our differences without throwing our people to the wolves."

Briacs rage seemed to give way for a moment of sad disappointment before he regained his posture, a rare crack showing the man beneath the machinations.

-"Why are you standing in our way? How could you raise your axe, our axe, against your own people?"

The question stirred his emotions. A virtual sea of bitter memories and injustices made against not only himself but every being that made its existence in the hills of the true folk.

-"Why? Because the madness of our way of life needs to stop. We live on carnage and bleed ourselves on the edge of extinction. What right do we have to put others to death whose only crime is that they have made better lives than ours in the same lands? How can we justify sending our old to die in the cruel jaws of the white wolf when there could be a way to save them? I haven't forgotten, Hod, and I never will."

-"Is that what all this is about? You want to punish me for the difficult choices we need to make as a clan? Then find another way instead of punishing your people. We need to still our hunger both when it comes to the body and the soul. I have said my peace. You have turned your back on your own people."

-"Uncle. See to our honored dead." Ulmar indicated the wrapped corpses.

-"Our honored dead. Not yours." Feeling no compulsion to be careful, Briac turned his back to them and waved at the edge of the forest clearly summoning more warriors. Several warriors of the true folk jogged out from the edge of the forest ready to do the chieftains bidding. Fear and resentment was clearly written in their faces at the sight of the Doomwolf opposing them. Still they quietly moved to the fallen warriors and started carrying them off in a slow procession.

-"Today", Briac stated pointing his mace at them, "we see to our dead. Tomorrow, we shall see to the blight that infects this land."

Ulmar stirred, taking one step forward. He wanted to stop him, force him to come to his senses and see the wisdom in Ulmars insistence that there could be a peaceful resolution. Briac, on the other hand, had his back firmly turned toward his nephew as he walked away.

Hild faced Ulmar with all the cool demeanor of a glacier, the only indication of life was her breath. They stood facing each other long enough that his comrades twisted slightly in discomfort. With the same slow movements of said glacier, Hild reached for an arrow, held it out in her outstretched arm and broke it in twain with a vicious snap. She let the pieces fall to the ground and backed away. As Hild moved toward the edge of the forest, catching up to Schilti, Ulmar picked up the broken projectile. The gesture was in his mind much like the woman always was; strong but unreadable. He still felt that he had lost her, even though her action could just as well meant a show of support. That train of thought was only a fool's folly.

36.

The village was too much of a running chaos. People were scared, upset, angry even, having been beset upon by a little known enemy without warning. This running around would only help his people. The villagers were tiring themselves out, like a buck running from a pack of wolves, they did not seem to realise that this was the time to rest and prepare.

-"It is time that I see to it that the preparations are made", Anahea half shouted at Ulmar and Aldred. "I will need your unconditional help, will you give it to me?"

The two of them nodded their response. A moment later they were hurrying along the street finding anyone who looked like they could be a member of the village militia ordering them to gather just outside the village inn. While chaos reigned there was no sign of Febe anywhere.

When enough of the militia had gathered, Anahea gracefully scaled a large barrel to speak to the gathered force.

-"Citizens of Penkath!! Hear me. We have been set upon by the old tribes that claimed these hills centuries past. I know that you are gripped by fear. I know that these are the lands that were promised to you and that you never asked for this fight. But, here we are facing danger together, we who sought to build the bonds of family will now twine the bonds of battle. This is not a fight that we can walk away from. The Barbarians at our doors surround us and will accept nothing short of your deportation or death. But we will prevail. We will stand proudly together, a cliff upon which these marauders will break. I ask you now to look to the leaders of the village. Trust in my leadership and fall in line to what the militia asks of you. All here that are not needed, tend to your homes, get some sleep. We will need your strength later. Any of you who are not yet part of the militia and who feel you want to enroll or help, report to either Merle or Nola."

Being done with her speech Anahea jumped down and started ordering the militia into position. A handful of militia were to stand watch on the outskirts of the village while the rest of them were to fortify the village. After the scouts left for their vigils an argument started amongst the group.

-"See here", Anahea tried illustrating her point by drawing in the dirt with a stick. "The village might be safe from the side that faces the river but it's still built like a bead necklace. The one that defends everything defends nothing which has never been more true than with our situation. See how the eastern part of the village spreads thin with many low buildings? We cannot hold anything further than Orvidius' house at the farthest."

-"And that's where your brain melts to mud silk-hugger,", the blond dwarf with the unruly beard hotly interjected. "If you leave these houses", the dwarf savagely jabbed at the dirt representing three of the most far away buildings, "then you might as well arm the barbarians yourselves with our heartfelt best wishes. I have stores that can in no way fall to the rascals."

Anahea took a moment to get a grip on her emotions before continuing.

-"What's in these stores of yours? And why can you not just move them?"

-"Move a small forge? And an anvil like mine? Unlikely. Even if you'd start grabbing and pulling at things that are of no use to you you'd ruin most of it by pulling it out. These things aren't meant to be uprooted."

-"What do you have in your stores?"

-"Just some basics, nothing you need to concern yourselves with."

-"You will tell me now," the Marshall demanded. The dwarf sighed deeply grumbling what could only be profanities and then conceding.

-"Maybe a hundred or so half finished blades and several hundred arrowheads."

A stunned silence was followed by a less than pleased Anahea, voicing her concern to the smith.

"Hundreds? What do you mean hundreds? Why would you... how could you even have a hundred blades just lying around your stores? How could you hold that back from me? What do you mean? Explain yourself."

The bearded smith absentmindedly kicked a rock over Anaheas' sketch in the dirt. He crossed his arms and frowned.

-"Look here, I was just doing research that's none of your business. They aren't even done, none of them. Most only have one side sharpened, no use to none. And arrowheads, they're just good business sense."

-"One side sharpened is enough. We bring what we can and then bar the houses, we still don't have the time to build defenses around them nor manpower to cover them. My decision stands."

Swearing iron curses, the infuriated smith toppled over several boxes and even a scrawny militiaman on the way to his buildings. Ulmar considered the prospect of the Tuakk and Marrodar getting their hands on a hundred forged blades and wasn't thrilled with the concept. He turned round, grabbed Aldred by the shoulder and dragged him after the dwarf. The apprentice muttered something in the style of "yes, yes, fine, fine," then let himself be dragged along.

They caught up to the dwarf after a moment jogging, though they chose to keep their distance, not wanting to get within punching range - just in case. Getting to the building they didn't even have time to follow him inside before the smith was yet again outside with a heavy chain in tow. Still fuming curses, the man from within the mountain summarily chained his door firmly shut, then proceeded to chain the other two buildings shut. The smith was red faced and sweating, while not giving a hoot about his passive entourage. Huffing he then swerved around heading straight for the Burgomeisters' house.

-"I suspect that our diminutive friend is going to make life somewhat interesting for our fair marshall."

-"He can try. Anahea will handle any interference from that old boar."

Aldred patted his companions shoulder in a way that greatly implied pity.

-"My dear hillman friend, do not underestimate the sharp claws of that woman."

Ulmar of course didn't, he was mostly hoping that they would be spared the additional struggle and chaos that was most certainly on its way. The two debated if they should follow the smith but decided against it instead going back to where they had left Anahea, both decided upon assisting with the construction of the defenses. The militia were now hard at work gathering barrels, chests, wagons and assorted furniture, piling up the wooden objects in the main street and then moving them into position. The Marshals' instructions had been simple and clear yet sufficient and the people of Penkath carried out her orders with efficiency. The basic idea was to construct an unbroken barricade that enclosed the more important buildings and would hopefully keep out the savage attackers. Ulmar felt sad at the sight of the defensive barricade that was growing in front of their eyes, it was far better than nothing yet the warriors of the True Folk were well accustomed to storming actual castles. Every clan with aspirations of survival except the Tuakk had constructed a tower or lesser castle to keep their people safe from inevitable invaders. An improvised barricade like this one would not prove much of a hindrance for his people. Ulmar knew that he had to do everything in his power to keep violence from ensuing, to stave off the savage bloodbath that would follow an all out battle.

-"Marshall Novamahe!"

The blond smith was back, content as a cat with a secret and holding a parchment in his hand. The Marshall was a bit too far away to be able to close the distance before the dwarf bellowed on.

-"I have here a direct order from the Burgomeister and the council of elders that you are to include my buildings into the defended and guarded perimeter immediately."

-"I've already explained why we can't."

The dwarf held up the parchment with a confrontative sneer.

-"And I've the order right here so start movin yar people to include my houses. Right now. On the order of Burgomeister Febe."

A silent and discreet nod was all the acceptance that the Marshal gave as she complied with the Burgomeisters' command. Happy to have his will done the dwarf marched over to his buildings with a pair of guards in tow. Anahea stood frowning as she started to draw a fresh map of the village in the dirt now including defenses of more or less the entire village.

-"We're spread too thin."

Ulmar probably didn't need to explain to Aldred, but he was upset and had to voice his concerns.

-"Let's focus on the now. How do we fix this?"

Ulmar took a few steps over to a pile of rough furniture choosing a satisfactory heavy chest to heave up on the barricade. He didn't have an answer.

-"Could be that with a little accident the buildings aren't all that important any longer. Like I don't know, a fire?"

Ulmar glared at the apprentice who was the essence of innocence in that moment. Seeing that Ulmar was less than thrilled about the prospect of arson, Aldred waved a bit, showing that he was past that specific idea.

-"So the marshall is intent on following the old bags orders and we can neither convince the smith to move nor accidentally burn the buildings to the ground. Then what?"

-"We defend the village. We build the barricade and man it. Nothing else to it."

-"Both you and I know that is a terrible plan Ulmar. We need more details. How would you go about attacking the village?"

-"If I think like Hild I'd focus on getting loot, regardless of Briacs' instructions. My people are starving, food is of the most importance. So I'd create a diversion, no, two diversions, by attacking up there by the inn. Mostly bows, javelins and torches. Then I'd send fighters in the dark here where we're exposed to the largest storage building I could find. That's what they'll do."

-"Fighting in darkness at the end of the world", Aldred said letting a flame the size of a finger dance along his hand, "I guess that's what I do now."

37.

The muffled shouts of battle didn't yield. Just as Ulmar had
predicted, The Tuakk and Marrodar had made a strike as
soon as night was upon them. They had rested and eaten
well at the inn, the militia on the other hand, had not
managed more than a moments' rest after seeing to the
village defenses. Such was the difference between the
untrained and the veterans in Ulmars experience, not really
what you do but how.

They were lying flat on their stomachs on top of large
boxes with a decent view of the surrounding room. It was
dark, tense and smelled of tar. They did not speak, did not
move, just waiting in the dark to see if Ulmar knew his
kinsman as well as he assumed.

Outside, the chaos continued. They could only hope that
casualties would be light, that his kin only wanted to keep
the village militia busy while Hild tried to strike from
another angle. With some strong-arming from Ulmar and
silvered words from Aldred Anahea had been convinced to
station the guards that should have been posted on the
barricade near the storage inside the building with them
instead. Ulmar hoped that would lessen the risk of
casualties. If he had read the situation wrong that act could
mean that the villagers could much more easily be flanked
and attacked from behind, a possibility that filled him with
cold dread. Aldred was close by, the heat of his body

reaching Ulmar through the dark. Maybe the magic that he wielded was ever present only barely contained by his mortal flesh, churning fire hot and strong. Ulmar believed so in any case.

A resounding crash shook them where they lay in the dark. It was starting to seem as if Ulmar was mistaken in his prediction regarding Hilds' plan. The militia members were stirring, itching to help their friends and neighbors. A rather large militia member named Gorgs was getting up from his hiding place, bent on getting somewhere where he felt he was needed. To move now would mostly reveal their hand if the warriors of the True Folk did show up. Citing a list of curses internally Ulmar got up and hastened over to the militiaman pushing him down again. The man seemed furious, meaning to challenge Ulmar but as he raised his head he froze. Something was moving. Ulmar was caught in an uncomfortable crouch, his back facing the sound emanating from the main door. There had to be several raiders in the building now. Gorg slowly drew his sword in anticipation of the struggle ahead. Ulmar was exposed where he crouched, it was only a matter of time before the raiders would spot him and perhaps even gut him before he could react.

In a split decision, Gorg lumbered into a charge, trampling Ulmars foot and in that same motion twisting his knee painfully. Wincing, Ulmar tried to get to his feet, only to find that the large guard had managed to gore his knee so that it seemed to have popped its socket. There was pain of course, excruciating, but what was more important was the fact that he was effectively immobilized. In a better world, he would have time to look over his injury or at least slowly straighten and realign his leg but he only had a moment or less to get into fighting shape. He didn't have that time of course. Behind him the raiders laughed at Gorgs clumsy attack as the guardsman bellowed. Aldred was on his feet, though no fire had enveloped his hands yet and the second guardsman was taking his first lumbering steps toward the raiders.

This could have gone better, Ulmar concluded. It would be a miracle if no one died, to be honest it would be a miracle if he himself didn't die in this botched ambush.

Ulmar rolled away from the fighting, only slightly hurting himself a bit further in the process. Wincing he crouched facing the raiders now. There were somewhere between half a dozen to a dozen of them. They had effectively disarmed Gorg, one raider at each arm and a kicking and punching Marrodar working his gut. At least the guardsman didn't seem to be mortally wounded, yet. The second guardsman was hesitating, no doubt paralyzed with the fear of a doomed battle. Aldred got up, letting flame pour out over his entire arms in a frightening fluid motion. The raiders were as taken aback as he himself had been at the first sight of witch fire, and reacted in much the same way. It was Bolbata, who in earnest had been open and welcoming to the Lowlander apprentice who threw the wicked handaxe at Aldred. It spun through the air too fast to properly register and impacted with Aldreds skull with a sharp sound. Rage flooded Ulmars veins as Aldred fell to the ground. His focus narrowed as he snapped his knee back into its socket, no longer concerned with the pain. Some sliver of conscious thought must have remained as he felt Kharagh slip through his fingers as he stood up. The raiders hadn't spotted him taking sport in working Gorg over so when the mass of Ulmars body connected with the group none of them had even a moment to compensate their balance. Swinging his arms wide he fiercely heaved the group of their feet. Gorg and five raiders were thrown from the door of the storage as Ulmar appeared in the space they had so violently vacated. Frightened, Bolbata stood before the rage of her clansman like a hare before a wolf. She slashed toward him with another handaxe, hoping to cripple the threat before true battle was joined only to see her axe literally bounce off the raging Ulmar.

The blow rippled through him but instead of registering pain, it felt good, fulfilling. Ulmar rejoiced at the feeling and longed to mete out the same. That sliver of consciousness that he had managed to keep back told him that he was in the early sways of berserking. Only through an effort of pure willpower could he pull back before he had ripped his own kinsmen limb from limb.

The axe had barely bounced off Ulmars body before his fist crashed into Bolbatas clavicle, shattering it with ease. While she was falling to the ground screaming her pain, Ulmar followed up his blow by headbutting a Marrodar to the ground. The raiders were breaking before his charge. Not quite quick enough, Ulmar caught up with a surprised Krat, grabbed him by the belt and scruff and in one moment of berserker strength threw the man over the barricade, a full seven feet up in the air. Ulmar had to crouch, catch his breath not to give in completely to his anger. More in control and shaking with the effort of it, Ulmar got to his feet again, turning back to the Tuakk and Marrodar he had wrecked through. The temptation of death and mutilation lay over his mind, spurring him to commit acts that he'd regret for the rest of his life.

The raiders were on their feet, rallying in a semicircle in front of him, ready to do battle with the feared Doomwolf. A warrior lunged a spear toward him, which Ulmar disdainfully sidestepped and grabbed with both hands. Growling he heaved at the weapon, using it to crash one raider into another with enough force that the owner of the weapon dropped it. Then the shaft became a vengeful club pummeling any that were dumb enough to face him. Thankfully the raiders ran as the lust for bloodshed was growing too much to control. Ulmar had to take a moment to calm himself. The shaking wouldn't stop, his mind and heart raced, his body was so much under the bloodspell that he didn't even hear the warriors roar their retreat. It was dark and cold. He almost threw up while shuffling back toward the storage where they had set their ambush, tired and spent by his own brand of fire.

Fire, he thought, Aldred. He forced himself to get to the Lowlanders side, stepping past the beaten heap of Gorgs body and into the dusk. He found him crumpled on the ground, unmoving. Bolbatas axe laid there, miraculously the blade hadn't cut into Aldreds body. Wondering if he'd be doing more damage than good, Ulmar lifted the man in his arms to carry him back to the inn. Aldred groaned. Ulmar felt a rush of relief, the man wasn't dead at least. Ulmar held him closer, hurrying through the ragged village.

Aldred wondered if he was getting used to getting clobbered in battle. It hurt, he was confused and his head was spinning but he was pretty sure that he should feel a lot worse. He was back in bed, a proper bed with only the most symbolic amount of lice, feeling very appreciative of lying down. There was a soft candle burning in the room highlighting the intimidating features of his hillman friend. As the light shied away from his eyes and cast deep shadows across his face Aldred wondered if there might even be something to the rumors that the man was possessed by demons.

-"Lowlander! You live! Quickly, recite the beasts of the forest!"

Aldred blinked trying to understand but failing.

-"I couldn't even do that if I was fully sharp and alert. Tell me, how did we fare?"

-"Better than we should have, but worse than I hoped. We won the night. Casualties were light and the True Folk didn't get much of what they were after. But two more dead and two others dying. This isn't a battle, this is a siege."

-"So what do we do now, my unbeatable friend?"

-"Now, I find Anahea so we can meet with Briac in the morning. We raise the banner of the goat on the hill in the same way we did before and eat away at his will to continue the siege like a river cuts into stone."

38.

Yet again Ulmar, Aldred and Anahea were poised on top of the small knoll on the outskirts of Penkath. They were tired and battered, not talking much, being that they were drained of the energy that would require.

Anahea was unscathed from physical harm even if she was haunted by fatigue, proudly refusing to yield to that same feeling.

Ulmars knee had swollen painfully, to the degree that it hindered his mobility. He would have to hide his injury during the talks with Briac or risk immediate attack. A show of weakness was all the true folk needed to throw caution to the wind and set upon the hapless villagers of Penkath slaying them to a man. Ulmar had been mulling things over desperate to find a solution that would work for all parties involved and he might just have happened upon something he felt would work if Briac and Febe wouldn't condemn them with their pigheadedness.

-"Anahea"; he started gently hoping to mask the uncertainty that plagued him, "how much authority do you hold over the actions of the village?"

The marshall didn't answer him with words instead just twisting and giving him a quizzical look.

-"I might be able to find a way to end the bloodshed, but I need to make some promises on your part, so what burden can you bear for peace?"

Anahea squinted her eyes slightly as she answered.

-"I do not like the idea of what such a peace could cost us. What do you intend Ulmar Blackaxe of the hills?"

-"I intend to barter peace, Marshal Anahea. What my people need more than anything is food and that you have in abundance, what your people need is protection from raids like these. Instead of being at each other's' throats this could be the dawning of a new age for both our people. So, do you have the power to give me permission to grant such a request?"

The marshall seemed anything other than pleased.

-"You do not know what these people have suffered to travel here to live under their own rule. You would barter away their independence and food that they can hardly spare so easily. If I agree I condemn these people to misery they fled, if I deny you, I condemn them to death."

-"Better cranky than dead", Aldred interjected.

-"Better cranky than dead," the marshal agreed and nodded. "Very well Blackaxe, do your best to negotiate peace and I will do my best to fulfill our promises. Please be careful what you promise though, your words will change peoples' lives."

Their goatskin banner was all that sounded for a while after that, its flapping not enough to keep away the tense silence that was between them. The Tuakk and Marrodar were on their way again, Ulmar could almost feel them. As the first rays of light shone upon the canopy of trees, the raiders raised their banner yet again. Breaking out in their roaring battlesong, the villagers that had been out on the street rushed to the uncertain safety of their homes. The silhouettes of Briac, Hild and Schilti sauntered toward the knoll. Just as before the raiders stopped within twenty feet from Ulmar and his companions.

This time the raiders didn't look as smug as before, though they were in no way battered or broken.

-"I ask you again for peace, Uncle. There is no reason why our people and the Lowlanders should have to resort to killing each other. Aren't these lands deadly enough without adding this war? Aren't the hills of the True Folk vast and largely uninhabited?"

-"Fool of a nephew. There isn't a valley or hill that isn't claimed in the lands of the True Folk. You keep spitting out your wish for peace and barter away what is ours for nothing. Tonight more have died and must be avenged with the blood of our enemies."

-"Why? The dead have fallen but why does their passing scream for blood? What if I could offer life for the living instead?"

A snarling Schilti took three strides toward the top of the knoll. The Marrodar chieftain swelled with rage, seemingly ready to throttle the lot of them. Reacting to Schiltis advance, Anahea lowered her spear menacingly which prompted the clansmen of the True Folk to ready their own weapons. Things were quickly getting out of hand.

-"Our dead scream for blood, for justice. Who are you to insult our ways and insult our honored dead? Blood must flow."

Raising his arms with palms facing outward in a gesture of peace Ulmar took a step toward Schilti.

-"The dead that fell here came in hopes of finding a way to feed the Tuakk and Marrodar and if you'll let me, I can make that happen without more warriors having to be claimed by the wolves. Think of your wives, your mothers, your old and your young. Isn't peace an option if it means that they might live?"

Briac placed his hand on Schiltis shoulder and more or less pulled him back into line. He then retook the word.

-"Why would we have to settle for scraps when we can take what we need and be rid of this blight upon our lands?"

-"Try your hand at violence and fail. If blood is all that you want we will help spill yours for every step you take towards our village."

-"Or you can claim tribute from the village and get what you want without having to spill any more blood," Ulmar hastened to fill in after Anaheas challenging statement. "As a show of good faith the village will provide food for you and your warriors today, a symbol of what is to come. Consider that, and see that there is another way, uncle."

-"You will feed us? As we stand with weapons in hand at your threshold you offer to help us regain our strength?" Briac laughed in disbelief at his nephews' radical proposal. "Then by all means explain your proposal."

-"Consider this. If you refrain from attacking the village any further, the villagers will grant the Tuakk and Marrodar a tribute of twice your weight in food every Solstice where at least a quarter of that is meat or dairy. Consider that, and I will arrange for the food to be brought to the edge of the village."

Ulmar could see that the trio were intrigued. With the time of the wolves now past, the most important concern was to find a way to feed the clans.

-"We will await this promised food. If it isn't delivered by nightfall, prepare to pay in blood."

Not awaiting an answer the representatives of the True Folk pulled back to the edge of the forest.

-"You may have promised too much, Blackaxe. I can't imagine that the council nor Febe will be quick to agree to these terms."

-"They will just have to agree, or die."

Aldred sighed walking up to the hillman and patted his back.

-"What a cheerful prospect, and see here is she now so that you can share this mirthful news with her. Good luck."

Behind them at the base of the knoll Ulmar saw that Febe had gathered a small contingent of militia and was awaiting their descent. He groaned internally at the prospect of butting heads with the Burgomeister again. There was no point procrastinating so he made his way down the knoll hoping that the marshal would back him up.

-"Burgomeister Van Vjanten, there is hope for peace if you'll only listen to me."

-"What have you done now?"

-"The True Folk agree to consider ending this bloodshed if the people of Penkath will in turn agree to pay tribute in the way of food to them. They demand twice the weight of their chieftain Briac in food, of which a quarter shall be meat and dairy and this is to be paid at every Solstice. I recommend that you agree to this offer and ask you to honor my promise that you will send food to them now as a show of good faith."

The Burgomeister stepped up to Ulmar and slapped him. His chin stung at the attack. From the look of it none of his companions nor the militia had expected that the old woman would physically assault the large and intimidating man. She moved to slap him again, to which he raised his finger in a silent warning.

-"How dare you, barbarian. We do not have much to spare and should not suffer the indignity to have to give it away. We worked hard for what we have, every day in these unforgiving lands and you just give it away."

-"It's that or death. I can do no better for you."

-"I know that. We all know that. We will do it but don't think I won't curse your name."

The Burgomeister left, taking her militia force with her.

-"I can't believe that went so well," Aldred pondered.

Ulmar didn't believe it either, he expected that there was trouble to come.

39.

During the day the militia were tasked to gather foodstuffs that were to be handed to the raiders who were hidden in the forest just outside the village. The muttering militia had made no effort to hide how they felt about the decision to feed those who had been responsible for murdering several of their friends and family. Yet after a while a pile of supplies grew at the foot of the barricade. There was bread, grain, vegetables and ale for a respectable force, all being organized under the watchful gaze of the Burgomeister. Ulmar was quickly re-establishing his depressing role as the outcast, to be hated, revered and shunned. A new village, new people even, yet same role.

When a sufficient amount of goods had been gathered the militia started moving it over the barricade to the collective groans of the village.

-"Chin up Ulmar, even if these people don't realise it this act might have saved them all."

Aldred was as lighthearted as always, a difference from his earlier life that he was truly grateful for. Now he was not really alone anymore.

As the villagers had placed their goods outside the defensive perimeter and pulled back, the raiders sent their own detachment to get the goods. Laughing and taunting the Hillmen took their time carrying the spoils back to their comrades.

-"We can't be lax tonight. This might still end in blood."

-"Figures," Aldred answered with a tired smile. "Seems like you people need a new pastime, this killing gets really tedious after a while."

40.

That night Aldred convinced him that they could keep
guard from the roof of the inn instead of patrolling the
village streets, in a vain hope of being at the right place at
the right time. He had discovered that they could easily
climb out onto the roof from their room and sit on the
rather slanted roof without risking falling off. So they had
gotten two steady steins of ale and some salted bread and
enjoyed the setting sun. Sitting there the view was quite
good lulling Ulmar into a false sense of security.

-"How is your leg?"

Ulmar poked at his swollen knee trying not to wince. He
considered just how honest he should be with the
Lowlander, after all he didn't want to worry him all too
much.

-"Good enough to run on, even if I'd prefer not to. How's
your head?"

Aldred fingered his impressive bump, while his gaze
wandered beyond the horizon. If Ulmar wasn't mistaken
he'd lie about it just as Ulmar had, probably even for the
same reason.

-"Head? Attached to my neck and fully functional. If it
wasn't for my precious souvenir one would never know

that I had blocked yet another blow with my skull. Noggin like a helmet, this."

To underline his point Aldred knocked on his head, as one would do on a door only to cringe with tears in his eyes. Ulmar just laughed at the display. He'd never have thought that lying would be anything other than a curse, even less that he'd actually enjoy doing it with a friend. Maybe the Lowlander was infecting him a bit with that concept of civilisation which Lowlanders were always so proud of.

-"Sometimes I wonder how it would have been to be born in your lands," Ulmar admitted, "I can't imagine a life nor land where people like you and the farmers tilling the fields of Penkath fit in. I like the idea of it."

-"All lives are worlds in their own rights and all worlds have their fates, laws, Kings and demons." Aldreds voice was almost sad, he touched Ulmars shoulder for a moment in an affectionate way.

Ulmar was expecting more but nothing followed his comrades' comment. He let it pass instead, taking in the Lowlanders' words. He just wanted this moment to go on forever but wishes in the hills of the True Folk are met with curses from demons. As he lay entranced the flames of several torches rolled out of the dark edge of the forest like a flock of angry stars. "Do you see..." was all that Aldred managed to say as they witnessed how the True Folk returned with war at their heels. From a hundred throats, ancient battle hymns erupted in the moments before the torches were tossed on, and past, the barricade. The militia had posted guards on that same barricade, now panicking and under attack their screams awoke those that had managed to steal a moment's sleep.

Not thinking just reacting, Ulmar rolled off the roof of the building to the sound of Aldreds surprised yelp. If it was training or just pure dumb luck that kept him from injuring himself badly, only the Dead Gods knew. Ulmar almost passed out as he broke his fall with a roll that echoed pain from his knee out into his entire body. With Kharagh in hand, he rushed for the barricade. A rain of arrows, torches and rough javelins hailed over the improvised structure, though almost all of them missed their mark. Almost. The poor militia members that had been guarding this part lay perforated at their post and on the ground by the barricade.

-"Black wolf gnaw on the skulls of fork-tongued traitors!"

The call echoed in many Hillman throats, every shout filled with outrage. Among the arrows and javelins, several rounded objects were flung, one of them landing in the mud at Ulmars feet. It was a head. It had to be a Lowlander head by the look of its short tended hair and smooth skin. Several lowlander heads lay in the dirt, decapitated swollen heads. Acting on surprise Ulmar examined one fleetingly to discover a swollen black tongue pressing out of the mouth of the murdered villager, while also having a strange sweet stench about it.

-"In the morning we come for you Lowlanders, and then we water the ground with your blood."

Bolbata had screamed her challenge in Avarossian, the Lowlander tongue. Infuriated, Ulmar looked around in the gathering crowd to find her. Aldred pressed to his side, Anahea was trying to arrange the villagers into some kind of vestige of a defense, and Febe was in turn trying to rally a gathering crowd. Snarling, Ulmar stepped straight to the old woman and grabbed her by the throat. Screams of dismay and disbelief surrounded him as he pressed the shocked Burgomeister to a tree.

-"What have you done?!" Ulmars bellow scattered the villagers nearest him. Anahea, Aldred and several militia were there, prying and pulling the strong Ulmar from the elderly woman. Momentarily shaking off the grapplers, he lifted the decapitated head so close to Febes face that she was nearly touching it.

-"You arrogant scheming fool!"

Ulmar let go of the Burgomeister and pushed himself free of his grapplers, keeping them at bay with the severed head.

-"You who are supposedly the leader of this village have condemned your people to death with your idiocy. Poison!" Swiveling the head around showing it to the crowd, he screamed yet again, "Poison! My people expected treachery and that's exactly what they got. You poisoned the food and they gave it to all these people to test it. You murdered your own people and now my people have no reason to not slaughter you all!"

-"I did only what anyone would do when beset by vermin, by mad beasts." The Burgomeister clutched her throat, coughing. "You snake among the roses, you are working with them to give away all that we worked for, even our hard earned freedom. No, that cannot come to pass. Now you sow the idea that your people hadn't already killed these good people, cut off their heads. No, we will not be fooled, and we will not surrender to fear of filthy Barbarians."

Tired and resigned, he didn't understand how any living breathing being could be this narrow minded.

-"I could have saved you all," he was no longer talking to the Burgomeister, instead, talking directly to the people he had hoped to save. "Believe what you will, but I wanted to end this, to save you."

Aldred pushed to his side and started leading Ulmar back toward the inn. No one stopped them, no one moved.

41.

Dawn was almost upon them. Ulmar and Aldred were standing outside the village barricade, Aldred holding the banner of the goat and Ulmar pacing to and fro. Aldred had been less than enthusiastic to be caught in the open this way, but Ulmar had been agitated to a degree that he was even less inclined to challenge him on the point. He didn't have a plan as such, he was just caught up in his own fury. He was tired of battles, blood revenge, blood oaths, hatred, murder and ignorance. He was tired of the eternal struggle of the clans and the madness they spread across the hills of the True Folk.

-"You don't have to be here," Ulmar growled inadvertently.

-"And miss this excellent chance of making a martyr of myself? Why should only you get that honor?"

Ulmar glared at the apprentice. He already knew that this was probably a lethal idea but he couldn't just let his kinsmen slaughter these people, even if their so-called leader had acted ignobly.

-"When they come I want you to keep back. This is between me and my kin. If I fall, I want you to make for the barricade and not look back."

Aldred didn't answer. In Ulmars mind he didn't have to.

The Tuakk and Marrodar warriors made no effort to conceal themselves this time. Unafraid, they walked out from the edge of the forest weapons in hand, murder in mind. They were spread out in a thin line, numbering at least a hundred strong. At their centre Briac, Schilti and Hild led the army of warriors. Ulmar started pacing, working up a battle-will, muttering promises to any spirit or ancestor that might be watching, reciting ancient battle hymns that felt right but he no longer grasped the meaning of the words. The villagers were manning the barricade under the supervision of Anahea. He could hear her commands even out here. She was competent, fierce and the villagers determined. Yet he knew that it would be too little to save them. The warriors of the hills of the True Folk had been born to do battle. A constant bloody battle against each other and the land that they had fought since the moment they drew breath. What was soft Lowlander flesh against that? Ulmar raised his axe, pointed at the oncoming horde, challenging them. The warriors hesitated at the sight of the legendary Doomwolf. Soon they were standing still at fifty paces, no one willing to be the first to test their strength against him.

The tension was excruciating.

One long moment after another, Ulmar faced them ready to stop any warrior foolish enough to take a step closer. With a slow deliberate stomp Ulmar began chanting one of the ancient battle hymns of his people, stomping, pointing, shouting and flexing he worked himself into a near frenzied state. He could feel the battlerage, the state of berserk building up inside him and knew he had to back down or he would lose control. Shaking with lust for violence, he let the razor sharp edge of Kharagh dance along his exposed skin leaving bright red streaks that trickled blood. Dancing on the edge of control Ulmar let out a primal scream that bounced along the hills echoing back as if generations of his ancestors stood at his back. In the midst of his scream hundreds of black birds took flight from what seemed like every tree, a cloud of black crows or ravens and as they did the howling of wolves could be heard in concert to Ulmars voice. At its crescendo the dark blade of Kharagh flashed with pure white light so bright it blinded all those that were watching for a moment. Had Ulmar not been so thoroughly caught up in the moment, he would have been taken as off guard as everyone else. The warriors of the True Folk cringed, cowered and backed away slightly from the avatar of doom.

-"Come then my kin. If you long for slaughter, I will grant your wishes. I challenge any that wish to raise their blade against this village."

 Ulmar took several long strides toward the hoard, the warriors closest to him did their best to stay their ground only shifting back a foot or two. With Kharaghs blade singing an ominous lament he dragged the axe across the ground drawing a long line. He then took several strides back roughly to the same spot where he had stood before awaiting their response.

None of the warriors of the True Folk dared move over the line in the dirt. Ulmar paced to-and-fro behind, ready to take on an army on his own.

-"Cowards."

Schilti had broken the spell. The warriors of the True Folk seemed to take heart, blinking away their fear like sleep from their eyes.

-"If the Tuakk cower from the blood traitor then the Marrodar will do what they can not. I know that Melkhar, brother of Karnae, is willing to take on the challenge."

A warrior that bore a strong resemblance to the fallen warrior Karnae raised his axe and stepped confidently over the line in the dirt. He then died.

It didn't look as if Ulmar could reach him from where he stood. When the Marrodar took the first step over the line, Ulmar spun while taking a step forward and then stretched out in a swooping blow where he only held onto the knob of Kharagh. The blow was struck so quickly that it could just as easily have been a lightning strike. Just like his brother, Melkhar lost his head, but, unlike his brother, he never got to launch a single blow against the Doomwolf.

Melkhars own axe spun off along the line of warriors coming to a stop several yards from Melkhars body.

At that point everything could go two ways. That little sliver of reasoning consciousness that Ulmar had kept from the fire of rage wondered which it would be. Would the True Folk become an enraged mob that fell upon him, ripping his flesh from his bones or would they fall back from fear of his gruesome reputation?

Briac stepped all the way to the line, stopping just a toes width from it. The chieftains' nostrils were flaring, his eyes wide and his face was red.

-"What have you done? What do you expect us to do? We were betrayed by the vermin that you keep to your chest. They tried to poison us. Poison! There is no worse way of feeding a warrior to the wolves. We will not idly stand back for an insult like that. They must die!"

Ulmar walked up to his uncle, staring him in the eyes, this time not wavering or backing down.

-"No. No more. Thirst for death and I will feed your hunger with our kin until the mountains shatter and the skies fall. I will plague you like the fires of Irogar himself. None of you died at the hands of that poison, she killed her own people. She, one frail and hateful woman that will be dealt with by her own for her treachery. You can talk or you can bleed. Now what will it be?"

Briac took a step back, turned to Hild and nodded.

-"No."

Hilds' gaze never left Ulmar, and her bow stayed slack. Briac violently gestured toward Ulmar.

-"No. We talk."

-"You have a blood oath to fulfill. Take the shot, kill him."

-"No. No more."

There was a murmur among the gathered warriors as their appointed general openly defied the direct order of her chieftain. The lust for battle had been replaced by confusion. Behind him he heard Aldred state "now or never" just loud enough for him to hear.

-"We offered a deal that benefits us all. I suggest you take it. Twice your weight in food every solstice and in return you see to the safety of this village."

-"No. That was before we were betrayed and now you expect us to protect them? No."

-"Uncle. There has to be a way to satisfy the clans. Thrice your weight of food. There has to be a way to resolve our issues without more bloodshed."

Briac went from furious to collected. It was obvious that he had found some price and Ulmar was certain that he was going to regret his desperate stance.

-"We demand more supplies immediately. We demand that the village of Penkath acknowledges that these are the lands of Clan Tuakk. Thrice my weight at the start of every season and I demand the crown of Trimboldumn."

-"The crown of Trimboldumn? That is not mine to give. How can you demand a thing that has been lost for an age? It is not even known where the crown is, you would have me chase legends."

Briac smiled a wolfish smile, the kind that always sent a shiver down Ulmars spine.

-"Ah, but nephew, I know where it is. I will give you seven days to return with the crown and then we shall accept your terms. Go now, nephew, and get the crown of Trimboldumn from Dead Mans' Rising."

42.

They made camp at the entrance to Dead Mans Rising. After the confrontation outside Penkath, Ulmar and Aldred had packed their belongings as quickly as they could and traveled straight for the cursed valley. They had been quiet and careful which had probably saved their lives as they found several signs of death delvers and goblins at every turn.

They had made it unscathed even if they had gotten to the valley much later than they had hoped. There was no helping it, they would have to take their chances camping there during the night and then delving into the valley in the morning. The time it took to travel had at least lessened their pains, Ulmar wasn't much bothered with his knee by the time they got to the valley.

It felt a bit strange to be back to that cursed place so shortly, even stranger to be using the same camp that the Tuakk had used. Much had happened since then. Ulmar looked at the resting Aldred, the stranger with locks of sunlight that had changed his life. Ulmar was now untethered, lost in life, a traitor to his people and somehow happier. He felt a little guilty that breaking the bonds of blood had brought him happiness, he tried defending his actions to himself by thinking that he was helping his people, making life better for everyone in the hills of the true folk. Would it have been another person that might have been the end of it, that reason was only the tip of the iceberg as he watched Aldred sleep and considered what had happened since he had left the clan he knew he was doing most of this for himself.

Usually True Folk would only venture this close to the valley in respectable numbers, keeping vigilant watch and having hot fires burning through the night. They didn't have that luxury instead relying on stealth and luck to keep them safe. They hadn't even made a campfire fearing that the light from the fire might entice the dead to leave the valley and drag them back to some twisted hell. Despite his fears dawn came without incident. They ate a meager breakfast and then started walking down the narrow descent into Dead Mans' Rising.

The way down was a treacherous goat path that twisted and turned. They couldn't see the valley floor for thick mist and it wasn't long before that same mist was so thick that they could barely see ten feet ahead of them. They didn't know what to expect in the gloomy terrain, not what they were looking for only that the crown of the ancient hero-king Trimboldumn was supposedly somewhere in the valley. Ulmar was aiming for that building he remembered might be somewhere in the valley from the time he and his kin had fled through there.

The ground was moist with only moss and fungi covering it, a muddy mess that reminded him of old graves. Aldred was trailing just behind him, nearly startling him into giving away their position as he put his hand on the Hillmans shoulder. Aldred crept up close and pointed into the billowing mist around them. Ulmars' eyes adjusted after time to realise what Aldreds finger was following, a dark shadow roughly the length of a man that was slowly yet utterly quietly moving ahead of them.

With Kharagh firmly held in both hands, he sneaked closer. It was indeed a man, a man he even recognized. With Hilds arrow still sticking out of his skull, Ourin of the Marrodar was walking away from them. Ulmars stomach churned at the sight of the once young lad. His flesh hung on the bones like leather belts, in some parts not even attached to the bones at all. The emaciated figure was covered in moisture, moss and fungi in a way that made him a thing of the ground. Ourin still had his unruly tuft of hair that was still just as it had been in life. It was hard to determine what injuries, if any, Ulmar had inflicted on the dead youngling after his death, though Ulmar was sure he had left Ourin in much worse shape than he was now.

A few steps covered the haunting figure in mist, making him a dark shape, a passing nightmare, moving away into some other part of the valley. It would be easy to repress the horrible visage, making him a guilty memory that tricked the mind. Ulmar knew better though.

Trying their best not to hurry they happened upon more dark figures in the mist. Fearing an encounter with the dead they stopped at every encounter to see in what direction the figure was moving and then plotted their course in an attempt to try to avoid them.

They could smell their earthy rotting presence every time they got close, a few times they glanced at other walking dead but so far they managed to keep far enough away not to be sensed by the things. They were getting closer though and there were a lot more of them. Either Ulmar and Aldred were getting closer to something around which the dead patrolled or the dead were hunting them. Realizing that no man could be so large the two companions happened upon their first structure in the valley.

A twelve foot high stone gateway adorned with strange complex figurative carvings that had a strange resemblance to the decorations of Kharagh. The gateway turned out to be a sort of arch standing alone along the path yet Ulmar only imagined that the empty gateway led them to the realm of the restless dead.

There was no time to linger at the arch, so the two pressed on, narrowly passing what once probably was a warrior but was now only a mass of walking bones. Only yards away from the first arch stood another arch identical to the first at which they stopped to determine if it was safe to move on among the dark figures in the mist. Feeling the pressure

321

of their situation they hurried on finding another arch and then another. The stone structures funnelled them deeper into the valley, only reinforcing Ulmars feeling of entering the underworld as the path gently descended.

There was a larger structure there. A large square formation at least twenty feet wide, hammered from heavy stone that was roughly in the middle of the valley. Standing by its foot the two companions were up to their ankles in wet almost watery mud that smelt of stagnation. There should be more water Ulmar concluded while feeling the rough surface of the constructed square, a fact that bugged him. There was no stream, lake or pond, just mud.

They scoured the surface of the structure for any sign of an entrance only to find more inscriptions and nothing else. The dead were getting steadily closer, Ulmar gave up looking for a way in and conceded to the fact that he had to make a stand here. So ends the tale of Ulmar Doomwolf of the Tuakk, a warrior no living man could kill that was dragged down into the pits of oblivion by the restless dead, he thought grimly to himself. At least he could hold his head high regarding the life he had lived, his only regrets being that he could not save the village of Penkath and his new but dear friend Aldred. Ulmar stepped a few steps into the mist, keeping Aldred behind his back, Kharagh firmly in his hands.

-"I don't know much of you, Aldred Brynnd Tollemack, I wish we had more time to get to know each other, but I am happy we had the time we had."

Ulmar would never have expected Aldred to respond with a chuckle.

-"If you don't plan on going running for the hills, you will have the time you require" Aldred whispered behind him. "I don't know about you but I'm not ready to be received into the eternal embrace of Vanenna."

Ulmar glanced at the Lowlander who was pouring over the pages of his strange book mumbling and gesturing at the stone.

-"A funny thing that people believe about magic, that it's this separated unyielding power that you use to beat reality", Aldred stroked the side of the stone in entrancing movements, "at the same time, they are completely correct and completely wrong. I see the arcane arts more like using knowledge and will to play after the gods rulebook, and learning how to cheat."

With a ceremonial air Aldred lifted his fist and knocked a single rapp upon the stone. Where Aldreds knuckles touched the surface, an intricate circle filled with spidery symbols flared up in fiery runes and a sharp crack reverberated around the valley. The seemingly smooth surface broke revealing the immense frame of a stone door that was moving at the speed of a rosebud opening in the sun.

-"What just happened", Ulmar queried.

Aldred smiled from ear to ear.

-"Magic", he informed Ulmar happily.

43.

The interior of the tomb was not at all as dusty as Ulmar
had suspected it would be, neither had he counted on it
having such heavy stale air that carried an aura of
foreboding. Aldred led the way with the flickering red light
of a tiny flame he had conjured out of the palm of his
hand. A narrow stairway had led into a small hall lined with
slim columns. There were more of the strange carvings all
over the interior of the complex, symmetrical symbols that
intrigued the eye.

So far they had come across two rooms at the end of long
hallways only to leave them before entering. When they
found a third room and were on their way from it Ulmar
couldn't contain himself any longer.

-"Why are we not searching every room? The crown could
be anywhere."

-"Traps. I've been in one of these tombs before, or rather
one very much like it, in Valeria. It's the kingdom's worst
kept and strangest secret that the land is scattered with old
ruins. According to official policy there has never been
anything in the lands before we arrived thirty two years
ago - don't ask, it would take too long to explain. Anyway,
there are tombs that bear a haunting resemblance to this
one and they are all littered with false sarcophagi and they
are all littered with deadly traps. With any luck we'll find a

smaller chamber with a false sarcophagus and a secret door to the real tomb."

They found the smaller tomb at last. They pressed past heavy brass doors entering a non descript room with a simple sarcophagus in a large niche at the back wall. Aldred immediately walked over to the wall in question to cast the same spell he had cast on the outer wall. Ulmar was uneasy, it felt like some dark malevolent presence lay over the tomb, and the further in they pressed the stronger it got. The dead kept to the outside so far, but in Ulmars mind it was only a question of time before they would stumble into the now very open tomb in search of the living. Whatever this was it felt different to the empty, shambling and ravenous things on the surface. This felt like a cold, calculating consciousness. He was tempted to stop Aldred from completing the spell but they needed the crown to stop the hostilities. Aldred knocked on the wall unleashing the red, fiery lines that ran along the now less than secret door. Swinging open there was a gust of air from the dark tunnel ahead, it felt much colder than the rest of the tomb. The air wasn't as foul but it still carried that sense of foreboding. They entered the corridor and walked into the room beyond.

The chamber was much larger than any other they had been in so far. It was easily fifty yards long and fifteen yards wide lined at the sides with the same square pillars as the entry hall had been. The hall was sparsely filled with all sorts of chests, equipment, statues and even a complete chariot. There was treasure enough to buy a city from what was haphazardly stacked around the hall, glittering gold and silver that would have entranced any adventurer that happened upon the mound. Entering Aldred increased the intensity of the flame giving them more light to inspect the hall. They stood a while basking in the sight of the vast riches giving Aldred the chance to ask about their quest.

-"Who was this Trimboldumn? I've never heard of him."

-"He was the last high king of the True Folk and my great ancestor. After his death the bonds between the clans of the tTrue folk were truly broken. It is said that he was tall and broad, with a deep booming voice and a shaggy beard and resembled a bear. He was the greatest hero of his age and his actions kept our people from falling into darkness when the world was in flames."

The objects around the hall bore the resemblance to Kharagh and the artifacts of old that had survived in some of the holds of the True Folk. Ulmar held out Kharagh comparing the Tuakk artifact to a thick russet colored carpet that was covered with intricate symbols. There was a definitive resemblance even if nothing could ever be an exact copy of Kharagh.

-"Better not touch that", Aldred whispered as Ulmar came close to the carpet.

-"I know, it's probably all cursed."

-"I was more thinking poisoned if it bears any resemblance to the tombs in Valeria. A shame really because I'm getting a strong vibe that a lot of this is imbued with magic of a sort I've never dealt with before."

They continued up the hall towards the only other exit, a nine feet high double door of copper that was green from age. While passing between rows of strange armor there was a flicker of darkness in the periphery of his vision. A strange thing indeed seeing that there was plenty of darkness all around the hall. Suspicious of what was happening Ulmar turned to study the area around a couple of the armors. The flickering light cast long dark shadows that tricked the mind, making Ulmar imagine a vast array of nightmares.

Then he realised that the shadows were moving.

Aldred screamed then the light of the fire went dark. He thought he had seen arms of shadow grasping toward him so he attempted to shift to the left only to be grabbed by something shockingly cold and strong. It felt as though terrible hands gripped his arms, forcing him to his knees. More hands pinned his feet and clawed at his throat. The numbing cold sucked the strength from his limbs, chilled him to the marrow. Ulmar realised that he wouldn't be able to fight very long against the terrifying attack. He might die cold in the pitch dark.

The hands slid over his throat and started to squeeze, another pair of hands moved over his mouth and nose starting to choke him. He was already groggy, losing consciousness was only a matter of moments away.

Several flickers of flame erupted from Aldreds outstretched hands. There were dark things all over him, shapes of impenetrable shadow vaguely humanoid wrestling the life from his body. As they were doing with Ulmar the dark things were choking Aldred.

Desperate to save the Lowlander, Ulmar stumbled forward wrenching his axe free of the things in the dark long enough to make a weak blow against one of the things in the flickering light of flame. There almost seemed to be mass in the thing as Kharagh connected with it, a numbing high pitched shriek tore into them as the thing slid off Aldred. Finding more strength when his attacker was dispatched, Aldred threw his arms back, raised his face skyward and let an inferno of flames wash over his body. Swathed in fire the monstrous attackers were rudely exposed, the few that were clinging to the wizard viciously burned. The same wailing reverberated from the now destroyed monsters and as it did the two companions realised that the wail was one without sound, a scream that echoed in their own minds.

The monsters could be seen now to an extent. Black forms that shifted in and out of the darkness that they were indistinguishable from taking on humanoid shape long enough to lunge at them. Their touch singed their skin with the cold touch of the White Wolf's breath leaving the area numb and weak.

-"Shadows!" Aldred screamed, "these things are made of shadows!"

Falling to one knee, Aldred held out his arms toward Ulmar. His own vision was fading, the monsters had robbed him of most of his breath and the cold pain was draining the life out of him. His vision was blacking out with flashing bright spots dancing in front of his eyes. Searing hot fire grazed his skin threatening to envelop him. Ulmar had misconstrued Aldreds intention, only glad to be given another chance of life. He got to his feet, angered, and leapt toward the nearest monster. Whatever the thing was, it had the same intangible qualities as a shadow as it glided between the inch wide gap between two ancient armors. The thing was efficiently out of his reach ready to strike at him as soon as he turned his back toward it. Frustrated he glanced and saw that Aldred was holding his own summoning fire to keep the things at bay.

Ulmar had had enough.

He raised Kharagh over his head and the hall bathed in a blinding white flash. The monsters wailed and were no more. Exhausted Ulmar slumped considering staying in the hall for rest instead he motioned Aldred to keep on.

-"That's the third time that happened. You're controlling it aren't you?"

Ulmar shook his head.

-"I have no more control of it, than a falcon controls a thunderstorm. Something has awakened in Kharagh. I can feel it, even if I don't understand it."

It felt good to put his unfinished thoughts into words. He realised now that he had felt it, Kharagh had changed and it all began when he fought the Hrimmkuningaz Trötl. He just didn't grasp how it felt different.

-"Strange..."

Aldreds confusion and worried demeanor concerned him. There was definitely something that disconcerted him regarding Kharagh, more so than the simple fact that it was a wicked two handed axe.

The large double doors resisted their intrusion for a while, becoming a hassle before they gave way, crashing broken, to the floor. The hinges had detached from the rock of the frame long ago, only the years of corrosion had held it in place. They had found the final resting place of High King Triboldumn the Bearfaced. That simple room was a place of myth that bound Ulmar back through the eons binding him closer to his people. Trimboldumns final resting place was a large marble sarcophagus that was completely devoid of markings and inscriptions save for a great bear carved into the marble roughly over where he expected Trimboldumns chest to be. Under that bear there was a short inscription of runes whose meaning Ulmar could only guess.

Placed on the sarcophagus, strangely enough, was a beautiful angular crown wrought in gold and silver. It was a fair guess that they had found the legendary crown of the High King. Why it wasn't buried with the king was beyond Ulmar, he was just pleased to find the thing and longed to grab it and be off. Before he had a chance to do just that Aldred slapped his hand away.

-"Might be poisoned or a trap", the apprentice mumbled.

Changing his position time and again he examined the crown from many angles creeping ever closer. He whispered incantations from his book, gestured and frowned. After the third time Aldred shook his head in confusion Ulmar just outright asked him of his progress.

-"What's wrong?"

-"There's no indication of a trap, I can't find any hint of a curse and it seems to be the real thing. I'd guess that it was brushed with poison in the very least but it feels too easy."

Ulmar shrugged, pulled out a piece of cloth and summarily just picked up the crown before Aldred had the chance to protest. At his companions' flabbergasted countenance, Ulmar commented.

-"It's done. Let's leave before Trimboldumn rises from his grave. I wouldn't want to face his wrath living nor dead."

The companions hurried out of the tomb, Ulmar was sure that they both had that uncomfortable feeling of that terrible presence, even though it had lessened somewhat after they had fought off the shadowy monstrosities. With every flicker of Aldreds fire, the shadows around them danced, making seeing an Ulmar attack at every turn. Still they made it up to the mouth of the tomb, stopping dead in their tracks a short stone's throw from the outside. Ulmar had been right to worry that the dead would enter the tomb. Just inside the doorway, swathed in mist, the bloated and half skeletal remains of a fallen warrior was standing as if at guard. There was no way of passing the dead thing without it becoming aware of them. They waited individually trying to devise a plan that wouldn't put them in harm's way only to fail. It seemed the thing had no intention of moving away, instead they heard the soft sound of shuffling just outside the doorway to the tomb.

They were caught between the risen dead and things of darkness, every moment bringing them one step closer to death or a fate even worse than that. Not having any other option Ulmar weighed Kharagh in his hands, started reciting a prayer to his ancestors in his mind and sped forward as quietly as he could.

How a man was to know if the risen dead had spotted his attack or the attack came as a surprise was unknown to Ulmar, but either way he had managed to strike at the thing without it reacting and with that savage blow he cleaved the thing from shoulder to groin. They stood at the door peering out into the fog seeing the dark outlines of the dead shuffling toward them. The sudden grip of a rough hand around his ankle made Ulmar jump. The cleaved corpse was still moving and dead bound on dealing with the living. With a grunt he cut off the hand and started moving to the right from the building. They were no longer trying to hide instead trying to make a run for it. The dead were after them, shuffling faster and correcting their course after them it seemed they had honed on to their essence.

Their path was blocked by a bloated repugnant shambler, its heritage impossible to determine under the years of decay it had suffered in Dead Mans' Rising. Aldred pressed his hands together and made churning rays of fire shoot out of his fingers as he gestured toward the thing. The moment of imagined victory gave way to despair as the only effect the spell had on the corpse was that it caught fire. With sickening sizzling bubbling and stench the fat and oils of decay fed the blaze, yet the dead thing just lumbered onward with its arms held wide in longing to grasp them into death's embrace. The two companions were driven by instinct or panic at the sight of the flaming abomination, each choosing a side and simply ran past it. The air warmed and sizzled as the dead thing attempted to grab at first Aldred and then him as they jumbled past. They ran for their lives in the thick fog, stumbling along the loose rocks of the steep wall of the small valley, their only shot of finding the entrance before the dead cut them off, hinging on them staying close enough to see it. It felt like they had been running for an eternity and still there was no end in sight. The dead kept getting close and only their speed saved the living from the ravenous horde. Ulmar knew it was only a matter of time before they would be cut off and knew likewise that there was no way he'd be able to fight his way through the ranks of the dead. Their only chance was to find the exit from the valley, an exit he had no way of knowing how close or far they were from.

Another swathe of mist hid another risen warrior. Honed reflexes meant that Kharagh connected with the corpse a moment after the thing stumbled out of the mist, cutting the things' legs at the knees. They pressed on with the decaying figure clawing after them with a look of pure hunger. Sharp, jagged nails dug into his ankle, the thing had managed to hit him despite Ulmars best efforts to avoid it. The wound throbbed after a single moment after its infliction, he could have sworn that it was the swollen feel of an infected wound. Enraged at the things' success, he swung round and cut off half of the things head in spite. His stomach churned at the sight of the thing dragging itself toward him, half its flesh loose and rotting, with half a head and legs twitching in the mud only slowed down and not in any way stopped.

There was a sharp incline of a slope on their right that might just be the trail that led out of the cursed valley. If he was wrong, they might become stuck in a pocket and overrun by the hungering dead but on the other hand they could not evade them much longer. He took the chance, spurring Aldred to climb onward. The apprentice was dripping with sweat and breathing hard. The softer life of the scholarly kind and the steel coat of chainmail had his companion at a disadvantage, at least when Ulmar compared their lives in his mind.

The two of them shuffled up and out of the valley. They had made it. In mere moments they would be in the relative safety of sunlight, an assumption that Ulmar made that he had no way of knowing if it would make any difference. Laughing from relief, Ulmar stumbled past a large boulder and came face to face with a drawn bow, an arrow pointed at his heart. Vroth stood before him with a content grin and let the string slip from his fingers. Grabbing Aldreds shoulder he pushed them apart sending Aldred hurtling to the ground beside the boulder and himself in the mud in the opposite direction. The arrow streaked between them a hairs' width from drawing blood. From the ground he found himself looking at Greldir who was keeling over coughing and shaking. The arrow that was meant for Ulmars heart had struck the young warrior in the stomach, a painful and horrible death for the young man. His innocence was somewhat lessened as Ulmar saw the war club that was slipping from his fingers. Apparently Greldir had been creeping up behind them in an attempt to kill them from behind.

Vroth was already readying another arrow, swearing at his ill fortune. Not having the time to bridge the distance between them in time Ulmar grabbed a sizable rock, flinging it as hard as he could at the pockmarked man. Missing the bow, the rock snagged the string making Vroth drop the arrow and smashed into the mans' groin. Vroth doubled over, understandably enough, but the small reprieve that he had bought was quickly gone as Herkeld stepped into view and very nearly skewered him with a nasty boar spear. Rolling around several times he was keeping himself away from getting impaled, but only just so. A blast of fire announced Aldreds entry into the fray. Hethweg rounded the boulder in haste, only barely keeping away from a gust of red fire. Sliding back to the surface of the stone, Hethweg waited for a chance to cut into the Lowlander as they spun round it in a deadly game of cat and mouse.

As Herkeld raised the spear high to make a vicious stab, Ulmar managed to first roll away and then roll on top of the weapon, forcing the weapon out of the warriors' hands. Herkeld swore having to draw a dagger and pouncing at Ulmar. A moment was all that Ulmar needed to regain the momentum. Kharagh found Herkeld quicker than Herkeld could manage to jump atop Ulmar. WIth a horrible spray of blood the Tuakk lost yet another warrior to senseless violence.

The screams of Hethweg announced her failure to keep from Aldred. The apprentice had simply stopped and then burst out flame at the first moving thing that came into view. Hethwegs arm up to her shoulder and the axe that she had been wielding had bathed in wicked fire searing the limb into uselessness. Disarmed and in horrible pain she simply ran from the ambush as fast as her limbs could carry her clutching the ruined apandege while wailing in pain.

Alone and facing a hopeless melee, Vroth drew a crude goblin sword and charged Ulmar bellowing his hate at the Doomwolf. Ulmar could easily have ended the fight then and there, utilizing Kharaghs superior range but instead he cut the axe into the ground and faced his kinsman unarmed. Vroth leered with the spark of victory and jabbed toward the now unarmed Ulmar, who with a twist of his abdomen dodged the blade, caught the arm with his left, disarmed him with a twist and grabbed Vroth by the throat.

-"Fool! It didn't have to come to this. There is still time to resolve this without more death."

Vroth spit at him while going for a dagger in his belt. Angered Ulmar grabbed the hand going for the dagger, pinning it in place and pulled Vroth forward and with a massive heave launched Vroth from the cliff and down into Dead Mans' Rising. Vroths scream of rage turned into screams of anguish. Ulmar imagined that the dead had caught up to Vroth and he tried not to imagine what was happening to the poor miserable soul.

He had known that only one of them would have a chance to live till summer. Now the Tuakk had lost three or, depending on Hethwegs luck, four warriors. Ulmar felt the stench of blood and wallowed in regret.

-"Did Briac mean to betray us?"

-"No", Ulmar answered without raising his gaze. "Briac wasn't counting on us surviving and if we did he would have wanted the crown. No, this doesn't have the feel of his hand."

-"I hope you're right. For all our sakes."

44.

The travel back to Penkath was made in mindful haste. They were both drained from battle, fear, lack of sleep and in Ulmars case, disappointment. With mixed feelings, they rested in the Dell of Turundar. Aldred professed his wonder that a farm like it would be abandoned in a land like that and, probably picking up on that there were things that Ulmar didn't want to explain about the place, he resigned into relative silence.

They made it to Penkath at midday. Briac had stood by his word, the village was unharmed by further attacks. Not having the will or patience to exchange barks with the Burgomeister they headed straight for the knoll outside the village. Not having the banner Ulmar simply let out a primal roar to announce his presence. The sound was a kick of two hornets nests as both the village and the forest buzzed with sudden movement.

Briac, Hild and Schilti made for the hill once again. The three of them seemed more rested, their wounds and blemishes healing and fading. They had the demeanor of a group of friends on a casual stroll more than warriors on route to a parlay. When the group had gotten within range Ulmar picked out his parcel and threw the crown of the last high king Trimboldumn at their feet. A mixture of awe and shock went through the group at the sight of the legendary object that no mortal eyes had beheld since the days of the great heroes of old.

-"I would be careful of touching it, poisoned." Ulmar casually cautioned as Briac stretched his hand toward it. The chieftain hesitated for a moment then picked up the crown using a swath of cloth, taking a moment to bask in the glory of the crown and then holding it high against the sky. The gold and silver gleamed in the light of the sun making Ulmar wonder why age had not dulled the gold nor blackened the silver.

-"You have what you want, now keep to your word. The village is kept safe as long as it pays tribute. You will not bully the village, you will not change the conditions of the tribute and you will not try to find ways to twist the meaning of the agreement. Do that and I will return and no matter the cost I will make you honor the agreement."

Briac was still completely focused on the crown. For a long moment it seemed that he wasn't even going to answer.

-"Don't worry son of my brother, if the pests keep to their word we will keep ours."

-"What?" Schilti awoke from his smug daze. "There can be no other future for these cattle than feeding the blade and fire. What drivel is this about giving our word to the likes of these?"

The challenging words ignited Briacs anger. The larger Briac pushed his massive mace in the ribs of the Marrodar chieftain.

-"You can follow me and rise to glory or get in my way and fall. The Tuakk will share the tribute from Penkath like brothers, so consider if you want to bleed and starve or do as I have decided and feed your people."

A lesser man would have buckled under the enraged attention of the Tuakk chieftain. The leathery Schilti pressed his chest against the mace instead and glared into his rivals face.

-"Step softly Tuakk. We will keep your word this time for the sake of our children but never think that we will cower under your words like beaten dogs. Push us and you will learn to regret that you never built a tower, only a wooden hall."

-"Step back," the Tuakk chieftain ordered. With great reluctance, Schilti stepped back in line.

-"You have the word of the Tuakk, you should know what that means."

Tired Ulmar nodded and walked back to the village, not giving thought to the fact that he was exposing his back to attack. He moved down to the barricade, clambered it in full view of the terrified guard that was supposed to keep out any hillman that got to it. Standing in his full height with the sun at his back he was an impressive and intimidating sight to behold. On the other side of the barricade a worthy assembly of villagers had gathered now witnessing this figure from their darkest nightmares. Ulmar held Kharagh for all to see.

-"You know me as the Blackaxe. I am Ulmar of the Tuakk, the Doomwolf and I've come to tell you that your battle with the true folk has come to an end. At the turn of every season you will gift the Tuakk thrice their Chieftains weight in foodstuff and in return the Tuakk will keep you safe from the dangers of the land. No clan will challenge the Tuakk in this. You will know peace once again. I give my word to both parties that this accord will be held and that peace will return, break it and I will return and let loose my ire."

The villagers of Penkath stood there like deer surprised in a clearing. None of them spoke, protested or moved.

-"We still have our room at the tavern. I will have drink and food and then rest while we can. Tomorrow we head for your mountain to deal with whatever evil has been birthed there", Ulmar explained with tired affection to his comrade. "This siege is over."

They stood on a rocky ridge and peered Northwards. He wasn't sure what the rocky outcropping was named, if it had any name but it marked the most northward Ulmar had ever been. Further and they would soon be entering the territory of the feared man eaters. The spectacular view was very much like many others in this land, small valleys containing small woods cutting like rifts in the hills. Yet a bit farther the dominating feature of the mountain that was called the throne rose above the hills of the True Folk. The mountain had the unique look of an actual throne or chair which had spawned a great many myths and legends. Among those that Ulmar had heard was that some thought it to be the throne from which the creator God had made the world at his leisure. Others thought that it was the sight where the gods meant to sit judgment over the actions of mankind before they fell. Others still believed it to be the seat that the King of Giants had chiseled out believing himself much larger than he actually was. Then there were stories of dragons, demons, magic and death. All Ulmar knew was that he felt disquiet radiate from the mountain, the stillness of a forest hiding from a predator.

-"It really does look like a throne. A huge snow covered dark throne for someone or something I'd rather not meet. I've seen it in the distance of course, but it gets very much more real this close up."

-"We'll get much closer, Lowlander. If we don't get eaten by the maneaters that is."

45.

Travelling north, there were ever increasing signs that they were entering territory claimed by the feared clans of the maneaters. There were much fewer animals and the few they spotted were very easily spooked, there were few signs of human habitation barring the crude markers that the man-eaters' had erected here and there in the countryside.

It had been many years since the maneaters had been bold enough to raid the Tuakk but after a Winter as the one they had endured, there was a risk that they would. Usually it was the clans further North that endured the maneater raids though.

Taking these facts in consideration the two of them travelled through forest and brush when possible, scouting out the way ahead as well as they could and stopped making campfires when they camped. Weather and wind made their trek a miserable one and only camping among the stunted trees kept them from getting sick in the increasing night rains.

A few days on the road they found the muddy footprints that in all probability belonged to a party of maneaters. The prints were rounder than a humans, not overtly so but enough to confirm that they were dealing with something other than men. The footprint was also considerably larger than a usual mans, not quite but almost twice the size.

-"Irogars fire! These have to be Ogre prints." Aldred was caught between excitement and confusion.

-"Half Ogre. Most of the maneaters are only half Ogre, even if some of them are true Ogres."

-"Oh well, why not sneak into the lair of man-eating Ogres. It's probably not the worst we'll do before this quest is over."

The tracks were only about a day or two old, meaning that the man-eaters might just be in the vicinity. They made a point of sneaking away as quickly as possible.

That night they made camp by a small brook that ran between two large spruce trees. The rain had hammered down a long time past sunset weighing down their improvised shelter consisting of a large woolen blanket tied between two trees. Small whiffs of mist rose from the valley floor lending a fey like quality to the campground. The food was wet, their clothes were wet, their boots and weapons doubly so. The only thing that was wet and brought them any satisfaction was the water in their waterskins, that they at least had in plenty.

A stubborn smell of smoke blended with the wetness growing from a realisation to a fact. If Ulmar wasn't mistaken it was cloudhead pine, the tall trees provided much wood but were notorious for producing large amounts of smoke and ruining the taste of any food prepared in its flames.

When the stench of smoke had grown to such a degree that there was no question if it was imagined or not the faint sound of large drums rose from somewhere far off in the night. The rhythmic sound spoke of a fast paced tempo that periodically fell out of sync.

-"Well, they're not afraid of revealing their position, that's for sure."

-"The maneaters rule these lands. There are several clans that live at the foot of the mountain who all compete for food and honor. They hate each other, and will ritually battle and murder each other in honor of whatever is on that mountain. It is told that they believe that if they offer the mountain enough blood, flesh and skulls that the man-eaters will be filled with unlimited power."

Aldred held out his hand catching a smattering of dripping water in his palm.

-"Are you sure we can't make a small fire? By the sound of it they're quite a bit far off and I'd give my last coin for a hot meal and the possibility of drying my clothes."

-"We shouldn't even be talking."

-"Might be worth becoming someones' meal just for some warmth and bacon."

They listened to the drums in the distance, the darkness of night slowly embracing them. Soon it would be so dark that they might not see anything other than maybe an outline or two. With the thick cloud cover the stars and moon would be no help at all. This might be as good a time as any to ask a question that had been nagging at Ulmar since they left Penkath.

-"If we are able to get past the maneaters and reach the foot of the mountain, what then? What's the plan?"

-"I don't know. This seemed so far in the future, I always figured that I'd have a plan when we got this far but now we're almost there and I don't have a clue.

-"It's a bad thing to not have a plan in a situation like this. But it's a worse thing to have a bad plan and stick to it. Since no one knows what awaits us, maybe it's better this way."

Aldred snickered.

-"I know several very experienced wizardly types that just spurted out their drinks without knowing why. A refreshing attitude that I wholeheartedly embrace. Thank you, my friend."

As they listened to the drums in the night they knew that the next day would be one filled with uncertainty and danger.

46.

The mountain had grown to such largesse that it was hard not to be aware of its overbearing presence no matter how you turned. According to Aldred it wasn't a particularly large mountain, but seeing that it was one of the few true mountains for many leagues, it seemed like the tallest and most impressive thing in the world. Ulmar on the other hand had never seen any mountain this close and found it hard to grasp that anything could be larger than the throne.

It was tempting to hurry in the soft dawn light, to get to the mountain and be done with it, but this close to the man-eaters that was next to suicide. Would it not have been for them they might make it to the mountain before noon. Now they would be lucky if they got there by midnight.

The terrain this close to the mountain was rocky and covered by forests of short Birchwood that was abundant in the hills of the True Folk, a perfect cover to move quietly and secretly. Ulmar wondered where all the signs of the man-eaters were, as they were supposed to live at the foot of the mountain. So far they had just happened upon paths and the markers not a single building, tool or table. There was hardly room for the clans as far as they could see.

Curious if Aldred knew anything more, he broke the silence to check.

-"Aldred..."

That was all that he had time to say as when he spoke a tall figure seemingly arose from the ground before them. Luckily they were already sneaking along fully certain that they would run into something so both simply lay down flat on the ground.

The individual lumbered slowly in their direction carrying a nasty stone warpick at the ready. It was a man of sorts. A horrible ugly beast of a man. Bald, muscular, with a mouth full of jagged long teeth. The man had features that were warped, speaking of something else than the race of man. Donning a mottley assembly of spliced pieces of clothing and fur to be able to cover his eight foot features, the individual was Ulmars inner vision of an ogre. A single hit of that pick would easily impale a foolish opponent, and he had no intention of ending up in the things stomach. Ulmar tried to slowly shift his body to hide but could only move about a hands' width for fear that he would be spotted.

From five yards away Ulmar could clearly smell the rank odor of the thing and hear its heavy breath. It stopped and peered out among the underbrush. He was tempted to look up, though doing so would expose his face and Tuakk lore was adamant that what you watched could feel your gaze, the last thing he needed was to risk gaining its attention.

-"All dead." The eight foot man growled out into the quiet of his surroundings. "All dead," it muttered confirming the words to itself.

A whipping crack next to him almost made him jump to his feet. The thick shrubbery was largely broken, its thicker parts lying uselessly on the ground. With broad swooping strokes the thing searched the underbrush with violence. Committed to his action and hoping that Aldred felt the same, Ulmar kept down, unmoving while the thing continued its search.

-"All dead", it repeated as it stopped. With equally lumbering steps it walked back from whence it came. He followed it from his hiding place as it seemed to take a step into the ground, walking down a stairway that was invisible to him. Waiting a while they then started creeping forward and to the side so not to run into the eight foot man again.

They found that they were at the edge of a sudden cliff. Running along the throne as far as the eye could see the cliff ran like a great ditch following the edge of the mountain. The sight was awe-inspiring and Ulmar doubted that the ditch was naturally formed even if he had a hard time imagining the titanic work that would have been needed to lower the ground along the mountainside. The slope wasn't exactly a free fall but might very easily turn into a thirty feet drop. There were a number of ladders, stairs and ramps that led out of the round trench on one of these the eight foot man was sitting guard ready to spring forth at any intruder that neared the lands of the maneaters.

Forming an enormous ring around the mountain was a veritable city of shabby small white stone houses in different states of disrepair. The squat structures had a foreign architecture unlike any of the houses in the holds of the true folk. It seemed likely that many had stood there a long time before they were settled by the clans of the maneaters.

The signs of the man-eaters could be seen everywhere, from the crude repair of the houses in the great trench to the rough wooden fences, tables, banners and equipment that littered the ground. It was impossible to know how many were living in the trench, if every house was occupied they could number tens of thousands, which Ulmar found very unlikely. Banners of maybe half a dozen different designs were haphazardly raised among the ruins of the strange city suggesting to him that there might be a dozen clans of man-eaters in the trench that hopefully didn't number much more than a hundred a clan.

There was activity in the trench in the form of a smattering of beings that wandered the streets, each group never straying too close to any other. The figures varied wildly in size, some not much larger than children and others even larger than the guardian that had almost happened upon them. From guessing on the size of the doorways of the buildings some of those broad and monstrous figures might be as tall as ten feet. Pointing the figure out to Aldred that had joined him on the edge of the trench he whispered "Ogre".

Further to the west they could see a large square open up. On that square was a large stone platform whose original use was a mystery. Now it housed a large square stone that vastly resembled a shrine that was discolored by large dark stains. Close to the shrine was a rough pit filled with what might be sticks or bones and lying on the platform next to the shrine were large blackened chains.

-"We might be able to sneak through in the areas between the banners, they don't seem to be guarding those very well. Then we just take it slowly and start finding a way up the mountain." Aldred pulled out the strange disc from his pack, the object seemed to shine gently.

-"Then we have this. The Saedr seal has been scratching at my mind for several miles now. I'm not sure how it's connected to the mountain but I'm sure that it's the key to getting into or onto the mountain."

-"It's a risk of course. You can see how the clans keep to themselves, they will be vigilant of intruders so we might well be spotted. But I think it's the best choice we have."

-"Ah choices, the spice of life."

47.

There was no simple way of getting down into the trench, any entry was either too open or they suspected that it was under guard. Choosing the safest option available, they climbed down the side of the trench with the help of a rope. Using a trick that he had learnt from a certain unsavoury acquaintance of his, Aldred thread the rope around a strong root, tied the ends together and then opened the knot on the ground. He then pulled the rope down and fastened it on his pack again.

They made for the nearest building expecting to be spotted at any moment. The squared buildings had both the advantage and disadvantage of being tightly packed with narrow alleys running beside them on all sides. If they could hear someone approach they could duck into said alley for safety, a pretty big if seeing how any that came close would most certainly be on top of them before they had the chance to react. Moving between the first few alleys they could hear the loud snoring of what could only be the man-eaters in the nearby buildings. So far they had a chance to get all the way through if fortune remained on their side.

Ulmar hadn't counted on the stench of rot that lay over the lands of the man-eaters. Waste of every kind was just unceremoniously dumped outside the lodgings without any effort to clear it. Carcasses of what he hoped were beasts, excrement, household goods and assorted broken things lined the walls of every occupied building, in different stages of decomposition. He knew that if it would come to it they would have to either hide in the waste or try to hastily maneuver through it, most probably ending up slipping and falling.

Through the intermittent gaps between the buildings they could just make out the tall mass of the throne, their dubious goal. Ulmar hoped against hope that fate would be kind enough to allow them to reach all the way, to get through the man-eaters so they could at last fulfill the first part of Aldreds quest. He just had the sinking feeling that they wouldn't be so lucky.

They stood in an area between two camps, or so they assumed, judging by the placements of several crude banners, peering out at the open street they would have to cross to get closer to the foot of The Throne. There was no smart way to go about it. They hadn't seen any place where the gap was tighter and to search for such a place would cost them a small eternity of time, every moment merely adding to the risk of them getting detected. Several groups of man-eaters were visible further up the street on both sides making detection more or less a fact, if they would be so bold as to risk it. Ulmar was fairly certain that if he moved quickly into an alley on the other side there was a slight chance that he might be able to fool them that he was just another maneater, an even chance perhaps. Aldred on the other hand was a dead give away. There was no way that the Lowlander with his golden locks, slender build and outlandish outfit could be mistaken for anything other than an intruder. Ulmar wanted to formulate a plan, pool their collective wisdom to try and reach a solution but was loath to speak again since the recent near encounter with the half-ogre guard.

Feeling that time was running out, he tried to convey without words to Aldred that they needed a plan. His quizzical appearance must have told the apprentice at least that much since he shrugged and made a pointing gesture towards the alley across the street. Ulmar was about to gesture that they should stay a while where they were, as they heard muffled shambling behind them. Time was up and without a better plan he shuffled forward, awkwardly stopping in the middle of the street clearly visible to the several groups up and down said street. He cursed his own hesitation, amazed that it hadn't gotten them both killed. No one was reacting. He quickly moved into the alley, stopping to wait for Aldred.

If Ulmars hesitation was a danger, that was nothing compared to the frustration of what Aldred was doing. Instead of hiding or running over the street the Lowlander had opted to open his book and stood there reading. Ulmar wanted to scream at him, calling him a fool and questioning why he wanted to get himself killed. This was clearly no time to read. He growled internally and readied himself to spring over the street in an attempt to pull him out of harms' way. Then Aldreds spell took effect. The outline of the Lowlander shifted and flickered like the air over a fire making him a blur against the background. It was a strange thing to try and follow his movements as he made it out into the street. Ulmar was very much aware of where he was yet still had difficulties following him. Would any of the maneaters catch a glimpse of him there was no chance that they wouldn't realise that something was very wrong but that was dependent upon anyone actually catching a glimpse.

The blur that was Aldred moved up to him and he could feel the man gently try to nudge him further into the alley. Collecting his wits, Ulmar backed quickly into the questionable safety of the alley, still managing to see the small patrol of half-ogres that would undoubtedly have caught them if they had stayed where they were. They were one step closer to The Throne and still undetected. Ulmar felt a glimmer of hope returning a smile to Aldred that was now becoming increasingly visible.

-" I didn't know you could do that", Ulmar whispered as quietly yet clearly as he could.

-"I was hoping I could," Aldred happily retorted, "I've never been good at that one so could just as easily have backfired terribly. Only lasts a couple of moments but on the other hand sometimes that's just what you need."

Ulmar encouragingly grabbed Aldred by the shoulders, unwilling to risk speaking again. It was bad enough they had broken the silence as they had. They crept onward between the buildings. They were clearly between camps and the alleys were all the much better for it. There was a minimal amount of debris and even less garbage lining the walls. The air was better and they had a clear view of the base of the mountain.

Peering from their alley position they scouted the last stretch. Like a small barrier that seemed to stretch all around the throne there was a small wall of assorted white junk that was ranging between ankle and knee high. The small wall didn't seem to have any breaks anywhere, just an elongated white pile that ran off into the distance. The barrier seemed to almost be a border between the lands of the maneaters and the foot of the throne. Just on the other side they couldn't see a single sign of the proximity to the maneaters. They exchanged wondering gazes not really knowing what to make of it.

-"Bones", Ulmar said at last, recognizing the telltale features of an empty socketed cranium. "It's all bones."

The dead had to have measured in the thousands to cover such a distance as it did. Some were clearly from all manner of beasts but there were more bones from the true folk heaped at the foot of the mountain than there had ever been Tuakk in the world. The sight dumbfounded Ulmar into complete inactivity. Were these all the victims of the man-eater tribes over all the years they had raided the tribes? How many generations of mortal kin had fallen to the predation of the tribes at the foot of the mountain?

Ulmar supposed that it was impossible to know, the sight of it was enough of an impossibility that was hard enough to fathom.

If he had had his wits he might have connected the increasing stench with oncoming danger as goblins have a notoriously bad sense of smell.

The ambush was quick and ruthless. Moving in from all sides were goblins that flung waves of rough nets over the companions whilst laughing murderously. The two companions were further set upon by the wicked creatures before they had fully understood their predicament. The goblins swarmed in, pummeling them fiercely with short clubs making it a mystery that the creatures hadn't broken and killed the companions during the first moments of this onslaught. Even given moments the goblins had gained the initiative not for a moment giving the companions the chance to get their footing. They were quickly beaten to their knees and then forced to cower into balls in the hope of protecting their bodies. Ulmar had lost overview of his surroundings, lost in the flashes of painful stars as a club pummeled his skull and the occasional glimpse of yellow crooked goblin teeth. There was something coming that he was fairly certain wasn't part of his imagination, heavy steps and a lumbering silhouette that were moving toward them.

A sinister rumbling voice taunted them.

-"Well, well, well... What's this then? Orogat so mighty that slaves come to him, give their lives to serve him. This makes Orogat happy, very very happy."

The voice belonged to the large figure that could only be a half-ogre. The figure stepped into view like a thunderstorm hides the sun, pinning Kharagh to the ground with his large foot. The creature laughed at their predicament which sent a brushfire of high pitched laughter through the ranks of the goblins who doubled their clubbing efforts. Orogat grabbed Ulmars shoulder with the grip of the Black Wolf himself and viciously dragged him to his feet. The half-ogre's breath smelt rancid as he huffed with excitement of his new slaves.

When Ulmar tried shouting, the words grated to a halt in his manhandled throat resulting in a gurgled whisper.

-"Maybe you make a good eating slave that struggles, much muscle, juicy muscles."

Orogat grabbed Ulmar firmly around the throat with his other hand and started squeezing the life from the warrior's body. He couldn't breathe, his lungs tried to gasp for air and nothing happened. He could feel the painful crush on his throat that was starting to cut off the blood coursing in his veins. He could feel the increasing tingling in his lips, cheeks and head. The half-ogre pulled him in closer in grim expectation, waiting for him to mouth his last attempt at breath. Ulmar pummeled the arms of the half-ogre with as much strength as he could manage but the course web of the nets entangled him, restricting his movement, his efforts did little other than spur Orogat on.

Ulmar refused to die here, not thinking he turned to instinct as he flailed helplessly in his attackers' grip. In desperation he lunged forward with an open palm, his arm whipping out toward the half-ogres face and managed to get enough of it through the nets to succeed with his attack.

Orogat roared in agony dropping Ulmar to the ground while stumbling backwards away from him. Ferocious and victorious Ulmar held out the half-ogres eye toward him in his open hand, the wicked smile of a wolf upon his bruised lips.

Orogat lumbered off, howling in anguish, giving him the moments he needed to save his life as Ulmar yet again grabbed Kharagh and with the ease of a broom cleaning spiderwebs cut the cords of the webs that burdened him. The goblins didn't understand at first what was happening to them as limbs were severed and heads split in moments by the ancestral axe of the Tuakk. The goblins scattered as quickly as they could, losing several more of their number to the sudden tornado of death that was reaping them furiously. Drooping and trying to collect his consciousness Ulmar stood in the midst of the carnage, on the verge of completely losing himself to bloodlust. His breath stung his throat as he gasped for precious air. Trembling he cut the cords of the net to help Aldred free and heaved the wizard to his feet.

-"Remind me to never get on your bad side, my frightening friend," he muttered trying to brush the dirt from his red robe.

-"Still. Undefeated," Ulmar proclaimed as he gasped.

-"As fundamentally impressive as it may be, I often feel that it is only when you fail at something that you can truly learn; but on a completely different note, we need to run. Now. It's a miracle that none of the other monsters have barged out and demanded our heads but I have the stubborn feeling that it is mostly a matter of time."

As if the world was trying to illustrate his point a vast amount of upset deep voices could be heard all around them in increasing strength. Hoping that they wouldn't leave a too obvious trail of blood the two of them spurted toward the nearest building that seemed intact enough for them to hide in. Bursting into the building it was only well honed reflexes that kept the two from attacking the inhabitants, cowering along the walls of the large room in the interior they found a group of people, frightened as they were they shielded themselves with their arms and moaned feebly. There was no time to do anything except close the door and hope for the best. The group consisted of several individuals both male and female of which several bore markings that identified them as being True Folk.

From the street outside the man-eaters were gathering together with a small swarm of goblins. Risking detection Ulmar opened the door just so he could peer out and hopefully hear some of what was going on. Two groups seem to have responded to the situation, both wearing the crude skin and bone outfits that the man-eaters he had seen so far seemed to prefer but there were clear differences in the groups markings. They gathered on opposite sides of the street and sent the goblins running to and fro in search of him and Aldred.

The half-ogre that had faced them walked into view; the brute was still clutching his maimed eye socket that hadn't stopped bleeding. Seeking approval from the largest Ogre in one of the groups he then stepped out into the middle of the street and bawled.

-"They took Orogats eye. Look, look what the dirty Hillmen did."

As Orogat released his hand several members of one of the groups started chuckling heartily at the sight of the empty socket. Orogats group immediately reacted, riled up, as they growled, protested and posed, making it very clear that they were ready for a fight. The first group was as agitated in mere moments frowning and swelling their chests.

-"No, no, if we fight Bekugag will take all our eyes. They are untamed in our home, we must find them."

The half-ogres words steeled the two groups resolve and the groups started searching in opposite directions. Ulmar felt that he had seen enough for now so he inched the door shut. The room was almost dark. He chose one of the nearest inhabitants who seemed slightly less skittish than the rest and who also bore the markings of clan Dregotalam.

-"You there, warrior of the Dregotalam, I am Ulmar, Doomwolf of the Tuakk. Who are you and what brought you here?"

The man hesitated and then straightened his back, almost meeting Ulmars gaze.

-"I was Lugaid and most of those you see before you are the pale shadow that remains of the great clan Dregotalam. Before last snow three of the man-eater clans came to our hold and crushed our clan. Our homes lay shattered while most of us have filled their bellies. We are all dead, some of us just haven't gotten so far. I don't know what you are doing here Doomwolf, this is one of the slave houses. If you have any wisdom you should hide till morning and then go back to the Tuakk and tell of the fate of the Dregotalam."

The clan Dregotalam was one of the few clans that was large enough to shield the Tuakk from the raids of the maneaters. The white wolf must have bitten deep into the land all over the hills of the True Folk to drive the man-eaters to utterly destroy the Dregotalam. Usually they would raid them, taking several but never so many that they wouldn't be able to recover. Maybe the last long winter was truly on its way if the man-eaters had been hit this hard. Without the Dregotalam, both the Tuakk and the Marrodar would face raids after next snow and would continue to be raided time and again till there was nothing left. Ulmar tried to shake off the grim news and instead focus on the now.

-"Lugaid of Dregotalam, as long as there are a handful of you left your clan lives on. Do not be so quick to throw yourselves to the wolves, fight and live as is the way of the True Folk. Why have you not escaped back into the hills, there isn't even a bar on your door."

-"I am no more," Lugaid croaked, refusing to look at Ulmar. "There is no bar because they don't need it. Any who are foolish enough to try to escape the man-eaters are hunted for sport and if they don't kill you then and there, you are made an offering to the god on the mountain. I may be dead already just as my clan are, but I won't choose to feed the thing if I can help it. The only thing I care about is keeping away from that fate."

-"Stand tall warrior of the True Folk," Ulmar growled more forcefully than he had intended, making the people in the room cower back. "Do not fear death as long as you have lived your truest. We do not bend at life's curses, we push back."

Lugaid crossed his arms as if hugging himself.

-"Just wait until tonight, they will make their sacrifices and then you can try your brave face."

48.

Outside the maneaters kept on hunting for the intruders that had so brutally attacked them in their homes. As they swept the streets and barged infrequently into buildings Ulmar kept waiting for them to enter the building in which they were hiding. He had placed himself so he would in part be behind the door when it opened counting on getting the chance to decapitate the unlucky creature that sought them. To his surprise no one searched the slaves' quarters. He wondered if the man-eaters were so indifferent to the people in the building that they could impossibly imagine them taking to arms against their captors or if the man-eaters were just doing such a poor job of searching for them. Whatever the case Ulmar was waiting for an intrusion that never came. During the wild hunt of the maneaters he had ample time to study the dirty miserable people, many who in part could be his own kin. For every miserable flinch, with every pained cower his heart ached. This was no way for any person, true folk or not to live, bunched together and fearful of every sound like animals waiting to be slaughtered. Whatever happened he decided that he would help them somehow, how could he not?

As the footsteps grew fainter and less frequent he decided that it was safe to talk to Aldred.

-"We have to help them."

Aldred wore an honest look of pain, clearly showing that he sympathized with the people in the building.

-"I'm sorry Ulmar, I really am, but we can't."

Ulmar was astonished at Aldreds words, he couldn't believe that the Lowlander would fight him on this.

-"What do you mean we can't? We can't leave them here to die. It's not even a choice."

-"Ulmar, please, look at where we are and what we're doing. How are we supposed to be able to help them? We need to get to the throne, we need to keep sneaking through insanely dangerous territory that I don't even know myself, just how we are supposed to be able to cross. We can't bring a baggage train of half starved prisoners and even if we do, please wait and listen to me, even if we do there is something up on the peak of that mountain that will probably spell the end of them all. Here they might live on."

He understood the wisdom in the Lowlanders words, it was a cold hard fact that any action from their part would spell the miserable death of the slaves. It was an uncomfortable truth that he had a hard time just utterly dismissing. Yet when he looked at them a righteous anger burned in his chest.

-"These are my people. Some here are even your people. Who are we if we choose to leave them to this fate?"

Aldred sighed deeply in contrast with his usual demeanor.

-"We are the living. It will haunt us, probably for the rest of our lives but we can't die here. You know, honestly know, that if we try leading them out of here we will be discovered and we will die. I know what I'm asking from you. It's not right, it's not fair. Still I'm asking because I have to. I need to find out what's up there, I need to bring that news back to my people. It's bigger than me, you and even all of us in this building."

Trying not to raise his voice Ulmar felt his temper lash out at Aldred.

-"Bigger than any of us? What do you actually know? Nothing. You speak of magic, of knowing that there's something there. You could just as easily daydream while casting chicken bones. These people are here now. They need us. They'll die without us. I will not let them live on in this misery while you chase mist-ridden nightmares."

Lugaid put his hand softly on Ulmars forearm. As they had argued he had completely missed how the man had crept up so close. Ulmar quelled a flinch and quenched the flash of a violent reaction.

-"You want to help us?"

Lugaid stared with pleading eyes, Ulmar hadn't understood how loudly the two of them had argued. He could only hope that he hadn't disclosed their location to the hunters outside.

-"You have a large soft heart, Ulmar of the Tuakk. One that I would never have thought beat in the chest of the one we all know as the Doomwolf. I thank you for that kindness but your friend is right. There is something on the mountain, something powerful and terrible. We who have been caged here have all felt its power grow. One wolf-ridden day it will come down the mountain trying to swallow the world. If you do not try and help your friend no one will know what is coming. Imagine that fate thrust upon your clan. If you learn what is coming you might understand how to fight it or at least get out of its way so we don't sleep in the mouth of the sleeping bears cave.

If you truly want to help us, grant us something else."

Lugaid opened his tunic exposing the naked skin of his chest.

-"Grant us a quick death, a warriors' death. We have all thought of ending ourselves but I cannot give in to doing it. Help us, release us."

Ulmar got to his feet feeling the massive weight of Kharagh in his hand. The slaves crept up to him, stretched out their hands pleadingly, held onto his clothes. Their eyes begged him for a quick release, terrified and tired eyes that were heavy with sorrow. It would be easy to grant their request, quick, merciful.

-"No."

His refusal made Lugaid hang his head, his body drooping at his feet.

-"I will walk up the mountain and stare into the face of whatever demon has made its den there. I do this for you all and for Aldred. Then I will come back down the mountain and I will take you from this place, all of you. By then Aldred will be able to get back to his people without me and I will be free to save you. I would rather die than leave you here one more day."

The people at his feet burst into tired tears. Ulmar knew that he wouldn't be able to take on the entire might of the man-eaters, he would most certainly die. If that was his fate he was content to face it with the strength he had lived his life. He was tempted to abate their expectations but there was a fragile shimmer of hope in the eyes of the slaves he couldn't shatter. He knew what his fate was and by the look that Aldred gave him he knew that Aldred fully understood the fate he had chosen. To Aldreds merit he didn't fight him on it.

The day crept into evening with more and more man-eaters awaking to the annoyed buzz that was the result of Ulmar and Aldreds incursion into the lands of the man-eaters. They had decided upon sneaking to the foot of the mountain as the man-eaters gathered to feast a while after sunset. It would mean moving through the city when most of its inhabitants would be awake, a risk they would take hoping to gain the element of surprise as most of the maneaters gathered by the open area they had seen while descending into the ditch. According to the slaves there was a real risk of running into crews of goblin man-catchers though Ulmar counted on being able to take care of such a group quickly. They said their goodbyes to the people of the slave house and crept into the night. Immediately they discovered that they couldn't move directly toward the mountain as their route was blocked by a post of full blooded ogres on guard. Maybe Orogat or this Bekugag were craftier than they had let on, maybe the man-eaters had figured out their plan.

Stealing two hide ponchos the companions moved on trying to blend in as meek slaves. They followed in the footsteps of a large and oblivious ogre hoping that no one would question their presence in his wake until the time they could break off and move back toward the mountain. Unfortunately for them the ogre headed in toward the open area and they were followed by a small band of very suspicious mostly human man-eaters. They could almost feel the glares of the brutes as they kept to their ruse. Any closer scrutiny would see them discovered, especially if they deviated from their oblivious ogre chaperon. Under and around the stone platform a small army of man-eaters had gathered with rapt attention on said platform. Mumbling discussions implied a great deal of suspense from the clans, though what was coming Ulmar could only guess. Great fire pits dug in the proximity of the platform were lit and over these there were crude iron frameworks from which large slabs of meat were cooking. It was hard to see from what beast this meat originated, making Ulmars mouth water despite his intentions not to be tempted, he had an uncomfortable suspicion that the meat was that of speaking beasts.

Several burly man-eaters waddled up on the platform dragging three captives between them. Suspecting their cruel fate the captives did their very best to fight and scream which only brought mirth and more excitement to the gathered man-eaters. Ulmar could hear several of them comment on the poor souls in the broken speech of their kind, it sounded very much like they were imagining how it would be like to eat them. A handful of man-eaters climbed the platform from the other side marching to huge drums which they immediately started to beat. Their tempo was unsteady but savage building up the already high suspense of the crowd. In unison the man-eaters at the foot of the mountain started to chant "Bekugag" over and over again, building in strength until there wasn't a single throat that wasn't chanting. A welcoming roar rippled through the crowd as a horrible twelve foot monstrosity stepped up on the platform. Bekugag, the seeming king of the maneaters was a thickly built massive ogre that shockingly had two heads. Both had a wicked leer, both painted and tattooed and both had the aura of a cruel cunning of a murderer. Bekugag walked over to the edge of the platform after a brief examination of the prisoners and there he lift his muscular arms to quiet his frenzied subjects.

-"Brothers." The echo of his own voice underlined the drama of the ogre and the message he was conveying.

-"We have been wronged," the first head stated.

-"Violated," the other head filled in.

-"Our weakness has lured invaders to our lands."

-"Invaders that walked our streets as if they were their own."

-"This cannot stand."

-"We do not allow weakness."

-"The god on the mountain hates the weak."

-"We have angered him."

-"So we must appease him."

The man-eaters dragged forth the first of the prisoners, a woman whose furious battle against her captors required three half-ogres to contain. Ulmar admired her strength, hating the man-eaters that much more for their sniggers and wicked glee. They chained her arms and pulled them tight so she was pinned into a sitting position. Bekugag stepped in behind her, grabbed her by the top of her head and then addressed the crowd again.

-"It should be the blood of the careless weaklings that flowed in her stead. I would have your heads and then crush your bones. You are lucky that the god on the mountain has no use for your blood." The two headed ogre lifted his heads' toward the peak of the mountain speaking directly towards it, "We give you blood, flesh and bones so you will spare us great undying one. We give to you so we are not crushed by the great one."

Bekugag stepped forward, brandishing a small obsidian blade, and Ulmar only had time to take a couple of quick steps forward before it was too late. Aldred tried to keep him from rushing in, pleading with him that they couldn't do anything to help the poor woman. Bekugag had already cut several massive gashes along the womans' throat and neck expertly missing the main arteries thereby keeping her alive longer. Cutting deep into the muscles of the neck the two headed ogre then tugged at her skull with a great roar that drowned out the pained screams of the woman. The skull was violently ripped from her neck unleashing a rain of blood that sprayed over the maneaters nearest the platform. They were already unchaining the headless corpse while Bekugag held out her head for all to see. In the background another terrified sacrifice was being dragged toward the chains.

Ulmar had lost himself to anger. Letting the foul poncho fall to the ground Ulmar locked his gaze upon Bekugag. There was no other in his world anymore. The ogres' gaze passed Ulmar at first then the ogre saw him for what he was. He raised his other hand and pointed toward the Doomwolf and screamed out.

-"Intruder. Take his head. There walks the intruder, bleed him in the name of the great one."

Gaining momentum Ulmar raised Kharagh ready to cleave his way through the ranks of his enemies. The first of the man-eaters faced him, saw his axe and scattered before him.

-"Glaubir, glaubir!" They bellowed.

Bekugag seemed taken aback by those proclamations but was quick to regain his composure. If his minions would not fight the aggressor he would have to. A chieftain of any kind in the hills of the true folk that was not willing to lead his people in battle seldom lived long. He dropped the skull of his victim in contempt and grabbed two large axes of his own. Striving for the initiative in the fight, Bekugag heaved his body off the platform utilizing his superior reach and drove a great axe straight toward Ulmars body. Anticipating the move Ulmar simply raised Kharagh and met the haft of the axe so that the blade neatly sliced through the wood like a scythe through grass. With deceiving speed the two headed ogre threw himself to the side narrowly escaping Kharaghs countering cut. A man of Ulmars size got shoved into Ulmar, a man that met a quick brutal end from the blow that he aimed at the ogre. Grabbing the foot of one of the iron cooking frames the ogre was yet again wielding two weapons and was immediately swinging wild vicious blows at the Doomwolf. Gracefully spinning and jumping over the blade he had found an opening in the ogres guard. Feeling that the end was nigh, Bekugag cast all safety to the winds and with a great flailing motion attempted to catch the Doomwolf in a dangerous crushing blow. Ulmars' only rational choice would be to retreat and then try to get back under the ogres guard before he had the time to launch another whirling attack.

Ulmar was not feeling rational. He was angered, filled with righteous fury. He didn't care if the blow would cut or crush him, he barrelled on putting Kharaghs shaft to his chest charging the axe forward like a battering ram. The blade sliced into muscle and bone with barely a stirring, then Ulmars own body slammed against the ogre's stomach as its heavy arms furled painfully around Ulmar. He had no idea if he had been cut or not, he was too far gone under the veil of rage to feel much of his body. Bekugag stumbled backwards revealing a massive wound in his chest just between his ugly heads. Taking into account the profuse bleeding, the ogre would probably not survive long past his encounter with the Doomwolf if he let him walk away. A short moment Ulmar was tempted to leave Bekugag in that condition, maimed and bleeding. That wasn't his way though.

-"I should rip off your heads, you coward."

Ulmar stated coldly just before he lifted Kharagh up for a massive blow that cleaved the ogre from wound to groin.

The tyrant of the maneaters was slain. Being the most vicious bloodthirsty of the clans, his people simply counted on his ruthless invincibility to reign over the lands around the throne. Now he had fallen in moments against the Doomwolf. The goblins and the more fainthearted man-eaters wailed and fled from death incarnate, the braver and more brutish howled in hate.

-"We need to run!"

The panic in Aldreds voice pulled Ulmar from the worst of his battlerage. They started running in the direction of the mountain trying to keep away from the frenzied ogres that pursued them. Ulmar laughed bitterly at the futility of it all.

 -"We can't Lowlander. I'm sorry I cost you so much."

Aldred shook and screamed.

-"We. Can't. Die. Here."

Pushing his arms outward and spreading his fingers he let loose a detonation of fire that roared out into the square. Somehow the scorching blasts of flame just missed Ulmar instead igniting several of their attackers. Screaming in primal fury fed by frustration Aldred spewed wave after wave of flame breaking the ogres assault and clearing the square. Exhausted he fell to his knees only to be scooped up on his feet by a still smiling Ulmar.

-"I guess if we hurry we might make it to the foot of the mountain and then I can hold them off while you start climbing."

Aldred grabbed hold of Ulmars beard forcing him to face him.

-"Could you please stop trying to find ways to kill yourself."

Not knowing how to respond Ulmar mostly laughed a hearty laugh and dragged his companion onwards. The ogres were closing in again. There wasn't much they could do to hold back the wave of fury that was on their heels but Ulmar felt he had to try. He hated that his refusal to let injustice slide by had been the end of them so he had to push forward, just try to get Aldred a little bit closer. They had made it past the last of the city and only the small bone barrier was between them and a rocky outcropping that Ulmar believed that he could hoist Aldred up on. From there it would be up to the Lowlander by himself to get higher so he'd better make this count. They moved past the strange barrier in a stride giving Ulmar the opportunity to build up speed till the outcropping. He lost his grip on Aldred, the Lowlander simply slid out of it. Ulmar dug his heels into the dirt to stop and turned.

The man-eaters, all of them, had fallen to their knees and were pressing their foreheads into the dirt. He had heard a clear scream, a command of some kind ring out over the angered voices just as they passed the barrier of bone and he realised now that just after that they had all shut up.

The companions stood there in stunned silence and watched the hoard of fierce fighters kneel unmoving in the dirt, some shaking like leaves from what Ulmar could only imagine was fear.

-"That's quaint." Aldred sounded more perplexed than amused. "We'd better get a move on before they come to their senses."

Ulmar put an arm over his friend's shoulders.

-"Looks like whatever we are about to face could be much worse than to die here."

Aldred turned around, took a couple of deep breaths and then took out the small disc that he called the Saedr seal.

-"Moment of truth," he said and pointed the metal object toward the mountain.

Nothing seemed to happen.

-"No boom or crack?" Ulmar asked with what he hoped was a humoristic intonation.

-"There," Aldred said, pointing to very discreet steps that were carved into the mountainside itself. "They weren't there a moment ago, it has shown us a way in."

Ulmar was hardly convinced that the steps hadn't been there all along and they just hadn't seen them. If that was the magic they had been waiting for he found himself thoroughly underwhelmed. Not wanting to give the ogres a moment more than was needed they made it to the stairs and started climbing. They were smooth, unremarkable while extremely hard to make out. When they had climbed a score of them they were no longer visible behind them at the same time they could only make out a score of them ahead. The stairway caressed the mountainside climbing quickly.

-"It feels wrong," Ulmar put his thoughts in words. "It's as if we're getting much further than the steps we are taking."

-"We probably are."

-"Who do you think built them?"

Aldred peered up toward the cloud covered summit of the throne.

-"You know, I wouldn't be surprised by now if it was actually built by some god. I hope not because whatever's up there is no friend of ours."

They kept climbing, step by step up the mountain feeling very exposed to the harsh weather of the lumbrian hills. Even if the winds tugged at them and rain streaked them they weren't as affected as they should be. Not being able to understand what was keeping the rain from their backs they kept climbing in silence.

49.

The view of the surrounding lands was spectacular and only became more grandiose every moment. There weren't many mountains in the hills of the True Folk, the nearest one might be on the border to Valeria. Ulmar imagined that the broken landscape was one or other of the places that he had travelled, though from this distance, it was hard to tell.

It started as something he imagined, he would look at the wall of the mountain seeing what seemed to be strange patterns. Trying to discern them did nothing, they just faded from his view. Keeping at it he came to realise that he was right, there were indeed subtle patterns on the wall, patterns that were like none that he had ever seen before. He tried putting his hand on one and following it only to be confounded by it and losing its intricate turns.

-"Look at this," he called for Aldreds attention, "can you see what I see?"

-"The patterns?"

Ulmar nodded his response.

-"I've been trying to keep from looking at them. I don't understand what they are, they're shifting."

-"So they really are changing?"

-"Yes. We'd better leave them alone."

Ulmar didn't agree with his friend, but chose to do as he was told, for they seemed magical and that was after all, Aldreds speciality.

Drops of rain turned to flakes of snow as they climbed higher. Ulmar growled a little internally at the annoying weather phenomena. It was all too soon to be grappling with the breath of the white wolf. He felt cheated to have to walk through the stuff yet again so soon. If he was honest with himself he wondered if he actually ever would want to experience snow again in any form or at any time. It saddened him to think of the end of the world when cold and darkness would swallow the last of the True Folk, the thought brought on by where they were headed.

There was a pillar of sorts that marked the beginning of a platform where the staircase turned. It was almost smooth, at least it felt that way, but over its surface more symbols could be seen. It was a clear indicator of something more, that they weren't just imagining things. Tired, broken and hungry they rested on the platform taking in the sight of the world. They ate in silence and then huddled together under a blanket for warmth. They were beset by a mix of emotions, a calm in the storm they were facing.

-"I don't know if I've actually thanked you for accompanying me on this fools' errand. Thank you Ulmar, I would have been dead many times over if it wasn't for you."

Ulmar let the soothing fresh breeze tug at his beard a bit before answering.

-"You expect to die then."

He never thought he'd utter that phrase and be smiling but somehow he was.

-"Well yes, obviously, but it's more than that. You've left your home, shielded me with your body, dragged me out of danger and even forsaken your own people on my account and I feel that merits a sincere thank you at the very least. It just needed to be said."

-"Do you know what is worse than death?"

Aldred mostly gave him a quizzical look not knowing how to proceed.

-"Lack of hope. It's the thing that makes me admire your folk more than anything. Without it you become me or my kin, wasting away, pushing death aside for another day and waiting for the wolves to win. Without hope, people are dead without knowing it, just waiting for it to catch up. That's a gift you granted me, hope. I don't know how you did it or what I'm hoping for but I feel it will course through me. For that I owe you my thanks."

-"Even if we die?"

-"Even if we die."

Aldred scooched over.

-"This is officially getting weird. A good kind of weird but still weird. Come on you unstoppable hopeful Doomwolf, let's kick the ass of a god."

Ulmar got up fully ready to give it a shot.

50.

They came to a portal into the mountain. The outer stairway that snaked along the mountainside hadn't deviated a single time, it just ran straight to this very open doorway into the mountain itself. It felt frighteningly dark on the other side of the threshold, carrying a feeling of some dark consciousness much like they had felt in Dead Mans' Rising. Etched into the portal were a new kind of marking, charred lines and symbols that were vastly different from the subtle shifting ones that shift in the stone surface. These inscribed circles seemed to have frozen the shifting ones into place, nullifying them to normalcy that creeped Ulmar out.

-"These are arcane sigils, magic circles," Aldred clarified to his untaught friend. "I've never seen them like before, they're raw, strange. I wouldn't trust them too recklessly, even if they seem powerful."

-"What are they doing there then?"

-"I don't know. Probably keeping this doorway from closing." Aldreds fascination with the inscriptions seemed to be merited, in Ulmars eyes they were just strange symbols. They had a strong character that he couldn't put his finger on, a beautiful pattern that was still very much just a pattern.

Not even knowing what they did they chose to pass them and hope for the best. There was a colonnaded hallway on the other side of the portal that was dark only to the extent that it felt foreboding. Somehow there was light seeping out that they could orientate deeper into the mountain. Feeling that they would feel better with more light, Aldred summoned flame into his palm as he had done before.

It turned blue.

He stared at his hand confused. Wrinkling his brow he increased its intensity but the flame was still a cool blue. Ulmar had heard of blue flame before, a hex sign, that witches or worse were close by. With a shake of his hand Aldred quenched the flame and tried a confident smile in Ulmars direction. The apprehension he was feeling seeped through.

There were doors to sleek empty rooms from the hallway they were following. They were in several sizes, some with spartan stone furniture and others in different shapes. They could only guess who had built them and to what purpose. They chose not to stop to investigate instead following signs of more magic sigils.

They were led to another stairway. This one was of grandiose measurements while in pleasing symmetry built of white marble that seemed to be strangely intermixed with the rock of the mountain. There were no lines, no indication of how someone had managed to fuse two so different types of stone. From further up the mountain, from the top of the staircase they could feel anxiety creep into them. Even if they were feeling the full weight of their intimidating quest this was something different, it was like a heat or cold radiating out of an object, external.

Step by step they climbed the stairway.

They felt faint, lightheaded. Not from what they were feeling just from something else. Ulmar kept fidgeting with Kharagh while Aldred crept on in a pose indicating that he was ready to cast magic at any moment.

They were here at last.

The stairway led up to a large round platform made of a sleek, smoothly polished stone that changed in color. Lines upon the platform crisscrossed to and fro in some kind of infinitely complex web of magical circles that hurt Ulmars head when he tried to follow. There were columns, two rows of them. Behind them there was no wall, they just opened out into the open air displaying large parts of the hills of the True Folk. Placed very precisely there were braziers that smoldered with blue fire. The flames grew stronger as the two companions entered the platform.

Opposite the stairway stood a high throne on a stepped platform that drew Ulmars attention as soon as it came into view. It was sleek, made from the same white marble as most of everything that was here on the platform, uninscribed yet impressive. It carried an aura of bombastic power.

Sitting on the throne was the body of someone. They stepped closer so they could get a better look at the individual. He was desiccated and withered with age. His long goatee and hair might have been unkempt yet were thick and dark. He might have been tall when he was alive and even in death he sat with a regal aura that radiated a man of power. His red robes were a strange mix between Aldreds, the markings and styles of the maneater clans and details that could not be anything other than from the true folk. There was magical paraphernalia aplenty worked into his outfit, making it very clear that whoever this was he had the image of a spellcaster.

-"No."

Aldreds voice was full of badly contained fear. The Lowlander took several shaky steps forward and summoned two burning spheres of intense blue fire. Ulmar didn't know who the man on the throne was but he felt fear from looking at it, a dead man that moved him in a way that few living could.

-"No, no, it can't be."

Aldred protested, shaking his head. He paced forward ready to unleash fire upon him. The dead man sat still with his hands firmly on the armrests, his hands tattooed and adorned with magnificent rings.

Then the dead man opened his eyes.

-"I would know that symbol, I would know it anywhere. Runes of power set in a burning circle. You are the mad mage, Irogar, the destroyer."

Ulmar knew the wandering wizard of the wilds from myths and legends. There were places he had seen that his clan claimed that the mad mage had twisted and destroyed. Unreliable, reckless and extremely powerful, the most widely spread story was that of Irogar riding in over the vales riding a storm of fire. Those days and nights entire clans had been wiped out. Ulmar had been a small child when the burning of the vales had occurred and some of them still hadn't recovered. It was as if the ash was tainted. How this dead thing might be that terror Ulmar did not know.

The dead mans' eyes fell on Aldred. There was a horrible inner glow emanating from them, a constant red glow that penetrated the dead flesh that still housed the sockets. Acting in desperation Aldred lunged forward hoping to let loose his flames on the thing before he had time to collect himself. With a nonchalant flick of his hand, Irogar did something. Aldred was screaming uncontrollably in pain. The fire that had never burned the young magic user was now eating into his flesh and setting his sleeves on fire. Horrible sizzling accompanied his howls of pain while he sunk to his knees. Ulmar rushed forward, smothering the flames with his clothes. In mere seconds the previously smooth delicate hands of the Lowlander were a bubbling ruined mess that smelt of burned flesh. Ulmar laid his still screaming friend on the floor facing the thing on the throne. In a matter of a birds heartbeat he would be able to close the distance and rip out the things unbeating heart and crush it in his enraged hands. An invisible wave rolling out from the dead man caught him in the beginning of his stride. It felt as if some terrible cold force had grabbed him by the lungs and wrenched the air out of them. Cold vapor poured out of his mouth when he discovered he could not inhale. The moment passed leaving him dazed but otherwise unhurt.

The thing that Aldred believed to be Irogar slowly arose from his throne. The fabrics from his robe clung to the seat releasing their hold with a long peeling sound, decomposing cloth stiffened with mold unfurled around the dead mans' legs. It was now standing taking on a guard of some sort, as how Ulmar imagined a spellcaster would become readied for battle. He tried getting up again, realising that the cold sweep of magic had not only robbed his breath but also felled him to the ground. The thing tilted its head slightly then wiggled its fingers like he was clawing something out of the air itself. Aldred was hoisted into the air spread-eagled, caught in a thickness of the air that had the look of smoke and mirrors. He convulsed in his bonds, Ulmar played the image over and over in his mind even if it had just happened. Another crippling pulse robbed him of his legs sending him crashing to the floor.

-"Eeee-roooh-gaaahr."

The voice echoed in their minds, a frail harsh whisper that dug in like glass. The berserker rage wouldn't do anything now, he was caught like a fish in a net at the total whim of the horror that they had awoken from its perch. Ulmar exhaled and focused, draining himself of hate, draining his fear and anger. He sought out a glimmer of light in his inner self, that feeling of calm and contentment he had been able to find while at the Lowlanders side. He grasped the feeling and channeled it like a shield over his very being. Unaware when he had closed his eyes he now realised that there was a white shimmer much like the shield he had imagined between him and Irogar, a white light glowed out of the silver runes of Kharagh.

The undead thing cocked his head and jabbed in the air. A blinding bolt of lightning slammed into the shield. The air tasted sharp as he wondered if the bolt had really been black or if it simply had struck his vision. The shimmering barrier fluttered but was intact.

-"Sssspelleeeater." The thing reverberated into their skulls with the power of a razor-flower unfolding in their minds.

Ulmar knew it was mostly a matter of time before Irogar broke his shield. He didn't even know how it had appeared or if he was at all responsible. Feeling Kharagh in his hand he noticed there was some kind of resistance as he moved it in the air, this was probably more of the axe's power that he had never known about. He rushed over to Aldred and somehow managed to call forth the blinding white flash that had saved them several times before. Aldred fell limp into his open arms. Ulmar ran, he knew he was no match to the dead Irogar so he hoped for the best and ran desperately down the corridors of the throne. He could still feel the thing like a cold fire in the back of his neck, a thing that was only growing in power. His legs pumped under him and he knew that he couldn't rest until they gave way. If he wanted to live, if he wanted his friend to live he had to keep going as fast as he could until they were off the mountain and deep in the valleys of the hills of the True Folk. Even then there was probably no hope of survival but he wouldn't squander Aldreds life, he had to push on. Time, pain and distance grew into an obscured mist that choked his mind. He could hear his strained breath and was aware of the hallways and corridors as he ran through them.

With blood on his breath and muscles screaming for rest he ran out a stone doorway which stone door was ajar. He had left the mountain, he was outside in the dead of night stepping into a beehive of sound. The man-eaters were running around in the city, flailing in panic. He didn't have time to consider it, he had to push through the city with the unconscious lowlander in his arms.

Expecting a goblin net or an ogre club to put a permanent stop to his efforts he ran past the barrier. The bones were shaking, dancing around. The skulls that were piled in the barrier turned to face him of their own accord, red pin pricks in their dark empty hollows. The maneaters continued to scream in anguish. He realised that it wasn't his imagination that the ground was shaking, it was actually shaking violently. Rocks and rubble broke from the cliffs above and the houses posing a lethal danger to anyone beneath them.

He almost ran into an ogre. The thing was flailing his arms and making noises as if it was choking. There was a red streaking mist that swelled out of its open mouth and whisked up into the sky above. The ogre trampled on leaving Ulmar standing with the broken apprentice in his arms seeing the scene before him for the first time. It was like a huge spider web or a horrible loom in work. Red moist streaks were being pulled out of the maneaters mouths and out into the sky and up to the top of the mountain. The savage clans in the trench were in gruesome pain on the verge of dying. A fitting apocalypse was upon the fools that had resided at the base of the mountain, Ulmar hoped it would be their end.

With red death and falling blocks Ulmar couldn't stay there. Ordering legs that he could no longer feel other than a source of pain he lumbered on out of the trench.

Ulmar awoke from unconsciousness stiff as stones. He had collapsed. Sleep or effort were to blame, the shattering headache he had was his prize. Aldred was there, he was still breathing. He was cocooned in his cloak again much like the first night after he had met him. He felt the Lowlanders brow confirming that he was burning up from fever. He should check his arms, his hands. He couldn't just yet. There were two chances of helping the apprentice survive, either the care of the villagers of Penkath or the expert knowledge of Kallabra. Forcing some water down Aldreds throat he realised that he had to push on, he had to get Aldred to either of them as soon as possible. The cloth clung to the apprentices' wounds and he lacked any means of helping him. So he drank deeply, ate a handful of food and picked up the wounded Aldred, who screamed abruptly before falling deeper into unconsciousness. The shaky trip through the hill-lands was probably a threat to Aldreds life but Ulmar felt that he had no choice. They had to press on, get away and get help. He ran through cramped valleys, through dangerous passes without scanning them for dangers and along freezing waters. He pushed himself onwards utterly oblivious of the world as he pushed onward until unconsciousness yet again claimed him.

51.

There were dreams. Such horrible confused nightmares. He
had a hard time telling where reality ended and dreams
started. He kept seeing himself standing at the precipice of
a large ridge with a clear view of the hills of the True Folk.
The world was covered in deep snow. He could even see
the great white wolf in the wind spewing down snow and
ice over all he could see. It was dark, so very dark. He had
to strain his eyes to be able to make out even the great
white wolf against the darkness.

There were fires in the vales. Red hungry blazes that licked
up every little flicker of life. In the shadows they cast he
could spot the silhouette of the great black wolf darting in
and out of where Ulmar knew the holds had to be.

The world was in its final time, he could see that. A
nauseating presence crept up beside him, it brought with it
that sweet stench of rancid infection. He glanced over to
see Irogar, as he had been in life, standing there. He was
biting Aldred by the scruff of his neck, hanging like a kitten
in the mans hold. Ulmar tried flailing out at him but his
arms moved so slowly that snow started to build up on
them. Irogar dropped Aldred to the ground putting his
hands protectively on his shoulders and waited for Ulmar
to catch up. Behind the long dead wizard great white
batlike wings appeared stirring up the snow into a blinding
swirl before his eyes. Irogar was gone for the moment. On

his right side the white wolf of winter approached its jaws dripping with ice, on his left side the black wolf of death and disease bared his sharp fangs, its mouth dripping with the ichor of the sick. He felt the tug as they grasped one arm each threatening to rip him into pieces. The great wings were back cold as only the white wolf could be. There were eyes between the wings, cold savage eyes that meant to destroy him.

-"Why do we need him?" A grating mighty voice muttered in his mind.

-"Because fate is woven", the voice of Irogar explained.

Behind Ulmar there was a growing light that bathed the world until there was only white.

He awoke cold and shaking. His first thoughts were of Aldred who thankfully was lying beside him. After a second wave of anxiety he confirmed that his friend was still breathing. He tried to get his bearings, discovering to his surprise that they were back in the valley of the Tuakk. The weather wasn't as cold as he had first felt so he felt confident that he could afford leaving Aldred where he was at the moment. He ran up to the hold only to slam into the doors of the building, it was locked. He ran for Kallabras hut, smashed open the door and found it empty. The old womans' possessions were neatly packed, her hearth was cold, it was as if she had decided to go for a trip outside the valley. Ulmar walked around the buildings and was met with more of the same. No one was here. There was no indication of combat or looting. It seemed as if the clan Tuakk had simply decided to gather the most important belongings and leave. He didn't understand it, it seemed impossible. Nethertheless it was what he found. He wondered if he might still be dreaming. Or maybe the malignant mage Irogar had cast some strange spell that made him imagine his life from the moments they were on the mountain.

He could not risk looking into the matter further, he had to get Aldred to someone that could look to his wounds. He could try Penkath but that was in the opposite direction from travelling to the Shimmering Tower. Should he look at the mans' wounds himself? Ulmar walked over to the lowlander and tried gently lifting the cape from his arms. Aldred convulsed violently, shaking uncontrollably long after Ulmar had let go of the cloth. This was beyond him, he suspected that the wound had to be cleansed with magic somehow. His heart shattered every time his friend convulsed in pain. No he had to move on, he had to get Aldred to the tower so they could be warned. Ulmar forced more water down the apprentice's throat and drank deeply himself. He ate as quickly as he could, stretched his stiff limbs and picked up his friend. He kept running as the sun moved across the sky. He ran into a valley fully expecting to be shot by goblins as he more or less ran into a pile of goblin gear. He realised that it was more than that, these were dead mangled goblins spread across the whole valley floor. He had no idea what could do something like that and didn't have the time to dwell on it. He had to keep moving.

He ran racing the coming darkness. His speed had long ago become a stumbling jog but he pushed himself onward. The taste of blood grew as his breath became more ragged. Still he didn't stop, didn't wait or hesitate. As dawn was on the lip of the hills his own sight grew dimmer. He knew that he was not going to make it. It was so far away, days or weeks. He just hoped that he would get close enough that he could find help for Aldred or just find Lowlanders and make them take him back to the tower. With that in mind he fell into darkness once again

-"Dumb and tenacious, like a dwarf." The wings with eyes spread their icy cold over them. Ulmar imagined the cold eyes once more looking straight at him.

-"Yes." The voice of Irogar whispered in his mind.

-"I have soon done my part," the winged voice growled.

-"Soon." Irogar whispered, sending iron slivers across Ulmars skull.

The wolves were there again, with Ulmar standing on the ridge of a hill. They were waiting for a sign, when they had it they would pounce and rip him to shreds. He was so cold. However he tried to cover his hide with cloaks and furs', but the icy cold seeped into the bone. Harsh wind streaked against him, the white wolf's breath no doubt. Far to the south there was a sparkle of a light so strong that it hurt his eyes, there was something in it but he couldn't make it out. He heard Aldreds voice say "I will never break" as he woke up again.

Aldred was laying with his back against a sharp stone. He knew this to be real because of the raw pain of it all. It was almost dawn. He looked over to his left and to his surprise the glittering facade of the Shimmering Tower rose over the surrounding hills and valleys. The sight of it almost made him cry. Crumpled on the stone beside him was Ulmar, the barbarian seemed worse for wear, ragged. He was fast asleep, a good sign at least.

Gazing out at the Tower was a shimmering see-through figure of a tall bulky man clad in the hodge podge robes of a self trained magic user. Even before he turned around Aldred recognized him for who he was. Irogar.

It was an image of how he had looked in life. Chiseled cheekbones, crooked nose and long hair that accentuated his goatee. If it weren't for the paralysing fear Aldred felt for him he would've considered him handsome. The dead mage smiled at him.

-"I always enjoyed fire as well," the words moved through Aldred like heated led. "Even if it is a childs thing to play with."

Coughing Aldred decided to confront the man.

-"What do you want?"

Irogar laughed, as he did Aldred could have sworn the sound was shattering his teeth in his mouth.

-"I want what you want, I want you to become my messenger."

-"Why?"

-"I want them to know that I have awoken. They need to fear again and I need them to know what is out here. When that is done I want you as my messenger to the world, you will serve me spreading the word of Irogar, the wild wanderer."

-"No. I won't do it," Aldred muttered fighting through the pain in his arms and skull to do it.

-"You will. Here."

Aldred was helpless to stop the dead mage from touching his forehead. It was as if there was an icy blade as long as the horizon that was burrowing into his mind. Convulsing he threw up gall as the blade wrecked his mind. And in it all he could feel the symbol of Irogar settle there.

-"I will never break." Aldred threw out in defiance.

-"They always say that." Irogar stated in passing.

52.

Ulmar carried the unconscious Aldred to the northern gate.
The Barbarian was smiling madly as he walked up to the
armored guards.

-"He has returned, he needs to warn you but you need to
heal him!"

The guards stormed up to the pair grabbing Aldred by the
scruff to identify him. Being a veteran of many years the
guard recognized the cocky apprentice in a moment.

-"It's apprentice Tollemack," he announced, "He seems to
be in bad shape. Inform the hospital and inform Lord
Sarsara herself."

The guards were already carefully sliding Aldred from his
arms. He was so tired but somehow he had made it. They
had done it.

-"I need to tell you. Irogar has returned."

The guards at the gate stared at the mad Barbarian with
fearful disbelief in the rays of the morning light. All the fool
did was smile and repeat; "Irogar has returned."

Johanna H.   Newport – Ireland.

Kieran Redmond, Ireland (Dublin)

Printed in Great Britain
by Amazon

63213628R00231